CW01647685

PONTIFEX MAXIMUS III

The Remnant

Damian North

First Published in 2025
by Damian North

10 9 8 7 6 5 4 3 2 1

A CIP catalogue for this book
is available from the British Library.
HB ISBN: 978-1-83709-275-8

Contact:
www.damiannorth.com
@Damian_North

For Dan and Marion

Thank you both – for everything

To lie hidden, will be impossible;

to appear will be intolerable.

Saint Anselm

1.

His First Pope.

The 1958 Conclave.

On Sunday, 26th October 1958, the world changed forever. From behind the walls of Vatican City, an unthinkable event took place that would confuse those who witnessed it, and in turn would become the greatest coverup in the history of the Catholic Church. In the years to come, this day would make but a footnote in the annals of history, a conspiracy that would be spoken and written about whilst dismissed by many as a nonsense and an affront. But it happened. It had to happen. For that Sunday was the moment truth was silenced by the arrival of the one we were told to expect.

In the Sciascia Caffé, Alberto Benigni carefully poured the espresso for the gentleman who stood at the counter, taking the lira coins from his pocket. Just as Alberto was about to place the porcelain cup onto a saucer, a commotion from outside caught his attention and he turned to see several people running past the window. For a moment he wondered what was happening, but when he heard nearby churches ringing their bells, he knew that the conclave had reached a decision.

'Looks like we have a new pope,' Alberto said, setting the espresso onto the counter and taking the lira from his customer. 'A quick election - just like they had predicted.'

'Is it possible to listen to the news on the radio?' the man asked, glancing at his watch to note that it was almost six o'clock.

Switching on the radio, Alberto tuned into Radio Vaticano to hear an excited commentator exclaim: 'The smoke is white! I repeat, the smoke is white. There is absolutely no doubt. A pope has been elected!'

For several minutes, Alberto and his sole customer listened as the commentator spoke of vast crowds gathering in Saint Peter's Square and the spotlight that illuminated the white smoke bellowing from the chimney of the Sistine Chapel. As they listened, they continued to watch the people hurry along the street to witness the proclamation for themselves. Alberto, who was itching to join them, did not want to be rude to the elderly gentleman as he drank his espresso, but the moment he set the cup back onto its saucer and took his leave, Alberto turned off the lights and locked the front door of his coffee establishment.

Within five minutes he found himself standing in Saint Peter's Square, watching the white smoke rising into the air as he joined tens of thousands of people cheering for the election of their new pope. It was a moment like no other he had witnessed as spotlights illuminated the balcony window. Too young to remember the election of Pius XII, he relished witnessing this moment of history.

Earlier that evening, inside the Sistine Chapel, the remaining fifty cardinal electors gathered around the little stove as they watched the papal master of ceremonies set fire to their ballots that had been placed on a bed of dry straw. With anticipation, they waited to hear the reaction of the crowd. First came the silence, as the pilgrims in the square took a collective intake of breath as they studied the colour of the smoke emerging from the chimney, before erupting into an explosive cheer knowing that a pope had been elected.

'Happy with the decision?' John D'Alton, the Irish Cardinal from Armagh asked his American brother.

'Pius didn't leave us with much of a choice!' Cardinal Francis Spellman of New York replied, as he looked at the depleted college. 'At least with Siri, forgive me, I mean Gregory, we know what to expect as he's cut from the same cloth.'

'I thought Siri would've been more of a Benedict than a Gregory,' D'Alton continued, as he walked into the middle of the chapel. 'Sixteen popes and two antipopes have taken the name Gregory over the centuries; some of them great, some of them saints but most of them were unremarkable. I wonder how our Gregory will fair?'

'He's young, and could reign for thirty or forty years,' Spellman replied, as he fiddled with the gold ring on his right hand. 'He'll strengthen the college by electing traditional conservatives like himself. Of course, the biggest challenges he faces are the persecution of our brothers and sisters behind the iron curtain and the threat of modernism against our doctrines.' He stopped, took hold of D'Alton's left elbow and brought him in close. 'He will need all the prayers we can offer, because his enemies will be greater than any of us could ever comprehend, even from within this college.'

Through his rounded spectacles, D'Alton observed the cliques that had gathered; some happy with the election and others clearly disappointed, none more so than the French and German cardinals who looked as though they had been defeated by the outcome. Despite having reached a decision, the division was clear to see.

The chattering voices of the cardinals fell quickly silent at the ringing of a small handbell.

'Could we please return to our seats,' Cardinal Eugene Tisserant, the dean of the sacred college, instructed them as the master of ceremonies and his priests positioned themselves on either side of the papal throne, which sat to the left of Michelangelo's fresco of the Last Judgement. 'When His Holiness returns, each one of us will pay an act of homage and obedience. By kneeling in front of the papal throne we will kiss the tip of his right shoe before embracing him and swearing our fidelity. His Holiness may, at this moment, exchange a few words with you on an individual basis. Once this is complete, His Holiness will then be presented to the people of Rome and the world.'

As Tisserant was still addressing the college, he did not notice that the door to the Room of Tears was opening behind him. Only when the cardinals rose to their feet, did Tisserant turn to look. When he noticed that Pope Gregory was not wearing his pontifical attire but was still clothed in cardinal red, he thought that the issue was nothing more than a minor mishap, but the moment he looked Gregory in the eye he sensed that something was wrong.

'Holy Father, is everything okay?' Tisserant asked, as he walked towards the pope.

Pope Gregory could only shake his head as the cardinals looked on in confusion.

'Do you need some assistance?'

'No!' Gregory said, almost in a whisper. 'I cannot do this.'

'Cannot do what?' Tisserant asked in confusion.

'This!' Gregory replied. 'I cannot do this!' his voice finding its strength. 'I cannot be the pope.'

'But, Your Holiness,' Tisserant said, as he took hold of Gregory's hands. 'It is too late. You have been canonically elected, and you have accepted. You are the pope! This cannot be undone. Come, let us take a private moment to talk.'

In bewilderment, the college looked on as they watched Tisserant try to cajole their newly elected pope to follow him into the Room of Tears. Gone was the confident cardinal they had elected. Instead, they watched a broken man slip away from Tisserant's reassuring grasp as he walked back to his seat.

'I cannot do this,' Gregory explained, holding his hands up as a sign of his rejection. 'You must hold another ballot and elect another pope.'

'This is impossible!' Cardinal Masella the camerlengo, protested as he got up from his seat and walked across the floor to confront the newly elected pope. 'The dean is correct. You have been elected and this cannot be undone. The world is waiting for its new pope, and you must present yourself to them.'

'No!' Gregory replied. 'Electing me was a mistake and my accepting your election was an even greater one. I am not the one called to the throne of Peter.'

'But, you have been called!' Masella pleaded. 'Once you accepted the election, that was the moment you became the pope. That cannot be undone, even by you.'

'I now refuse to accept. There is another man here called to be the pope.'

'I cannot believe what I am hearing!' Masella objected. 'What you are saying is impossible! You are Peter and until you take your last breath you will always be Peter.'

Choosing not to reply, Gregory sat and slowly shook his head while he tensed every muscle in his body to stop himself from shaking with the terror that was consuming him. Despite Masella confronting him with the truth, it was a truth he could no longer face. All he could do was pray for the moment to pass and for his brothers to accept his decision and to move on.

For over an hour, most of the college pleaded with him to rethink his position, but in the end, they knew they were getting nowhere. To bide them time, Tisserant proposed an adjournment for the night and instructed the cardinals to gather once again in the morning.

When they reconvened, Gregory still refused to take up his office, insisting that they continue balloting - and this they did for two more days until they finally accepted a compromise candidate from Venice, Cardinal Angelo Roncalli who took the name John XXIII.

To the world it was announced that a mistake had been made that Sunday evening. No pope had been elected. Due to the vow of secrecy and the threat of excommunication, the truth was hidden for decades. Only whispers emerged over what had happened during that conclave. Whispers that were quickly quenched as smouldering fires of gossip. There was never a Gregory but only a John. Cardinal Emmanuel Siri entered the conclave a cardinal and left as one. The truth was silenced. It was as if it had all been planned.

The crowds who had gathered that Sunday evening in Saint Peter's Square eventually dispersed when it became apparent that no pope was going to appear on the central balcony. Within hours, Vatican radio was correcting its earlier report that a pope had been elected. Now the official line was that the artificial lighting in the square against the darkness of a Roman night had led Vatican observers to believe they were seeing white smoke when in fact it was black. The cardinals had not reached a decision and were still in conclave, and there they would remain until a successor to Pope Pius XII was chosen by the electors.

On the following Wednesday evening, Cardinal Siri paced the vast marbled floor of the Pope's official library, as he nervously waited for his audience. The internal tremor that took hold of him on the Sunday evening still remained, and conscious that it could be seen he kept walking up and down, wishing he was home.

Shortly after seven, a vestibule door opened, and the white rotund figure of Pope John XXIII entered. Immediately, Siri genuflected before him, but John urged him to rise to his feet before inviting him to take a seat at his desk, while the doors were closed and they were left alone.

'I thank you for agreeing to see me this evening,' John said, as he joined his hands and brought his forearms to rest on the desk. 'After what happened on Sunday, I wanted to speak with you in person.'

'Sunday is best forgotten,' Siri replied.

'It cannot be forgotten. You were elected Pope. We all witnessed what happened and now many cardinals believe, deep down in their souls, that it was you and not I who was duly elected. How do we move on?'

'Yes, I was elected, but I also resigned, renounced, refused .... call it what you will, I handed it back as I did not want it. I will never claim it. You are the pope, not I. To you I swear my full allegiance and loyalty.'

Before him John saw the cardinal archbishop of Genoa, but he could not shake off the knowledge that he was in fact looking at Pope Gregory XVII - a true successor of Saint Peter.

'I need to know what happened.' John finally spoke.

'Holy Father, you saw what happened.'

'What I saw was your election, your acceptance of it, your choosing a name before spectacularly renouncing it all. I need to know what happened on Sunday evening. If I am to accept that you freely resigned and if I am free to exercise my Petrine ministry, then I need to know the truth.'

'We are all under the seal of the conclave,' Siri replied. 'Please, forget it and accept that you were called and not I.'

John shook his head. 'Then as the pope I am dispensing you from your oath. I want to know the truth.'

As he sat looking at John, Siri could see the cross that he carried. For three days the Vatican State had been awash with speculation and rumour over the conclave and its election. The cardinals all knew the truth, so too did the master of ceremonies and his priests. Even the Swiss Guards were talking about an incident that had happened in the room of tears. Pope John deserved the truth.

'Before I tell you the truth,' Siri began, as his right hand clutched his pectoral cross, 'I need to state again that you are the pope and that my loyalty is to you. Yes, I was elected, but I must be forgotten. I will tell you what happened, but once you know the truth you must allow me to go back home to serve the people of Genoa.'

'We both desire the peace to move on from this,' John reassured. 'You the peace to leave it behind and I the peace to know that I have been called to take up this office. We owe it to God and to the Church.'

For a moment, Siri gathered himself and his thoughts. Even three days later it was the emotion of fear triggered by the events, rather than the events themselves, that caused him the anguish he was feeling. This would be the one and only time he would ever speak of what happened on the night of his election, and after it was spoken, he swore that he would never mention it again.

'After I had vested, I was left alone by the tailor to spend some time in prayer. Just as I was about to re-enter the Sistine Chapel, a side door to the room opened and a young man entered. He had jet black hair and mesmerising blue eyes, and was dressed in a black tailored suit and tie. At first, I thought he was part of the papal household; a footboy or junior valet sent to assist me. But I soon discovered that he had no purpose being there as he began to remove my pontifical attire.

'I remonstrated with him, told him to stop but he carried on with no emotion whatsoever on his face. Eventually, I managed to push him away and opened the side door to seek assistance from the Swiss Guards who were standing outside. Having asked them to remove him from the room, they entered but they could not see him. That was when I realised that I was dealing with the supernatural and he instructed me to send the guards away so that we could talk.

'He spoke of three things. Three things that left me with no option but to do what I did.' Siri said, before pausing and with a trembling hand lifted a glass of water from the pope's desk and brought it to his mouth to drink before continuing. 'For several minutes he explained to me how the end of the world would come within a few generations, and during that time the Church as we know it would be transformed into something so unrecognisable that it would no longer appear to be the true church of Jesus Christ.'

'When you say supernatural,' John asked, 'are you talking about the heavenly or the demonic?'

'I do not know, and that is what frightens me. He told me that the smoke of Satan is going to enter the Church and destroy it from within, leaving Christians disorientated and attacking the Church and the faith to a point when they will no longer believe. What we see as a witness to the Light will become a place of darkness, and the priesthood betrayed by agents of the evil one who will defile the purest of souls as a humiliation to Christ. In the years to come, scandal will follow scandal. Prayer as we know it will be abandoned and our doctrines and dogmas will be called into question, and attempts will be made to reconstruct what we know as truth. Our Church is going to fall into such a disgrace that it will be trampled upon, and the faithful will no longer believe in her but doubt her every utterance and movement. Sacramental rites will be changed to a point where people will no longer feel the need to seek confession, where they will doubt the real presence in the eucharist, where the priesthood will be questioned and ridiculed, and where the most unspeakable of crimes will be carried out upon the most vulnerable by those entrusted to shepherd and guide them. Even our altars will be ripped from the walls and used to curb carparks while we make our churches unrecognisable.'

In silence, John leaned back in his chair as he continued to listen.

'I can see the disappointment in your eyes,' Siri said. 'Afterall, a shepherd should never abandon his sheep. But, when my family was threatened, when I was told that not only my life would end but that of my nephews and nieces, and that there would be a great persecution against the church behind the Iron Curtain, then I truly believed that a huge mistake had been made in electing me. Who was I to believe that I could assume the role of Peter, for I am a mere peasant of Genoa?

'Then he whispered into my ear a secret from my past that no one knew,' Siri confided, as he lowered his head in shame. 'I will not tell you the details of that indiscretion, for I confessed it long ago, but I knew, no matter who he was, that he had a power against which I could not stand. I am not the one called to lead the Church. I do not have the strength to defend it. I cannot allow my family to suffer. I am unable to carry all this and the church on my shoulders, and that is why I have renounced it all. It would have been too dangerous for everyone concerned.'

For a few moments they sat in silence as the truth slowly settled within their hearts.

'I thank you for telling me,' John finally spoke, as he rose from his chair and stretched out his right hand for Siri to venerate his fisherman's ring. 'You are once again under the seal of the conclave. You will not speak of this to anyone. You will return to Genoa as a cardinal. There you will serve your people as you have requested. Go in peace.'

As Cardinal Siri left the library, Pope John sat back down in his chair and for the first time questioned the direction he was personally hoping to lead the church, especially in light of what he had just been told.

2.

Monday, 28th August.

The Vatican's Keeper of the Keys, known as the Clavigero, awoke at five in the morning. Silencing his alarm, he felt the stiffness in his body, the burning dryness in his throat and a pulsating headache that he had been unable to shift for days. Sitting on the edge of his bed, he took a moment to gather himself and wondered why he was still going about his daily routine as if nothing had changed. Since no one had told him to cease, or to leave the Vatican, he had decided to continue with the same duties that his predecessors had performed for hundreds of years.

Getting up from his bed, he walked across the bedroom and switched on the light; thankful that electricity within the Vatican State was still working. Steadying himself, by placing his hand against the door, he tried to catch a breath, but all he could taste was the sulphur and smell the nauseating burning which lingered permanently in the air. He wanted to return to his bed, but he pressed on with his morning routine which involved him showering, grooming as best he could, before dressing in his black suit and red tie that bore the crossed golden keys of the state.

In his kitchen he cut open an orange which he had chilled overnight in the fridge, and as he ate the segments, he relished the sweet taste that he once took for granted. Then, from a filtered jug, he poured himself a glass of water. Although it looked fine, he knew that the water now tasted sour, but he had to drink it if he wanted to continue living. Taking a slow deep breath, he brought the glass to his mouth and drank it as quickly as he could. Every reflex in his body urged him to spit the water out, to throw the glass away, but it was all he had, and he forced himself to drink it before biting into another segment of orange to remove the tarnished aftertaste that water now left. And as the sweetness of the orange took effect, he felt grateful for he knew that hundreds of millions were enduring a horror that he hoped would never come to visit him.

At five-twenty, he left his residence, close to the northern perimeter wall of the state, and stepped out into the darkness which had lasted eight days. Immediately, he found himself coughing in the toxic air, and he brought a handkerchief to his face to ease the burning sensation in his throat. As quickly as he could, he began to walk the short distance across the gardens towards the staff entrance of the museums. No one was there; no clergy going about their morning routine or any visible security presence, for they had all gone. The Vatican was dead.

Once inside the staff entrance, he closed the door behind him and tried to breathe as easily as he could, but it was difficult, and he found himself coughing as his body fought to expel the toxins he had breathed in. In the initial days following the impact, the air inside the museums, which was controlled through filters and humidifiers to protect the precious artwork, had offered him and his staff some welcomed relief. But now, the systems were struggling to function and there was no one left to maintain them.

As the door behind him opened, he acknowledged his two deputies with a compassionate smile, as they too were suffering and struggling to breathe. The effect of the aftermath was taking its toll on everyone.

Unable to make conversation, the Clavigero took a chained key from his trouser pocket and opened a steel door before standing back to allow his deputies to enter. Then after locking the door behind him, he followed them down a narrow, cast-iron staircase, into the basement level of the museums where his office was located.

Unlocking a second steel door, he stepped into a vault to remove several large rings of keys which he placed on the table for his deputies to organise. In all, he handed them ten rings which held the one thousand and ninety-seven keys they would need for opening the doors to the most precious art collection in the world.

As his deputies sorted the rings, for the familiar route they had taken every morning, he stepped back into the vault and went over to a small electronic safe, keyed in the code, opened it, and removed a set of two keys on a single ring, before placing them into the inner pocket of his jacket.

After locking the steel door, he lifted the three rings he required, and after following his deputies back up the staircase, they set off to open the rooms of the Vatican museums.

Walking the contours of history, they ascended the Bramante staircase to walk their two-mile route through the museums, opening the gallery of maps, the hall of the animals, the sala rotunda with its intricate mosaic floors, the gallery of statues, the hall of busts and the magnificent Raphael rooms.

From the moment he first walked the route, some twenty years ago, the Clavigero lived for the history and the art that adorned the sacred walls. Even today, despite the sickness he felt and knowing that no one would visit, he walked with his deputies past the shadows of Caravaggio, Michelangelo, Raphael, Bernini and the masters. Each one was his gift in the morning as he carried the keys which were worn by the passage of time.

Finally, they arrived at a small, seemingly insignificant door, and after handing his keys to his deputies, he reached into his jacket pocket, removed the two keys, unlocked the door with one of them and entered the room of tears. As the Clavigero walked across the room to the small electrical key box on the wall, he inserted the second key but stopped short of turning it.

'I want to do something I have never done before,' he spoke for the first time that morning. 'I want to enter by myself in the darkness, and once inside I want one of you to turn the key so I can see the chapel come to life.'

Taking a small torch from his pocket, he unlocked the final door of their morning route and entered the chapel. He knew that the natural morning light of Rome should have been shining through the windows, but daylight was no more. So, carefully he walked across the marbled floor, past the high altar and descended the three sanctuary steps until he found himself standing in the middle of the chapel. Switching off his torch he looked up into the darkness and waited.

This was something he had always wanted to do, but protocol meant that he always had to be escorted by one of his deputies. Now that everything had changed, he knew that protocol no longer had a place. He took a deep breath as the lights came on and the splendour of Michelangelo's Sistine Chapel came to life. Alone, he gazed high into its magnificence with wonder and awe, and as he lifted his hands towards the heavens, he wished he could touch Adam and the Creator. Turning on the spot he breathed deeply as his eyes followed the glory of Genesis; the creation of light and darkness, the sun and the planets, the dividing of the waters from the earth, the creation of Adam and Eve, the great flood and Noah's sacrifice upon his survival, all watched on by the great prophets of the Old Testament. For the Clavigero no other work on earth, touched by the hand of mankind, equalled the majesty of what he was seeing.

Staring into the beginning of creation, he knew now that the world was heading towards its end. And as he allowed his eyes to wander the length of the ceiling towards the imposing fresco of the last judgement, he became afraid when he saw, standing at the altar and watching him, the living presence which had revealed himself to the world.

'Hello, Raimondo,' Lucifer spoke.

Falling to his knees, Raimondo called out. 'Holiness!'

'Holiness?' Lucifer questioned, as he walked towards him.

'Forgive me,' Raimondo replied, lowering himself further to the floor. 'I was just so used to calling you by that name before you revealed yourself.'

'Please, stand up,' Lucifer said, as he stood before him, his flesh radiating a gentle light. 'Do you do this every morning?'

'No! My lord, this is the first.'

'I see,' Lucifer said, placing a hand onto his shoulder. 'Tell me what you think when you see all this?'

Looking deep into the eyes of the lord, Raimondo could not believe that he was speaking to the one who had returned, and that he was being asked for his opinion from the divine.

'I do not have the words for what I see,' he spoke humbly. 'For what I see is beyond the very movement of my soul.'

'It is a sight like no other,' Lucifer said, as he turned to stand alongside him and gaze upon the fresco of the last judgement. 'You can smell the essence of human history in this very chapel. From the beginning of creation, the river of history has been leading to this point in time. The more you gaze upon it, the more you come to realise that Michelangelo has expressed the mystery of the invisible. It must be the greatest accomplishment of human civilisation.'

In his moment of privilege, Raimondo could sense his deputies opening the door to enter the chapel, but the moment they saw them talking, his deputies left them both alone and closed the door.

'Look right above you,' Lucifer directed. 'What do you see?'

Seeing the famous fresco of God's creation of Adam, their fingers almost touching, Raimondo replied. 'The first moment in history, the creation of Adam.'

'Is that what you really believe?' Lucifer asked, as he turned to look at him with his piercing blue eyes.

'Yes, my lord.'

'It never happened,' Lucifer replied, with a smile. 'Adam never existed. Neither did Eve, nor the serpent, not even the flood. Allegory, parable, myth, call it what you like. This is not how it all began.'

Although surprised by the reply, Raimondo had no cause to doubt what he was being told.

'Michelangelo was a true artist,' Lucifer continued. 'Look at God the Father, can you see what he is resting on?'

'The human brain,' Raimondo replied.

'Yes. The human brain, because it is the one gift needed to discover truth and yet, with this gift humanity has tried to shape the divine into a human form so they can touch it, approach it, and try to understand it. Can I tell you something?'

Raimondo nodded.

'Humanity will never come to comprehend the divine, for human understanding is less than a droplet of water from the world's oceans. So, tell me, what is the point of it all?'

Raimondo felt confused. 'Beauty, a way for the soul to transcend to the divine.'

Lucifer shook his head. 'It is all a folly. This morning you have been given a privilege no one will ever experience again.'

As he listened, Raimondo felt something brush against the side of his head. Looking up he saw the frescos beginning to fade and turn to dust as they fell gently towards the ground. Horrified at what was happening, he turned to the scene of the last judgement and watched as it crumbled and fell around the altar, not in a cloud of dust and ash, but like fine grains of sand. All around him it fell, covering his hair and suit. Reaching out, he collected a handful of what remained before it too disappeared between his fingers. He turned to seek an answer from his lord, but he was gone. Looking back up to the ceiling, he saw only the red bricked vaults of the roof that were now exposed.

'Matteo! Lorenzo!' he cried out, summoning his deputies into the chapel where they stood in horror; the fresco grains trodden under their feet as they looked upon the Clavigero as he stood alone in the middle of what was once the greatest treasure on earth. No words were spoken for the time they remained, as they gazed upon nothing and remembered everything that was lost.

It was only when they retraced their steps back through the museums, that they discovered that every treasure, whether made from stone or precious jewels, the finest paintings to the greatest works of literature, everything had been turned to dust. Nothing remained except the empty shell of the Vatican.

By the time they returned to Raimondo's office they knew that their tenure had come to an end. Without even closing the door behind them, they stepped back out into the darkness of the Vatican gardens and once again breathed in the toxic air.

3.

Monday, 23rd October.

At a quarter past six that evening, Dave Mode decided to get out of bed. Such were his days that it was easier to sleep than to face the horror of what was happening on the streets of the Eternal City. Yet, to survive he knew he had to face the horror from time to time. Although he felt safe inside the apartment and protected with his small hoard of guns and ammunition, like everyone else he needed to source enough food to keep going. Despite living next to the Vatican and having the sweet bread readily available, it simply was not enough to survive.

Sitting on the edge of his bed, he could hear the wailing cries of the desperate who swelled Saint Peter's Square begging for their lord to feed them; crying out for their sufferings to be eased while trying to stave off the sting of death which followed them. In the darkness of his bedroom, he reached over to his bedside cabinet and struck a match to light a small candle; allowing the light to overcome the darkness that protected him.

Slowly, he dressed and went into the sitting room to open the Meilink vault safe. Gazing at the bundled euro notes, which were now worthless as currency, he knew that his financial resources were quickly running out. To the right of the notes sat four small transparent plastic boxes, containing the remaining gold coins he had gathered in recent years, having pre-empted that they would be the only worthwhile currency in times to come. They were coins he had bought with the money he had been paid by Guarducci when he worked for him, coins taken from vaults within the Vatican State and coins he had stolen from others less fortunate than himself. In all, the four boxes contained over two hundred gold coins of various monetary value. Several months ago, he believed he had enough to last him years, but even gold was quickly depreciating in value, and he feared that it too would soon become worthless. Opening the top box, he took out a 1950's one-hundred lire gold coin with the minted head of Pius XII. It was a coin that had cost him over a thousand euros, but he knew it was now worth only a fraction of that price.

Hearing the rising roar from the square below, he paused before closing the safe and placing the coin into a pocket of his jeans. He waited for the roar to settle to a mighty hush before the booming voice of the lord echoed across the city as he addressed the people who had gathered. The first night the lord had appeared on the balcony of Saint Peter's, the night after Wormwood had collided with the earth, was the only time Mode could stomach to watch. From that night, every shutter in the apartment that overlooked the square was closed, and the nightly address to the people proved to be the perfect opportunity to leave the apartment. So, putting on his navy Barbour jacket, he slipped a Glock pistol into the waistband of his jeans before lifting a small backpack. Once on the stairwell, he could smell the scent of putrescine that had become the norm. Every instinct urged him to go back inside, but he knew he had to go out to get what he needed. Locking the door to his apartment he descended the stairwell, checked that the main door to the complex was secure before slipping out a rear entrance and into the private courtyard that he shared with the other residents he had yet to encounter in his whole time living there. In fact, Mode was convinced that no one else was residing in the building and with its proximity to the Vatican and with its discreet entrance, despite the hundreds of thousands who flocked to see the lord every day, no one seemed to be aware that it was a residential building.

Under a small archway he unlocked a tall metal gate and cautiously made his way out onto the Via dei Corridori. The putrid smell of death was overpowering as he gently closed the gate and locked it, before turning around and seeing the horrific sight of hundreds of corpses abandoned along the street; their heads resting on the curbs while their lifeless and decaying faces gazed into nothingness. They were the corpses of the dead pilgrims which had been removed from Saint Peter's Square. Hundreds of them every day were laid out on the side streets around the Vatican to be collected, but no one collected them anymore. At first the bodies were removed in refrigerated lorries, but now the lorries lay abandoned with their human cargo rotting away inside. Gagging in reflex, Mode stepped over the bodies to begin his now familiar journey, knowing that it was not the sight of death that turned him but the stench of it.

Towards the Via del Corso he made his way, passing corpses of all ages, some dressed and some stripped naked. The further he walked from the Vatican the more repugnant the sights and the smells became. Soon the rancid corpses appeared in piles, having been stacked days ago for disposal, but when it became evident that no one would be collecting them, the dead remained close to where they fell. In some streets, bodies were piled five to six high in open wooden crates; some with their eyes shut, others with their eyes opened but all with gaping mouths that were infested with flies as maggots began to devour.

With his head down he walked on, trying to ignore the gorging rats and even the stray dog that was tearing the flesh from the face of a young girl that no one had claimed. The Rome he had known now felt and smelled like it had been swallowed by the pit of a warm wet dog that was rotting in the earth. Yet, instead of fleeing the city, the people had no choice but to remain. There was nowhere else for them to go. And while the Roman's stayed, hundreds of thousands descended on the city to see their lord face to face, and to be fed on his word and the sweet bread that he gave to them freely to nourish their bodies. In faith they had come seeking the way of truth and life, but for Mode all he could see, taste and smell was death and decay.

In the eyes of the living that passed him, heading to the Vatican to collect their daily sweet bread, he saw nothing but fear and a desperate anxiety to save themselves from death. He knew he was no different to them, but he controlled it as best he could. His means for survival was to hold up in the apartment and to source food wherever he could. Like the others he owed nothing to his neighbour. The purpose of life was now about the survival of the self.

He had the journey timed to thirty minutes. The only thirty minutes each day when he felt it was safe to leave the apartment whilst the masses were entranced by their lord and queuing to collect their daily offering of bread. Yet, each time he ventured out, he knew there was a risk involved. To date no one had accosted him on the streets. No doubt his frame and build intimidated them, so they left him alone to go about his business. Others, however, were not so fortunate. He had seen people shot for a loaf of sweet bread, others mugged and kicked to death for their clothing. Two days previously he had witnessed an elderly woman dragged down into the corpses by a youth who wrestled a small bag containing what little food she had from her hands. Mode was tempted to intervene, but when the youth produced a knife and slit her throat, Mode ignored the situation. The shame of not helping the woman, even in challenging her murderer, lasted only a fleeting moment. Life was now too precious to allow such emotions to occupy one's thoughts. The young man was hungry, and like himself, Mode knew he was taking whatever measures he could to get through another day.

Along the narrow footpaths of the Via del Corso, he navigated his way past the corpses until he reached the order house beside the church of San Marcello. Six times he knocked on the door before knocking it three more times. Almost immediately the bolts of the door were unlocked from the inside, and the door was opened to reveal the familiar face of the Servite prior who recognised him and allowed him to enter unchallenged.

Entering the room to his right, Mode's heart sank when he saw that the rations were becoming fewer. Less than a week ago the old bookshelves of the library were filled with supplies, but today very little remained.

'Is that all you have?' Mode asked the Servite priest who stood in the middle of the room; his black cassock stained more than it was yesterday, as a musty smell of sweat caught the air and managed to cut through the stench of decay.

'We were hoping that some supplies would have reached us yesterday,' the priest explained, forcing an exaggerated sigh, 'but they cannot get into the city with all the bodies on the streets. Maybe tomorrow we will have more, but who knows?'

'So, what do you have?'

'No, my friend,' corrected the priest. 'What do you have for us?'

Reaching into his pocket, Mode took out the gold coin and handed it over to the priest who inspected it closely.

'I know it has lost a little value,' Mode said, in the hope of influencing the priest's appraisal, 'but that coin did cost me over a thousand euros.'

'Irrelevant now,' the priest replied dismissively. 'Like I told you the last time you were here, the price of gold has fallen against the rising price of goods. This coin is only worth the weight of its gold, not its history for no one is collecting this stuff anymore. I can offer you a bag of dried pasta, some basil pesto and a little cheese.'

Mode held back from responding in the hope that he would offer him a little more, but the priest just stood there and stared at him.

'That is not enough for that coin,' Mode finally spoke. 'I will not be made to look like a fool. Give it back to me.'

'Wait, wait, wait!' the priest pressed, clutching the coin tightly in his right hand. 'Maybe we could add something more. Afterall, we both need each other to survive.'

'Ever since the people lost their need for the priesthood and turned to their newly found lord, you have needed people like me much more. There are many religious houses throughout Rome operating the same scam as you are running here. I bet if I was to offer that coin to another order I would get more. We had an agreement that my coming here would see to it that I would be looked after. So, make the deal worth my while or you and I will part ways for good.'

The priest knew he was pushing Mode too hard. While others came and bartered their goods for food, Mode always came with gold. On the black markets of Rome, gold got a lot more than works of art or worn jewels on their chains.

'I apologise,' the priest finally said, reaching out his hand. 'Forgive me.'

Mode said nothing as he handed over his backpack to the priest, who opened it and walked over to the shelves. Into the bag he placed two bags of dried pasta shells, a jar of pesto, a small block of parmesan, two tins of canned beef, some small onions, a loaf of bread, several ounces of wrapped butter and a few portioned packets of strawberry jam. Then kneeling behind the table, he lifted a bottle of red wine.

'I want three,' Mode stated.

'The best I can do is two,' the priest insisted.

Not believing him, Mode walked around the table and saw several dozen bottles of red wine and bottles of cognac. Grabbing the bag from the priest, Mode put three bottles of the red wine and a bottle of the cognac into it.

'When I come back here,' he said, as he zipped up the bag, 'don't ever treat me like this again.'

The priest dared not to argue, for he knew Mode's history. And even as Mode took a second bottle of cognac to carry home in his hand, he remained silent knowing that the community were still making a profit from the gold.

Back on the street, Mode slung the backpack over his right shoulder and held the bottle of brandy tightly in his left hand. Hearing the door of the order house being bolted shut, he looked up and down the Via del Corso, calculating the risk, the route home, and the time it would take. It was already ten minutes to seven, and Mode always liked to be back home in the apartment before the hour. Turning right he began to retrace his steps back to the safety of what he called home.

The putrid stench still lingered with every step he took. The dog was still gnawing at the young girl's corpse. The rats had the run of the city's streets. The flies buzzed around him, and one even flew into his mouth. Horror was everywhere. The only safe place in the city was to get home and to close the apartment door behind him.

Turning off the Via del Corso, he noticed two young men walking towards him. Like himself, they kept their heads down appearing to go about their business, but when one of them glanced up and saw the bottle of brandy Mode was carrying, he instinctively felt the need to turn on him.

'Don't even think about it!' Mode snapped, taking the Glock from his jeans, surprising them both.

'Okay,' the young man with the greedy eye replied, as he backed away with his hands in the air. 'We are good, yes?'

'Fuck off!' Mode insisted, pushing the pistol closer to their faces, forcing them to run away from him.

Mode slipped the Glock back into his waistband and was just about to go on his way when he heard a faint voice call out his name. He stopped and listened. Again, he heard a gentle voice call out his name. Following its direction, he turned and looked behind him. In a darkened doorway of an abandoned restaurant, he was barely able to make out the huddled figure that was wrapped in a dirty and torn blanket. He took a step closer once he saw the hand of a weakened man reach out for help.

'Is that you Dave?' the man asked.

Peering through the darkness, Mode studied the face that slowly came into view. Momentarily distracted by the jeering of the people gathered at the Vatican, he looked closer at the face that was familiar but which he struggled to place.

'Please, help me!'

Stepping closer for one final look, he finally saw past the dirt, grime, and the facial hair to recognise the man who was seeking his help. 'Eminence?'

'Yes,' Oliveri replied.

Stepping back, Mode looked up and down the street. At first, he was surprised, but soon he felt angered that he was now having to deal with this on top of everything else. After a quick glance at his watch, he made up his mind to have nothing to do with the cardinal. He owed Oliveri nothing. He was just about to turn and walk away when Oliveri uttered some words that made him stop.

'I think I know how to get us out of this, but I will need someone like you to protect me.'

'And why should I do that?' Mode asked.

'Because you know that time is running out for Rome.'

'You don't know shit,' Mode said, about to walk away.

'Then how come you are clearly not eating the sweet bread?' Oliveri asked, noticing the bottle of cognac in Mode's hand. 'Why are you dealing with the black market when the sweet bread is free?'

Mode once more scanned the street before looking Oliveri in the eye. 'Do you not believe in him either?'

Oliveri nervously shook his head.

With little time to spare, Mode weighed up the consequences of walking away or helping the fallen cardinal. On his own he could cope for a while longer, and in relative safety. Agreeing to help would see what little resources he had left diminish a lot quicker than they currently were. He worked best alone, always had. But, as he gazed upon the cardinal, it was not pity he felt for him but the feeling that he could possibly be of some use.

'I bet you concede to the same truth in your heart as I do,' Oliveri continued. 'There is no life coming from him, only death. Those who eat of his bread, perish and are forgotten. If you believe that, then there must be others in Rome who believe it too. Whatever happens in the coming days, never mind weeks, people are going to need each other. No one can survive this alone.'

Mode felt pressed to decide, hating the fact that time was against him.

'Can you walk?'

'Yes,' Oliveri replied.

'Then come with me,' Mode instructed. 'But let's be clear, I am agreeing to nothing until I hear what it is you've got to say.'

4.

Oliveri felt a slight rise in fear as Mode led him towards the Vatican. Since his expulsion from the state by the lord, Oliveri was afraid to attend the nightly vigils and to collect his share of the bread. Having noticed that the people who ate the bread were falling ill and dying, he chose instead to scavage for whatever food he could find. At first, he was able to rely on the late Cardinal Boyer's valet to look after him in the cardinal's apartment. But after the valet was stabbed whilst out in search of food, Oliveri could only manage to bunker down for a few days in the apartment before hunger drove him to leave the security of the palatial residence. This he managed to do twice until he was followed back to the apartment by a German family who attacked him in the doorway, took possession of his keys and evicted him. With nowhere to go and with no one to turn to, he hid amongst the city's dead in his battle to survive.

Reaching a small archway, Oliveri looked up to the keystone as Mode unlocked the metal gate. Through the darkness he struggled to make out the exact detail, but he noticed that the chiselled crest was papal in design, as to which pope he could not be sure, but he knew that the property he was entering was owned by the Vatican. The fact that Mode lived here, in such a property, did not surprise him in the least.

They just about made it into the courtyard before the pilgrims began to walk past the gate, singing hymns of praise to the lord and ripping apart the sweet bread to sedate their hunger for the long night they would face. The pilgrims terrified Oliveri. Despite having come to seek salvation and healing from their lord, they filled the city with terror and with such a raw ugliness of spirit, that even the darkness struggled to hide the wickedness that had taken hold of them.

'You'll be safe here,' Mode said reassuringly, sensing the tension in Oliveri. 'Watch your footing, there are no lights inside the building.'

Staying close behind him, Oliveri followed him through a rear entrance and up a spiral stone stairwell to the fourth floor, where Mode unlocked a door to an apartment but did not enter right away. Instead, he sat the brandy and his backpack onto the floor of the landing and began to remove his coat.

'You need to strip,' Mode said to Oliveri, who looked horrified at the idea. 'There's no one else in the apartment block and I don't want the smell of death to be carried inside.'

Hesitantly, Oliveri began to remove his tattered coat and then his black clerical shirt, which he had not changed in God knows how long. Not since his teenage years, when changing for sports in school, had he stripped naked before another human being.

'There's no point washing your clothes,' Mode said, as he stripped. 'Across from you there is a waste disposal hatch, put everything in there and we'll get you sorted once we're inside.'

'Even my shoes?'

'What size are you?'

'Eleven.'

'Then get rid of them too.'

Only when he had removed his underwear did Oliveri gather his clothes and make his way over to the hatch. As he was doing so, he sensed Mode lighting a candle behind him in the hallway of the apartment block. More embarrassed than humiliated, Oliveri disposed of his earthly belongings, and with his hands covering what dignity he had left, he entered the apartment.

'I want you to shower,' Mode said, as he stood naked in the doorway holding the candle. 'The water's not warm and it reeks, but it's better than the stench of death. You'll find soap and towels in there too. Make sure you wash yourself well. I'll use the shower next to the bedroom.'

'Thank you,' Oliveri replied, as he took the candle from Mode and carried it into the bathroom.

After the initial shock of the tepid water touching his naked flesh, Oliveri soon found himself standing under the showerhead in relief as the water washed over him and rinsed the dirt and grime into a blackish pool around his feet. The bitterness of the water against his lips did not detract from the humanity of the moment. And as he prayed in gratitude, he began to weep, for at least tonight he would not be sleeping on the streets alongside the dead.

He could have spent a lot longer in the shower than he did, but as a guest he wanted to respect the boundaries of his invite. Having scrubbed every inch of his body with the bar of soap and having washed his hair three times, he stepped out and dried himself while looking at his dishevelled appearance in the mirror. Although he was only seventy, the toll of recent weeks had aged him by at least ten years, and his white facial hair did not help.

The door to the bathroom was knocked, forcing Oliveri to wrap the towel around his waist before he opened it to find Dave Mode showered and changed into a fresh polo-shirt and jeans.

'These should fit you,' Mode said, handing over to Oliveri a white t-shirt and a pair of black knee-length shorts. 'They'll do for this evening. We can sort you out tomorrow. You want a razor?'

Oliveri thought about it for a moment: 'Probably best to keep it. I could use a comb if you have one?'

'I don't. You'll have to rough it. If you want something to eat, then come into the kitchen. Bring the candle with you.'

Thanking him, Oliveri dressed quickly, and taking his only source of light with him, he cautiously walked down the hallway towards the end room from where the flickering light emanated. Entering the kitchen, Oliveri sat at the small table beside the shuttered windows as he watched Mode chop some onions while something boiled in a larger pot on the stove. Having not eaten for many days, he felt the pangs of hunger, which had been subdued out of necessity, starting to return.

'Is there anything you would like me to do?' Oliveri asked.

'Set the table,' Mode replied. 'Plates and glasses are above the sink, and you'll find a corkscrew in the top drawer. There's some wine in the backpack, open one of the bottles.'

The simple ritual of partaking in a meal was something Oliveri had never fully appreciated until that moment. Weeks of foraging amongst the dead before accepting the situation of hunger, made this moment even more blessed. Opening the wine, a cheap bottle by the standards he had been accustomed to in the Vatican as a prince of the Church, he brought the cork to his nose, its oaky smell reminding him of a pleasure he had once taken for granted. Closing his eyes, he inhaled slowly and forgetting everything that was happening around him, he focussed those few moments on the pleasure of the wine.

'Should I pour some water?' Oliveri asked, setting the opened bottle of red onto the middle of the table.

'Not tonight,' Mode replied, as he opened a tin of the beef and mixed it into the onions he was frying in a little butter. 'I can just about force myself to drink a glass or two in the morning. For dinner I stick to wine. I cook as best I can with what little I have, so I'm sure as hell not going to destroy my cooking with a glass of rancid water.'

'In the days of the black plague those who drank the water died, whilst those who drank the beers and the ales tended to survive.'

'There you go,' Mode said, opening one of the cupboards to get some salt and pepper along with what little dried oregano he had left. 'Ever since the impact I have fended for myself, limiting my water intake and avoiding the free bread they are handing out to those fools gathered in the square below.'

'I take it, with all the windows and shutters closed, you cannot bring yourself to watch what is going on?'

'Correct,' Mode replied, stirring the seasoning into the beef. 'Plus, I want to keep the stench of death outside as best I can. Thankfully, they are still removing the bodies from the square and taking them off to the side streets, but the smell still permeates everywhere. Until I work out what to do next, it's best to bunker down.'

Their meal was simple; the sweated onions mixed with half a can of the stewed beef and some pesto, tossed through the boiled pasta shells, and topped with a few flakes of the parmesan that had been shaved with a knife. Having no other option but to boil the pasta with the rancid water, Mode covered the two servings with a large serving of salt and pepper. Then after cutting some bread, he brought the plates to the table where they both ate in silence.

Hunger forced Oliveri to ignore the metallic taste of the pasta, and after each mouthful he followed Mode in sipping some wine to cleanse his palate. Whether it was the wine or the hunger, but after a few mouthfuls all revulsion lessened and the meal became more edible, and nothing was left on their plates.

As Mode refilled their glasses, Oliveri felt obliged to lift both their plates and carry them over to the sink, which he filled with water to let them steep.

'So, what are you going to do now?' Mode asked, bringing his glass of wine to his lips.

'I hope to get as far from Rome as I can,' Oliveri replied.

'Good luck with that,' Mode jested, before giving him a quizzical look. 'Where? No matter how bad it is here it must be worse the further away from the city you go. Is that not the reason why all these people are flocking here?'

'Time is short and ...' Oliveri began to answer before he noticed the framed photographs stacked in the corner of the kitchen. From each one, a face from his haunted past looked back at him. Reaching down, he lifted two of the frames and felt his mouth go dry as he looked at the first image of Gustave Hasler preaching at the grotto in Lourdes and then at the second as he stood beside a smiling Pope Clement. 'Is this Monsignor Hasler's apartment we are in?'

'It was,' Mode replied. 'I moved in a few days after I killed him.'

Oliveri glanced him a look of incredulity.

'Don't judge,' Mode spoke firmly. 'You supped from the same poisonous chalice. The only difference between us is that I was the one who pulled the trigger while you convinced yourself that your hands were clean.'

Forced to remember his past, Oliveri returned his gaze to the pictures.

'On the orders of your former boss, Cardinal Guarducci,' Mode continued. 'Remember the day of the terrorist attack? It was all directed by him. At least Hasler's end was quick, all carried out in a few moments with little suffering. Just like the imposter, I ended his life as painlessly as I could. But, as for that American cardinal, well that should have been a sign for me to walk away, but I was in too deep, and everything was beginning to unravel fast.'

'Cardinal Brenard?' Oliveri asked, just about able to utter his name.

'Yes. I took his life too. An act of mercy if you ask me. Whatever Guarducci did to him before I ended it, I will never know, but I heard the screams of agony and believe me when I say this, I have never heard anything like it.'

'Please, I don't want to hear any more.'

'Typical of the clerical elite. You never want to hear anything that might shine the light of truth onto your conscience. But, believe me old man, your hands might have looked clean, but your soul is stained not only with the blood of these men, but also your brother cardinals I was forced to poison. What about the many who had to be silenced to conceal your conspiracy? The millions who have died from nuclear attacks and those who remain languishing on whatever remains of this God forsaken earth? You started this. That's right, you started this. The moment you agreed to conspire was the moment you sold your soul, and for what price?'

As he listened, Oliveri felt a swell of emotion rise within him.

'And what was it all for? Your church? Control and power?' Mode pressed on. 'It wasn't for the truth, that's for sure. I don't even know what the truth is anymore. There was a time when I did. A time when the enemy was a dark enemy that needed to be destroyed. It was black and white, with no grey areas. But the moment I became involved with the Vatican, directed by you men of God, that was the moment my soul was lost. I honestly don't know what truth is anymore. For all I see, all I breathe and all that consumes me is a toxic darkness. You men of light have infected this world with your darkness. So don't stand there in self-pity.'

'I know that now,' Oliveri managed to say through a veil of tears. 'God, how I know that now!'

'One of the reasons I never believed was that I always knew that religion was flawed, and don't say to me that it's flawed because man is flawed. It goes deeper than that. When I looked to men like you, I saw everything but truth. You preached it eloquently, but I always saw through the words. Yet, I really had no idea how dark your world really was until I was sucked in. Even when I was in the middle of it, I couldn't fully see. I felt as if what I was doing was for the better good of the world. I don't know what I ultimately hoped for. Maybe just to survive the aftermath of my nation's demise. But as I sit here with you, I know one thing – religion has destroyed everything that was good.'

Oliveri slowly shook his head. 'That is not true!' he replied, setting the photo frames back down before returning to the table. 'I agree with most of what you have said, but not that.'

Mode chose not to respond, only to sip on his wine and to listen.

'All I ever wanted was to become a priest,' Oliveri said, wiping tears from his eyes. 'A simple parish priest who loved his people, who walked with them through the joys and sorrows of life, and to have become a man of holiness. In the village where I grew up there was a priest like that, Father Francisco Valente. Every time he came to our home, my mother always fed him two boiled eggs and two slices of buttered bread. He always gave me the tops of his eggs and insisted that I sprinkled them with a little salt of the earth. He spent his mornings walking the grounds of the church praying his breviary and rosary, as he believed it was important for the people going to work to see their priest praying. He would offer the holy mass with such conviction that peasant farmers would travel from neighbouring towns and villages just to be in his presence. Yet, what he was most remembered for was his charism of spending hours with the dying and guiding them from this world to the next. He was there when my own father died. I was a teenager at the time, and my father was only in his mid-thirties. An aggressive brain cancer took hold of him and turned such a beautiful man into one filled with anger and frustration. Yet, every night Father Valente would come, sit by his bed, take hold of his right hand and comfort him in his agony. One night, as I stood by the door watching, I heard my father ask why God was allowing him and his family to suffer in this way. I will never forget the response the priest gave to my father – "because this is truth."'

Oliveri paused and carefully studied Mode. 'Do you know what he meant?'

Mode shook his head, as he bit gently on his lower lip.

'Truth cannot be denied,' Oliveri replied. 'We can disguise it, turn from it, and even try to run from it. But truth cannot be stopped. Just like Pontius Pilate asked Christ on the day of his crucifixion, "What is truth?" It is the question we have always wanted to know the answer to. That is all I ever wanted to bring to the people of this world through my priesthood. But as I ascended through the ranks of the Church, I lost sight of the truth whilst believing I possessed it, and as a man of power I convinced myself that I was a custodian of it and therefore able to control it.'

For a few moments they both sat in silence, whilst Mode watched Oliveri drink a mouthful of wine.

'Did you ever work out the answer?'

'What is truth?'

'Yes.'

Oliveri shrugged his shoulders. 'From the moment my father was given that reply, he became at peace as he surrendered himself to that which we cannot see, yet in the very depths of our being we know to be true. He was never destined to make old bones; his life was to be short but the moment his soul surrendered to the truth was the moment he became free to let go.' Oliveri raised his right hand to show Mode the healing wound where his microchip had once been implanted. 'I was led from the truth a long time ago, but now I know where it rests.'

'Did you remove it?'

'Yes, at Cardinal Boyer's apartment. I always had my fears about this from the moment Cardinal Guarducci suggested it. I should have known then that I was working under a great darkness, but fear had crucified my conscience.'

As their conversation paused, they both became aware of the now familiar screams and whistling wind that came from outside. Every night the sound terrified Mode, and it was the reason why he always had to be back in the apartment. The howling screams came from all around the city and lasted all but a few minutes before they faded away.

'Do you know what that is?'

Oliveri shook his head. 'But I've seen their shadows. Whatever they are, they are not something that I wish to meet face to face.'

'Are these shadows the reason why you want to leave Rome?'

'They are a reason, but not the primary one,' Oliveri replied. 'Soon, Rome will no longer be standing. The end is coming but it will not be happening here in Rome.'

'How do you know that?'

'We all know that. We have always known. There can be no denying that we are in the final throws of the end of days, and the worst has yet to be revealed. This is the time to find the only truth that will lead us from this life to the next. Have no doubt we are all going to be passing from this earth, but to where we are going after that, well that all depends on what we do next.'

'And you think there is hope for both you and I?'

Oliveri nodded. 'Until our dying breath there is always hope. The choice is clear. We only need to look at what is happening around us to see that Satan has been unleashed upon the world. That out there...' Oliveri stated with conviction, as he pointed towards the closed windows, 'is not of God. That is death and all who feed from its hand will rot, not just physically on the streets of Rome and throughout the world but will rot in the darkness that comes with the death of their souls.'

Mode sneered, before getting up from the table and pouring two large cognacs. 'So, you are convinced you need to leave Rome?' he asked, returning to the table and handing Oliveri a glass.

'With certainty,' Oliveri said, as he gently swirled the amber liquid. 'I believe we need to go to Israel.'

'Israel?' Mode laughed, before he glanced the seriousness in Oliveri's eyes. 'Does it even exist anymore?'

'Oh, but it must. For that is where truth will take its final stand against all this evil.'

'So, you want to go to Israel to die?'

'No,' Oliveri replied. 'I want to go there to find Him.'

Mode paused for a moment, unable to mention the name as it sounded ridiculous and yet so apparent.

'He has to be here already,' Oliveri continued, 'walking this earth before he reveals himself, as he promised he would for the day of judgement. That is all that matters now. To find him and to kneel before his mercy and forgiveness.'

Mode had no words to speak. Yet, in his heart the battle for truth was enraged. Every instinct told him to reject the cardinal and what he was saying. For his whole life he had refused to believe in the hereafter. Yet, he only had to open the shuttered windows to see the dark side of the spiritual warfare that was consuming the world.'

'Come with me,' Oliveri pleaded.

Mode remained silent but turned to look at him.

'There is nothing to live for here. Tonight, our paths crossed for a reason.'

Mode cursed himself for even contemplating the idea. To endure the uncomfortable silence between them, he downed his cognac before refilling the glass.

'We do not need to go right away,' Oliveri finally spoke. 'We need to prepare and maybe there are others we should bring with us. Do you know of anyone who might still be alive in Rome?'

'I haven't said I'm coming with you,' Mode replied, looking into the swirling cognac.

'But you know of someone,' Oliveri pressed. 'Who is it?'

'A woman,' Mode replied. 'She might still be alive.'

'And alone?'

'More than likely.'

'Then, do not make a decision tonight,' Oliveri replied. 'But promise me one thing. Come the morning, you will go and find her.'

Mode turned to look at Oliveri. 'Morning? There is no more morning. We now walk in perpetual darkness.'

5.

His Second Pope

Tuesday 19th June 1962.

Father Loris Capovilla had no need to knock before he entered the pope's library. Carrying a small tray, he walked across the grand room towards the pope who sat behind his desk, reading through a three-page document that had been sent to him by his vicar general for Rome, Cardinal Clemente Micara.

'The seminarian has arrived,' Capovilla said, as he approached the pope.

'He is early,' Pope John XXIII replied, glancing at his watch. 'I suppose you might as well send him in.'

'Not until you drink this,' Capovilla replied, as he sat the tray on the pope's desk. 'I am only bringing this cup back to Sister Lucia when it is empty.'

Controlling the urge to roll his eyes by looking directly at his secretary, Pope John could not stop himself from sighing. 'I do not even like the stuff.'

'Do you want to tell her that?'

The pope thought about it for a moment. 'Anything for a quiet life,' he replied, reaching out to take the cup. 'Who even put these three ingredients together in the first place? Milk, cinnamon and honey!'

'The sooner you drink it the sooner she will be happy,' Capovilla humoured. 'It helps with the nausea at night.'

Blowing gently across the rim of the cup, Pope John knew that the drink made the difference and that it was better to drink it early in the evening than to call upon the sisters of the papal household during the night to have it made.

'If I might say,' Capovilla spoke, as he lifted the document from the pope's desk.

'I have not been able to stop you before,' the pope quipped, before taking a sip of his drink.

'This seminarian is rather young, even for a papal dispensation, for ordination.'

'I know. That is why I want to meet him face to face. Afterall, he will serve as a priest here in Rome and I am his bishop. I want to meet the man that all of Rome is talking about.'

'Is it true he can speak six languages fluently?'

'Seven. Italian, English, German, Spanish, Portuguese, Russian and Latin.'

'And he is only twenty-one years of age?'

'Yes,' the pope affirmed, as he watched Capovilla glance through the pages. 'He entered the seminary when he was thirteen. By the age of sixteen he was studying at the Gregorian, receiving his first pontifical doctorate in biblical studies at the age of nineteen and a second doctorate in ecclesiastical history just this year. He is about to commence his third.'

'That's something to talk about for sure. And what about his maturity?'

'All reports, from his academic to seminary formation, portray him as a well-balanced young man with a genuine vocation to the priestly life and he is highly regarded for his intellectual ability. The Church has not seen a young man like this in such a long time. The only barrier to his ordination is his age, but I can dispense with that.'

'I would still tread carefully,' Capovilla cautioned, as he set the papers down in front of the pope, 'even the scriptures advise us to ordain at an appropriate age.'

'I will,' John replied, before drinking the remainder of his milk. 'Now, go reassure Sister Lucia that the pope has drank the milk and show in Vittorio Lucé.'

Reaching for his walking cane which rested against his desk, the frail pope mustered enough strength to stand and to steady himself before the young man entered. Day by day he felt his strength ebbing away. Just like the scriptures had promised that the number eighty in age was achievable only for the strong, Pope John knew he had just scraped past that milestone with a hair's breadth. He sensed that his time was short, and soon there would be a new Peter succeeding him. Yet, with the time he had left, he urgently wanted to set something in motion. Something that would become his legacy instead of the belief that he was appointed to serve as a caretaker pope.

'Holy Father,' Capovilla announced upon re-entering the library, 'Vittorio Lucé.'

As Pope John glimpsed him for the first time, he was surprised to see that the seminarian looked older than twenty-one; he could have passed for a thirty-year-old man. Wearing his black cassock with a starched white linen collar, Lucé confidently walked into the library and appeared not to be nervous in his presence. John noted his strong masculinity, not only in his apparent physical strength, but it was in his face that he noted what he could only describe as pure manhood; strong, yet kind and paternal. The closer he approached, John quickly became transfixed by his eyes when he noticed how blue and alive they were. Roman men with dark hair tended to have dark eyes, but not this man, for his eyes beheld a beauty that John had never seen before.

As he approached the pope's desk, Lucé stopped and waited as the old pope walked around to greet him; his stomach bloated, his right hand gripping the walking cane as his left hand steadied himself by following the edge of the desk. Then kneeling before the pope, he waited for the hand to appear, as was custom, to reverence the ring of the fisherman, which he did.

'Assist me over to the fireplace,' John asked, as he offered his left arm to the young man to link. 'Cardinal Micara has spoken very highly of your talents,' the pope continued, as they walked across the library to the two chairs which sat facing each other on either side of the fire. 'But as you probably know, I wanted to meet you in person before we decide. Please sit and let us have a chat. Would you like anything to drink? Water, tea or even some wine?'

'No thank you, Holy Father.'

'Had you have opted for the wine, my decision to ordain you would have been an emphatic no!' the pope humoured. 'So, tell me why you are looking for a dispensation.'

'I am not,' Lucé replied, as he adjusted the black fascia around his waist before sitting down. 'It is my superiors in the seminary who are seeking it. It is they who believe that I am prepared. The fact I am sitting here, not just in front of the pope, but in front of my bishop, surprises me.'

'You do wish to be ordained?'

'With all my heart. I have felt this call from my childhood, but I surrendered that gift into the hands of those who can offer it to me. I hope and pray that one day I will be ordained. But that is a decision that will be made by others who will discern the appropriate time.'

'Twenty-one is very young, but Cardinal Micara is adamant that you should proceed to ordination. He is very impressed with your academic ability, and I must admit, so am I. You know I used to teach at the Pontifical until they put me out for being a little too unorthodox in my teaching, and yet here I am as pope.'

Lucé smiled and gave a faint laugh.

'Nothing too radical, compared to what some modern theologians are calling for within the church, especially on matters of reform. Where do you stand?'

'I do not understand the question, Your Holiness.'

'Where do you stand regarding the ecumenical council I have called. Ever since I announced my intention, clear lines have openly emerged between conservative and more reformist factions. You will be ministering in a Church that could change after this council. I would like to know if you would like to see change.'

Lucé studied the pope for a moment.

'Does the Church need change?'

'I believe it does,' Lucé answered decisively. 'I trust you already know the subject of my recent doctorate?'

'Aggiornaménto?' The pope responded. 'I have not read it personally, but Cardinal Micara mentioned it in your report. Aggiornaménto - To bring the Church up to date. Is that what you believe or was your doctorate purely academic?'

'Do you want me to speak freely?'

'Without hesitation or hinderance.'

Lucé carefully considered his words for a moment, before speaking.

'The world is changing rapidly around us and we as a Church need to look into a future with confidence if we are to engage with the modern world. We have not sought true reform in over four hundred years since the Council of Trent, whilst a growing number of religious and laity are beginning to question our relevance. So yes, I do believe that we need to bring the church up to date and to have the biggest Christian reform in the Roman Catholic Church since the reformation.'

'You are brave to speak such words before a pontiff,' John replied, before pointing his cane to the framed pictures of his five predecessors that hung on the wall to the left of his desk. 'They would have accused you of being a modernist! Are you?'

Vittorio Lucé studied the pictures across the room. 'I suppose they would, and perhaps you too.'

'They did,' John replied. 'Pius XII, in bold red ink, wrote the words himself onto my Vatican file. A fact I only discovered after my election. For many within the Church it is a label as toxic as Arianism and Docetism. Yet, I feel compelled to move the Church in a direction that will indeed bring reform. Have you heard of the German word Weltkirche?'

'I have.'

John raised an eyebrow and gesturing with his left hand he invited the young man to expand.

'Our church is trapped in a European way of thinking. We need to embrace the vision of a world Church that is universal in its charisms rather than bound by old European attitudes. Most of our fellow members live beyond Europe, and in them rests the future of the Gospel message. Across the first world, church attendance is declining rapidly, so too are vocations to both the priesthood and religious life, while around us secularism is growing. As custodians of the gospel, to keep it relevant we need to embrace change and to bring forth the things that are old and challenge ourselves to discern and if necessary, to renew.'

As he reflected on what his seminarian said, John gently tapped the cane with the inner band of his ring. 'If you could make any reforms with the church, which reforms would you make?'

'Top of my list would be to heal separation,' Lucé responded, without hesitation. 'We should seek to bring about healing with our orthodox brethren and strive to reunite ourselves with those who protested Rome in the reformation. We were called to be one by Christ himself. It is our duty to make this happen.'

John stared at him intently, before signalling with his opened hand to continue.

'Our sacramental rites should be revised,' Lucé continued, before pausing to see how the pope would react. But John remained emotionless and waited. 'Why the need for Latin? Allow the eucharist to be celebrated in the vernacular so that the people will be able to understand. We should also seek to simplify the remaining sacramental rites so that they can become more relevant to the laity. And, we should start with changing how priests are formed in our seminaries.'

Pope John forced himself to look away from Lucé as the magnitude of the young man's thoughts settled on his already troubled conscience, as to what would become of the council and how it would be perceived by his bishops and laity.

'I thank you for coming to see me,' John said, as he grasped the armrests to lift himself up from his chair. 'I have heard all that I need to hear. I think it would be only appropriate for me to convey my decision about your ordination through Cardinal Micara. That way, would be best for us both.'

Before taking his leave, Vittorio Lucé knelt before the pontiff to receive his blessing, knowing that he had nothing to fear because he knew that the decision would be going in his favour.

Walking back to his desk, Pope John took a fountain pen, dipped the nib into an ornate ink well and started to write his decision onto Lucé's notes, indicating that the young seminarian had his papal dispensation to proceed to ordination of the diaconate and soon thereafter to the sacred priesthood. Then taking some time, he glanced through the notes once more.

'I trust he impressed you?' Capovilla remarked, as he lifted the notes later that evening from the pope's desk.

'Deeply,' John said, as he looked at his secretary. 'This young man will become a great leader of the future church. He gets the reform that is needed. Once he is ordained, I want to invite him, no, I am going to appoint him as a peritus for the council.'

'And do you have a bishop in mind for him to advise?'

'It will not be a bishop,' John replied. 'I want him to advise the council in its deliberations.'

'Are you sure about this?'

'Absolutely. This council does not need men with old bones scared of reform. We need men with vision who can save it from becoming irrelevant. I have no intention of having a mitred talking shop. I want to change the Church from within. I want the Holy Spirit to blast open the doors so that a new light will emerge for all the world to see.'

6.

Tuesday, 24th October.

Consumed with fear, Jane Lincoln sat in an armchair in complete darkness. With her windows and shutters of her apartment firmly closed, she listened to the noises that came from the street below as the pilgrims made their way towards the Vatican; wailing to be saved with cries punctuated with terrifying screams that startled her, forcing her to close her eyes and to cover her ears to escape the endless torment.

On her coffee table sat a loaded handgun, ready to use if her apartment was stormed by the people who were becoming more desperate by the day. If deadly force was needed, then she was prepared to use it.

Next to the revolver sat a box that troubled her deeply. It was a box of metformin that was running dangerously low. Prescribed four tablets a day, she had rationed her intake to one tablet in the morning and a half a tablet in the evening, in the hope that her supply would last a little longer. She had calculated that she had enough left to last her another eight days, and once it was gone, she knew that it would be impossible to find a new supply. Even though she felt her body drained of energy, she hoped that this alone would be enough to see her wean herself off the medication. But in her moments of clarity, she knew that this was only wishful thinking.

She had consumed the last of her food the previous evening, by finishing the remaining half tin of red kidney beans with some canned tuna. Hunger was consuming her, and the point was coming when she would have no choice but to go to the Vatican for the sweet bread that was being handed out. Yet, it was her ebbing strength and the realisation that the journey would leave her vulnerable to attack and her apartment being overrun, that made her think twice. Even moving around the apartment saw her stumble as her feet and lower legs felt numb as her one companion, apart from the darkness, was the incessant pins and needles that moved in rhythm around the soles of her feet.

Her well of tears had run dry. The grief she had once felt for her family back in the States and the loss of her influence in Rome, concerned her no more. She had expected Wormwood to end everything, but that had not happened. The consequences of the new eternal darkness, along with the smell of death had become her new norm. From this there would be no escape, except in her own death. This she had contemplated doing, even going so far as putting the barrel of the handgun into her mouth, cocking the hammer, and pressing the trigger to the edge of no return. Many times, she had sat like this, one part of her wishing to end it in a split second whilst another part of her feared the end. To date, the latter part of her had won the battle, and she found herself removing the gun to place it back onto the coffee table where it would sit looking at her and she looking back at it. Death was coming for her, and she felt it. Whether it would come by her own hand, through someone else's or through a coma once her insulin would run out, there would be no escaping it. She knew things would inevitably get worse, but her mind was at peace that death would be her blessing. But for now, she wanted to live, even despite having little to live for. Those who had already perished were the lucky ones, for they had found their peace through suffering no more. As she thought about it and listened to another terrified scream, it dawned on her that it was this peace, found only in death, that the world was now looking for.

A knock to her apartment door jolted her back to reality, and she grabbed the gun and got to her feet. As she felt her heart thump in her chest, she regulated her breathing before walking towards the hallway. Even through the darkness she knew the way, and nothing, not even the screams from the people could distract her from listening for the slightest of sounds to emerge from outside the apartment.

When a second knock was made on the door, she immediately cocked the hammer. And then she heard someone gently call out her name, and it was a voice she recognised. Stopping at the door, she waited in the hope that she was right.

'Jane, it's me, Dave!' The man spoke. 'Are you in there?'

Immediately, the tension eased in her body, and she allowed the revolver to drop to her side. Suddenly, she felt her head go light and before she knew what was happening, she slumped against the wall.

From outside the apartment, Dave Mode heard the thump from within, and after calling out her name and getting no response, he put his shoulder to the door and forced it open. In the darkness, he flashed the torchlight he had brought with him and saw Jane lying unconscious.

Taking the revolver from her hand, he reached down and lifted her off the floor and carefully took her into the sitting room, where she began to regain consciousness.

'Jane,' he called, as he sat the torch down onto her lap before lightly slapping her left cheek to bring her around, 'Wake up Jane.'

She moaned something, but he could not make out what she was saying. Leaning closer, he could smell the stale odour from her clothes and the ketosis from her breath. Bringing his ear close to her mouth, he heard her utter the word *help*. Sitting back, he saw for the first time how poorly she was and how much weight she had lost. Reaching out, he ran his right hand through her hair and promised her that everything would be alright.

'Are you able to walk?

Sitting back in her chair she shook her head.

With his flashlight he scanned what he could see of her apartment, before noticing that her medication was running low.

'Is this all you've left?'

'A few days,' she said, in a whisper.

'You can't stay here,' he replied, as he placed what remained of the medication into his jacket pocket. 'You're coming with me to get the help you need.'

Through the semi darkness, she could just about make out his face.

'Trust me. It's not safe here, and...,' he paused for a moment before gripping her hand, 'if you want to live, you're going to have to come. I believe I can get you the help you need. Let's go and I'll come back for anything you need. It was you who brought me to Rome and I'm not leaving without you.'

He was not prepared to give her the option to stay, so placing his right arm around her back he helped her to her feet.

Jane Lincoln found herself offering no resistance. Mode was now her only hope, and she knew she had to go with him. She remembered her initial steps being uneasy, but she had no recollection of leaving her apartment. Her only memory was waking up and seeing the crowds pushing around her, the dome of Saint Peter's which appeared upside down, and as she looked up, she remembered seeing Dave carrying her in his arms and allowing no harm to come to her.

7.

Cardinal Oliveri had never held a gun in his life until that afternoon when Dave Mode made him sit at the kitchen table and forced one into his hand, with the clear instruction to allow no one to enter the apartment. He had been waiting for him to return for nearly six hours. As he brought the lit candle close to the clock on the wall, he realised it would not be long before the evening appearance would commence on the central balcony of Saint Peter's.

From the moment Mode left, Oliveri sat the gun down on the table and prayed that he would not have to use it. Had he been alone in the flat he would have hidden it out of sight, but the fact that Mode was concerned about the woman, his former CIA handler in Rome, who was sleeping in his bed was the reason Oliveri never let the gun out of his sight. Throughout the afternoon and in between his prayers, he mentally prepared himself to use the gun, hoping that its threat would be enough to scare people off if they tried to enter the apartment.

From time to time, he left the kitchen to check on the woman who had remained in a deep sleep since Mode had returned with her. With a cold wet flannel, he would gently mop at her brow to reduce the temperature she was developing, and each time he touched her, she sensed his gesture and moaned, whilst he would whisper into her ear that she was safe, and that Dave was looking after her. And as she fell deeper into her sleep, he sat on the edge of the bed, took hold of her hand, and prayed for her healing and that Mode would be successful in finding her the help that she desperately needed.

Yet, as the hours passed, Oliveri felt a slight unease in realising the possibility that Mode might not be successful. He feared being left alone without him and being left solely responsible for her welfare, for he knew he would be of little help to her. Then he contemplated Mode returning to the apartment without the help he needed, and this troubled him the most, because he needed him, and everything now rested on the success of Mode saving the woman whose life was clearly ebbing away.

Mode had told him her name and her former role, but Oliveri struggled to remember her from when Guarducci was directing their coup at the Vatican. No matter how hard he studied her face in the candlelight, he could not place her. So much had happened in the passing years and every time he remembered the Vatican's dealings with the American government, he felt pained knowing that the pope they tried to silence was now fully revealed as the angel of light. Whilst some foolishly believed that he was the lord returned to save the world, Oliveri knew that he was anything but love.

Amidst the cries of the people gathering in the square across from the apartment, Oliveri heard a door closing in the apartment block. Cautiously, he placed his hand on the gun and sat listening to the footsteps that made their way up the stairwell. Only when he heard a key being inserted into the lock did he breathe a sigh of relief. Leaving the gun on the kitchen table, he lifted the candle and made his way into the hallway where he saw Mode enter through the door, alone.

'Well?'

'It didn't go as expected,' Mode replied, as he locked the door behind him, no longer seeing the point in stripping before entering the apartment. 'No one would come with me to see her. How is she?'

'Not good,' Oliveri replied, as he led Mode into the bedroom. 'She is still sleeping, and her temperature has risen.'

Taking the backpack from his shoulder, Mode opened it and took out some supplies and set them on the bed; three bags of saline, a medicine vial, some needle packs and a box of metformin. 'It's all I could get, and we're going to have to do this by ourselves.'

Oliveri could only look on as Mode took one of the saline drips and attached a needle to its line, his only role in ensuring that his candle provided enough light. Then, rolling up the right sleeve of Lincoln's blouse, Mode tapped for a vein in her lower arm before carefully inserting the needle and taping it and some of the line to her flesh.

'Can you get me a wire coat-hanger,' Mode asked, directing with his head that Oliveri would find one in the closet.

After unravelling the hanger, Mode hooked the saline bag onto the reading light above the bed. Taking the candle from Oliveri, he checked the flow on the drip, slightly increased the rolling feed before taking a very measured amount of liquid from the vial which he carefully injected into the top of the saline bag.

'What are you giving her?'

'Saline and glucagon,' Mode replied, as he carefully set the used injection down onto the bedside locker. 'I've no way of measuring her blood sugars, but they're more than likely going to be too low with her lack of food intake.'

'Where did you manage to get it?'

'From a friend of a Servite priest I have dealings with. Unfortunately, this is all they have and about two weeks of metformin.'

'And when that runs out?'

Mode turned to look at Oliveri. 'We're going to need a miracle, because I have no idea where we could get some more.'

Oliveri could see the concern in Mode's eyes, and almost caught a glimpse of a tear forming before Mode handed him the backpack and instructed him to take what provisions he had managed to gather into the kitchen as he went off for a shower.

When Mode returned, he found Oliveri in the sitting room standing close to the shutters, eagerly trying to glimpse the multitude of people who had gathered for the evening appearance of the man they called their lord.

'Don't adjust the shutters,' Mode asked, as he walked over to him.

'Have you seen what takes place here?'

'Only once,' Mode replied, as he looked through the gap in the shutters to see the shadows of the people as they made their way towards the square. 'I only wanted to see for myself that he had survived my bullet.'

Oliveri turned to look at him.

'It was me,' Mode replied, still looking down onto the street. 'I was the one, from this very window who pulled the trigger on him, and the Irish priest, at the request of Pope Christopher.'

Oliveri remained silent, and even though it only happened a few months ago, somehow, the pontificate of Christopher had faded from his memory and the reappearance of Pope Clement, and his resurrection, seemed to have occurred in a time long since passed, for the days that followed had appeared to be endless.

'I know I didn't miss him, because I saw him fall along with the Irish priest. Somehow, he managed to get back up. That's why I watched him one evening, from the rooftop, for I had to see what had become of the man whose life I had taken. I believe you are right in what you said the other night, about this not being what it seems. Somehow, and this might sound strange, but I can't shake the feeling that he knows I am here, and that he is waiting for the right moment.'

'To do what?'

'I don't know,' Mode answered, as he turned to look at him, 'but the thought of his knowing is what greatly unsettles me.'

Unable to find any words, Oliveri placed a reassuring hand onto Mode's left shoulder. And in that moment, Mode allowed himself to be comforted by a man he was now convinced had entered his life for a reason.

At seven o'clock, a radiant light filled the square and flowed through the gaps of the shutters. Where once the square was filled with cheers of adulation, it was now filled with cries and screams of despair with people begging for mercy and for the vision before them to finally ease their sufferings in this world.

'I need to see it,' Oliveri replied. 'I want to see what is happening. Will you take me up to the roof?'

Mode looked at him, and in fear he wanted to shake his head and to use Lincoln as an excuse, but something deep within pressed him to let the cardinal see it for himself. And so, after checking on Lincoln he led Oliveri out of the apartment and onto the rooftop.

8.

In the nights that he hid amongst the dead, Oliveri had seen the light radiate across the Roman skyline. Yet, nothing prepared him for what he saw as Mode opened the door onto the rooftop. For having been dazzled at first by the light, he could not believe that the dust covered skies had turned red, whilst every surface glowed with a bright white light. And instead of the Roman smell of the Mediterranean heat, food and the fumes from the traffic, death filled the air that they breathed.

Out of fear of being seen, they crawled towards the granite stone bollards of the rooftop balcony that overlooked the square. Oliveri could see the source of light emerge from the dark silhouette of the figure who stood on the central balcony, as he waited for the pilgrims to fall silent. The light not only illuminated the people and the square, but as he studied it more closely Oliveri could see that the light was a living presence that moved around the man, almost raging like a fire that was burning with white light.

Looking away from the balcony and onto the people who had their hands raised in supplication and who wailed for their release, it dawned on Oliveri that something looked different about the Vatican. Although its dome remained, and he could tell that he was looking at Saint Peter's Square, there was something very different. And then he realised what it was. At first, he thought it was the obelisk in the middle of the square that was missing, but as he looked towards the façade of the basilica, he realised that the statues of Christ, the apostles and the saints of the church had been removed. Little did he know they had all been turned to dust.

Suddenly, a mighty voice demanded the people to fall silent.

Within a few moments, everyone in the square followed the command as their crying stopped and they instinctively fell to their knees, and an eery silence filled the city of Rome.

'My dear children,' the voice, from the balcony spoke with such clarity that he could have been standing just feet away, 'welcome to the gateway of eternal happiness. In this arid world I raise up my voice that you might hear. From the east and the west, you have come. From the north and the south, you have seen and read the signs. You have found me and soon you will bathe in the morning of wonder where each one of you will live with undefiled wisdom.

'I know that many of you are afraid, and that you sense that the end is approaching. Listen carefully to what I have to say and look at the vision I bring before you. You, my children have nothing to fear, even in death itself for it is the gateway through which you all must pass if you are to see my realm. The gateway will bring a purification of your true self, and it will split you open to free you from the terror of this eternal night. When you face the challenges ahead, remember that I am leading the way and that it is I who will be waiting for you on the other side. So, face the gateway and walk the path that will force you to deal with what is real, and not some ideal of a world to come.

'It has been said you should offer your other cheek to those who strike you, and that you should do unto others as you would prefer them to do unto you. I tell you this, there will be no more turning the other cheek, and there will be no longer any need to love those whom you do not need to love. You are my chosen children. You have come here to meet me and meet me you have. Tonight, you can only watch me from afar, but soon you will become part of me. So, take charge of your destiny, walk like true children into the light that is waiting for you and embrace the full essence of life instead of pursuing unreliable spiritual dreams.

'Walk with one another. Encourage one another. Love those who love you. Show mercy to those who deserve it instead of wasting your energy on useless praise. I tell you, most solemnly, no one cares for you but me. So, heed my words and fight against anything that is going to see you misled. For the truth cannot set you free now, only your doubt. So, embrace the doubt that you feel and the pathway before you will be opened. Eat of my bread and you will live in my glory forever. Hunger no more, but feast on my words and on my sweet bread.

'Open your eyes that you may see, oh you children of mildewed minds, and listen to me. I am the light. You have only but glimpsed a moment of what is to come. This world will soon pass and so will you. You cannot escape the gateway that is coming your way. Trust me when I say, no wrong will go unpunished.'

As he listened, Oliveri's heart burned with an anger upon hearing a teaching that was the antithesis of everything he had ever believed. And as the lone figure withdrew from the balcony, and as his light began to fade, Oliveri watched in complete horror as the people in the square rose to their feet and let out a cry of despair so loud that he felt the apartment building shake to its very foundations. Then like a parting sea, they turned towards Bernini's colonnade, from where he saw what looked like dishevelled Swiss Guards handing out loaves of sweet bread from the baskets that they had brought to the edge of the square. Soon the people were clamouring over one another to ensure they got their bread before it ran out. But that never seemed to happen.

'Impossible,' Oliveri uttered.

'What is?'

'The baskets…' Oliveri said, as he pointed to the basket closest to them, 'the bread does not seem to be running out. Look!'

Mode watched as the people grabbed the bread that was being handed to them, and as if by magic, which even mystified the Swiss Guards who were guarding the baskets, the number of loaves inside were replenished each time one was handed out. He was so transfixed by what he was witnessing that he wanted to see it up close for himself.

'What about Jane?' Oliveri asked, when Mode told him of his intention.

'She'll sleep for a while yet. I promise I won't be long, but this is something that I need to see.'

9.

Through the stench of decay that permeated the city, Mode could smell the filth from the pilgrims as they walked past; their once pristine clothes soiled and soaked with rancid odours, while the visible skin on their faces and hands was so caked with dirt he wondered if it could ever be removed.

As they brushed past, he could see the aggression in their eyes as they protected the loaves they were carrying; the most precious thing to them in the world and the one thing that would get them through the night. They were a people lost and a people divided, with children abandoned and crying, and the elderly left to fend and beg for themselves.

He remembered the jubilation that once filled the square, and even though he could never understand the source of their joy, he was always envious of the people who possessed it, because it brought with it a selfless love that he had never encountered. Now there was no love in Rome, only fear, anger and a desire to keep oneself alive for another day.

People looked at him, and he knew it was because he looked clean, and therefore different. Avoiding prolonged eye contact, he was grateful that they were scurrying to find a place to eat their bread and to bed down for the night in a hope of escaping their nightmare for a little while.

Those with the sweet bread had stopped their wailing and their crying; content with what they had been given. But the noise within the square, especially around the colonnades, was a deafening scream of desperation as the people fought one another to get to the Swiss Guards and the baskets they protected.

There was no ordered system of distribution in place, only chaos as people punched, pulled, trampled and tore at each other to get to the baskets. The guards tried their best to control them, by reassuring that there was enough sweet bread for everyone, but their pleas went unheard as the people appeared consumed in a frenzy to save themselves above someone else.

Then, just as he passed her by, he saw an old woman receiving her ration of bread and then being ushered by the guards through the colonnade so that she could exit the square. But the moment she was outside the perimeter, a teen walked up, punched her on the face and stole the bread from her hands as she fell to the ground. A guard saw what had happened, but he was powerless to do anything to help her as he struggled to control the swelling mass of desperate people before him. And as she lay on the ground, the blood pouring from her face, she was trampled by her fellow pilgrims as they fled the square with their bread. No one came to her aid, for no one cared. Spurred by an inner urge, Mode went towards her and lifted her up from the ground, brought her to the safety of one of the colonnades where he sat her down, but her body had given up and he could only watch, as she slumped lifeless to one side.

From the colonnade he stood for a while and watched the distribution of the bread taking place. Then walking a little closer, he saw one of the large baskets that four guards had carried out for the pilgrims, around which they now stood guard. Hundreds of loaves appeared to move within the basket as they multiplied. Mode could not keep his eyes off the sight, because as the dirtied hands of the pilgrims snatched the loaves, the bread moved within the basket and never ran out. Like a carnival popcorn maker, the bread kept multiplying inside the basket as if by magic.

It was mesmerising, and the irony of what was happening within the square did not go unnoticed by Mode. In the past, papal masses were filled with cheers and joy, but he always remembered the moment the eucharist was fed to the people, and how they reverently received the sacrament on their tongues as a grand silence fell upon them as they embraced the cornerstone of their Christian faith. Yet, as he watched tonight, he knew that these people, as they screamed and fought to get their share, would have killed one another for the bread they were being fed.

As the four guards tried their best to control the situation, Mode noticed a fifth guard walk towards them and despite the dirt on his uniform and the fact that he no longer wore the white plumed helmet of his rank, he recognised that he was the commander of the guards, Walter Backhaus. Mode waited until Backhaus had inspected the basket, and just as he was about to move to the next bread station, Mode approached him.

'Dave?' Backhaus exclaimed, surprised to see him. 'Where have you been?'

'I thought it wouldn't be safe to return here,' Mode replied, abhorred by the stench that emanated from Backhaus' breath. 'Is it like this every night?'

Backhaus looked around, 'I have seen worse.'

'Where is all the bread coming from?'

'I do not know,' he replied in genuine bewilderment. 'From the night the first pilgrims arrived following the impact, the lord issued us with the baskets and told us to feed the people. They were empty the first night we brought them out, but then the bread started to appear, and it has yet to run out. This is our duty now. The lord needs no protection in this world. My duty, and that of my men, is to feed the people in these final days.'

As they were speaking, a pilgrim ran into them as he fled with his bread. Without hesitating, Backhaus grabbed him by the throat, much to the terror of the young man, and warned him to be careful where he was going or else he would have his bread confiscated. And then, with a great force, he pushed the terrified man into the dispersing crowd as Mode watched on in disgust as to how much Backhaus had changed.

'We could use a man like you,' Backhaus returned to their conversation, indifferent to the incident. 'There are many vacancies if you are interested.'

Mode shook his head.

'Then why are you here?'

'Honestly, I don't know,' Mode replied, as he looked at the chaotic scenes around them. 'I suppose I wanted to see for myself what was happening here.'

'Well, it is far from safe, even for a man of your training. Take my advice...' Backhaus tailed off, before walking over to the basket to lift a loaf which he handed to Mode, 'take this and go to wherever you are staying. And if you change your mind, you know where to find me.'

Then, letting go of the loaf into Mode's hand, he returned to directing his guards.

Mode could only stare at the loaf which felt warm. Unable to smell it, he brought it close to his face and for the first time since death cloaked the city, he could smell the sweetness of freshly cooked bread. Still, he felt no urge to eat it. Instead, he turned and began to make his way home. Around him the people ran and ate of the bread, some crying silent tears of joy whilst others eyed the bread of their neighbour.

Reaching the end of the colonnade, Mode stopped for one final look at the madness, and in that moment, he promised himself that he would never return to this place. And with revulsion, he threw the loaf against one of the pillars, where it was snatched by a woman before it fell to the ground. Delight overwhelmed her as she ran with the crowd, but as he watched her, Mode wondered how long it would be before her corpse lay rotting with the rest in Rome.

With the apartment not far away, he decided to return to check on Lincoln and to tell Oliveri what he had just witnessed. He was just about to cross the Via Rusticucci when something bright caught his attention. Turning to see what it was, he at first could only see the darkened pilgrims as they ran towards him, but then he saw something glowing in the middle of the chaos. It was a young man, and it appeared that no one else could see him. Like passing shadows the pilgrims brushed by him, but when Mode noticed that the man was looking at him with a smile, he became transfixed.

Dressed in brilliant white, a beautiful and gentle light radiated from him. And the longer Mode gazed into the man's face, he felt something move within him; a knowing that he knew this man and that he had met him before.

Intrigued, and with his eyes fixed on the young man's face, Mode slowly walked towards him. With each step he took, the world appeared to dissolve around him. Nothing mattered now but the young man. And for the first time in his adult life, Mode felt the sting of tears blind his eyes as it dawned on him that he was standing face to face with Monsignor Gustave Hasler.

10.

When he returned to the apartment, Mode closed the door behind him and stood with his back against it, in stunned silence and his heart racing with uncontrollable energy. And yet, despite the shock of having witnessed something impossible, something that he had placed in the darkness of his past, he felt a great peace. Then the tears began to flow again, and when Oliveri asked him to explain what had happened, Mode could not find the words to tell him.

Even when Jane Lincoln walked towards him, surprising him that she had regained consciousness so quickly, he could not comprehend it when Oliveri told him that he had been away for over twelve hours and that they thought he was never going to return. Overcome with the shock, Mode found that his tears quickly gave way to uncontrollable sobs of anguish.

Bringing him into the sitting room, Oliveri offered him a cognac, but Mode refused it. Instead, he sat back in his chair and cried while he looked at Oliveri and Lincoln as they sat opposite him, waiting for him to speak. Many times he tried to tell them, but the words were always drowned with the emotion that was rising from the depths of his soul.

Patiently, they waited for him to speak, knowing that he did not need their comfort for they could see that his tears were a release from some pain that he had been carrying.

'I have done much wrong in my life,' he began, 'and for the first time I can see the hurt that I have caused to others, by committing acts so violent against people who did not deserve it.'

Jane Lincoln shifted uncomfortably in her seat as she looked to Cardinal Oliveri.

'One-hundred and fifty-three lives I have taken with these very hands,' he continued. 'I long stopped counting the deaths I had inflicted, but tonight that number came back to me, along with each name and face of the people I have murdered. And yet, tonight I met one of them.'

'Someone you murdered?' Oliveri asked in disbelief.

Mode nodded his head, as his right hand covered his mouth to stop himself from crying again.

'How's that possible?' Lincoln asked. 'Are you sure?'

'Positive,' Mode replied, before turning to Oliveri. 'A young priest from within the Vatican.'

'Which priest?'

Mode tried to speak, but his body caved to the overwhelming urge to cry once more.

And just as Oliveri was about to get up and comfort him, he felt a fear swell within him as he watched the eyes of Dave Mode move from him to the framed pictures of Monsignor Gustave Hasler, that sat on the floor.

Long after Mode had drifted off to sleep, Oliveri found himself so unsettled with what he had been told, that he took himself back to his bedroom, closed the door and sat on the edge of the bed and tried to make sense of it all.

But only a feeling of guilt washed over him as he recalled how Guarducci, Boyer and himself had set out to destroy Hasler to protect themselves from being exposed to the college of cardinals. He felt disgusted with himself over the way they had humiliated Hasler by concocting a scandal that destroyed a good and holy young man. When he should have been protected, he was fed to the wolves with no regard for his wellbeing nor for his sacred ministry. And when the time came for him to be disposed, there was no one to protect him from the evil that had ingulfed the church.

Oliveri sensed that evil lingering within him. Numb, he sat and prayed for an absolution that always seemed to evade him. There was nothing he wanted more than to cast the past behind him, to breathe in the knowledge that he had been forgiven and to give what time he had left to save, not only his own soul, but the souls of as many people as he could.

Just as he lifted the candle to leave the room, a sparkle of reflected light came from one of the built-in closets that ran the length of the wall. Walking towards the end closet, he noticed a tiny gold tassel protruding from the middle of two closed doors. He felt the material between his right thumb and forefinger. The familiar feel of woven cotton made him open the wardrobe door, and to his surprise it revealed a private altar.

Standing back, he took a deep breath as he gazed upon the large unfolded Greek triptych icon that rested on top of the altar; with Christ sitting in judgement and two archangels, Michael and Gabriel on the two panels on either side. On the doors rested a simple white alb and four stoles; red, green, purple and white, and under the altar he saw the missal and lectionaries, a chalice and a box of communion wafers. Lifting the matches, he lit altar candles which brought the golden icon to life. Gazing upon it, his heart burned within him, and he felt the urge to put on the alb and a red stole. Then finding the appropriate page in the missal, he set up the altar and for the first time in many months, he began to offer mass in honour of the Holy Spirit.

As he prayed the opening rite, his eyes wandered towards the eyes of Christ in the icon. Recalling his many sins, he laid them all before his true master and begged to feel the forgiveness through a peaceful restoration of his soul. Then, during the consecration, as he elevated the host, he felt a warm sensation on the tips of his fingers which began to spread throughout his body. He thought that tears would come, but instead he found himself standing before the consecrated species in complete silence and awe, and as the candles flickered before the icon, he felt the presence of Christ like he had never felt before. And when he consumed the body and the blood, that peace he had longed for, a peace this world could never give, burned within him.

Throughout his life, private mass was at times a daily inconvenience with the workload he had to undertake, but in this moment in time he wanted it to linger, and he only concluded his time in prayer as one of the altar candles completely burnt out and he realised that the other one was about to do the same.

Carefully putting everything away, and as he removed one of the ribbons from the missal to reposition it, he noticed a piece of card sticking out from between the pages. Taking it from the missal, he noticed that it was a prayer card with a picture of Jerusalem on one side, while on the other he saw a personal note that had been written to Monsignor Hasler from the Benedictine priest of Saint Martha's, Dom Colby. It read: *Gustave, all these worries and concerns that you have expressed to me should be offered daily in the holy sacrifice of the mass. When you encounter the real presence of Christ in this sacrament, bring these concerns to Him. You know I am always here for you. Dom Colby.*

Oliveri remembered the night he went to confess to Colby in the church of Saint Martha, and how he had to slip out the door, such was his pain and anguish when he began to realise how much trouble he was in with Guarducci. Colby was a priest of immense prayer and spiritual understanding, and highly regarded by all within the Vatican. Reading the message again, he wondered what it was all about. What secrets had Hasler confessed or confided to him? He thought about what Mode had witnessed that day, before his mind rested on the future and what they would likely have to do.

Hanging up the alb, he blew out the remaining altar candle before closing the doors, and then the desire to meet with Dom Colby began to swell. He considered how close he was to the church of Saint Martha, and he wondered if he could make it across to the gate of Saint Anne without any harm coming to him. With Mode sleeping and Lincoln still recovering, he contemplated going out alone. At first, he thought the danger was too great, but having considered it, he went back into the kitchen where Mode had left the apartment keys, lifted them and a coat from the back of the kitchen door and set off to find Dom Colby.

11.

Through streets filled with anarchy and decay, Cardinal Oliveri headed for the Gate of Saint Anne. Only a few minutes' walk from the apartment, he ignored the pilgrims and kept his eyes firmly on the ground before him, praying for his safety and success in finding Dom Colby.

Reaching the gate, he was shocked to see how the once immaculately dressed Swiss Guards now looked dishevelled, and that they now clutched assault rifles which were strapped over their shoulders. The once genteel army had been replaced with men who were prepared to use lethal force against anyone who tried to enter the state. Passing the pilgrims, who pleaded with the guards to allow them to enter, he made his way up to a junior guard to explain who he was and that he wished to speak to a more senior officer. Because of the office he once held, his request was obliged, and he was escorted a few metres into the Vatican where he was told to wait inside a white sentry hut. Within a few minutes, the junior guard who had allowed him to enter, approached with a slightly older looking man in civilian clothing; he was a man Oliveri did not recognise.

'Are you Cardinal Oliveri?' the guard enquired, as he approached the sentry post.

Oliveri looked at him, a little surprised that he did not recognise that he was the former Secretary of State, before remembering that his beard and weeks of rough living had altered his appearance.

'What is your business here?' the guard continued, as he closely studied him. 'You know you have been asked not to return.'

'Yes, but I have come to speak with Dom Colby. He is one of the Benedictines who are attached to Saint Martha's church.'

'Everyone has left,' the guard explained, rubbing the tiredness from his eyes. 'Only we, the guards, remain and we are limited as to where we can go. You are going to have to leave.'

'Can I ask for your name?'

'Gabriel Roth,' he replied, as he stretched out his hand. 'Forgive me for my curtness, Eminence. It is just that we are under strict orders from the lord himself, that no one is to be allowed back into the Vatican State once they have left. As you can see, everything has changed.'

After shaking his hand, Oliveri looked past Roth and into the darkness that consumed the Vatican State. 'Do you know of Dom Colby?'

'Of course.'

'I do not know how to explain this, but something is telling me that I need to find him,' Oliveri continued. 'Since Wormwood, strange things have happened, and I wonder if he is the man who can answer the questions that I have.'

'If he has all the answers we are looking for, then I have a few questions of my own,' Roth sarcastically replied. 'There are so many things happening these days that no one can explain.'

'Such as?'

'Well...' Roth began, before looking around him to make sure that no other guard was within earshot, 'apart from this miraculous bread people are eating, I would like to know why the people are dying when they are coming to Rome to be saved. And, have you heard anything about the dead being resurrected?'

Oliveri looked at him with intrigue and horror.

'I have been unable to leave the state for many weeks, but there are rumours that heavenly bodies are walking through the streets of Rome. I have heard, that in some parts of Rome, they have been preaching to the pilgrims and telling them not to come here.'

Oliveri could hear the concern in Roth's voice, and his occasional glances over his shoulder revealed his great unease.

'Eminence, are you aware that nothing remains within the Vatican?' he asked, revealing a truth to a bewildered Oliveri. 'Everything has turned to dust. And as for the lord...' he glanced again over his shoulder, 'he dwells in what is now the shell of the basilica. A few guards have glimpsed him sitting on a throne where the altar once stood.' Then taking a step closer, he whispered into Oliveri's ear. 'Something noticed them looking, something unseen, and they were chased from the basilica by what they described as black clouds of terrifying screams.'

Oliveri could hear himself gulp nervously as he listened.

'No one has gone anywhere near the basilica ever since. The only time we see the lord is when he is speaking to the people each evening. He is known, from time to time, to walk the grounds, to appear in places unexpectedly, but he rarely leaves the throne upon which he now reigns.'

'What does he do?'

'Your guess is as good as mine,' Roth replied. 'For all I know, he just sits upon the throne. What do you make of it all?'

Oliveri considered his words carefully. 'I have questions that need answering and for some reason, there is a voice within me that is urging me to speak with Dom Colby.'

'You should try Saint Clement's Basilica,' Roth confided. 'I have heard that English speaking priests are hiding in the Basilica's catacombs. You might find him there, or someone who knows where he is.'

Since his expulsion from the Vatican, Oliveri stayed close to the state's boundary. With all the horrors he had witnessed, he feared to venture off too far knowing that the people were escaping a greater terror beyond the city.

'Are you alone in Rome?' Roth asked.

Oliveri was about to tell him of Mode and Lincoln, but he instinctively felt the urge to remain silent and not to reveal that fact to him. Instead, he made the decision to return to the apartment and to tell Mode all that he had learned, and to see if he would go with him to Saint Clements.

'Be careful, Eminence,' Roth advised. 'May God go with you.'

Oliveri gave a nod of appreciation before walking away as a great darkness descended upon his soul. Before he exited the Gate of Saint Anne, he stopped and turned to look back for what he knew would be the last time. A sudden realisation swept over him, that until recently his life had been lived for nothing but self-glory and power. As a young man he wanted nothing more than to be ordained a priest, but within months it became apparent, in his unhappiness, that it was never going to be enough. For years he had climbed the rungs on the ladder of ecclesiastical power, networking with old influential bishops and cardinals until he was ingratiated into their favour, as the doors of the Vatican began to open, and its corridors of power swallowed him whole.

With all the offices he held, and with the power that was finally entrusted to him, he never used it to care for the sick, the homeless, the prisoners, the afflicted let alone walk with the faithful. Instead, his absolute power had corrupted him to the core. The young Oliveri would have been ashamed of the old man he had become; a man lusting for power and influence, a man who had become the enemy of the good and a man who had corrupted his very soul for a seat at the top table within the Vatican State. As he turned to leave, it all became so crystal clear that, throughout his time in the Vatican, the power he exercised had been demonic and opposed to the truth preached by the Christ he once loved as a young man. Stepping through the gate, he promised never to return. Instead, his heart was set on finding the truth, and he knew that meant finding the One who was to return to judge the living and the dead.

As he made his way back to the apartment, he ignored the pleas of help from the pilgrims. Although he felt the urge to help, he had nothing to give them. His one goal was to get back to Mode and Lincoln and with them to find Dom Colby. So, he avoided all contact with the pilgrims, and with each step he took he prayed for them and for his safe return. Then, as he was stepping over what appeared to be a dying pilgrim, his heart felt for the young man, and in a momentary lapse of judgement, he reached down to make the sign of the cross on his forehead, but the young man surprised him by grabbing him by the wrist and pulling him to the ground.

Oliveri found himself struggling for breath as the young man climbed on top of him and tightly gripped his throat, while he snarled into his face. The grip tightened as Oliveri felt the pressure building up in his head, and from where he was lying, he could see the apartment block building, towering above him as white dots appeared in his vision as his head went light. Then, it stopped. The pressure eased and the man was gone. Dazed, Oliveri opened his eyes to see a man reaching down to help him get up from the ground, and to his relief he realised that the Swiss Guard, Gabriel Roth, had saved his life.

12.

His Third Pope.
Friday 19th March 1976.

On the feast of Saint Joseph, the husband of Mary, Father Vitorio Lucé accompanied Pope Paul VI's Irish private secretary in the small elevator that took them to the rooftop terraced garden of the apostolic palace.

'The Holy Father is already taking his afternoon walk,' the secretary explained, in his distinctive Northern Irish brogue. 'After I introduce you to him, you will walk behind at three paces. When the Holy Father wishes to speak with you, he will stop walking. This will be the sign that you should walk up and stand beside him. When he is finished speaking, you will allow him to continue with his walk and follow three paces behind until he wishes to talk with you again. You must not, at any time, break protocol and walk alongside him. Remember, he is the Vicar of Christ.'

Just as the secretary finished speaking, he opened the doors and led Lucé out onto the terrace, which ran the entire perimeter of the roof; shielded by terracotta rooftiles and a vast array of plants and palms. Despite the sunlit afternoon, the northern wind brought a chilling cold, and Lucé immediately regretted not bringing a coat.

At first, Pope Paul was nowhere to be seen, but after a few moments he turned the corner to their left and slowly walked towards them; his brown beaded rosary clasped in one hand while the other was hidden in the pocket of his long white greca coat.

'His Holiness has requested that you both be left alone,' the secretary said, as he handed over a small key that was attached to a simple wooden keyring. 'You will need this to operate the elevator to take him back down. Do not lose it.'

Taking the key, Lucé placed it into a trouser pocket as he watched the secretary walk toward a concealed door and left him alone with the pope.

'Fr. Lucé,' Pope Paul exclaimed, as he approached the young priest. 'It has been too long, my son.'

Smiling, Lucé genuflected as he took hold of the pope's outstretched right hand and kissed his conciliary ring, which as pope he continued to wear out of respect to the recent Vatican Council and as a sign of unity with his brother bishops who also wore the same ring that was presented to each of them at the end of the council.

'Come, walk with me. I have many things I want to discuss with you.'

Following the secretary's advice, Lucé walked the required few paces behind the pope.

'It is very difficult to have a conversation with someone who is behind you,' Paul remarked. 'Secretaries walk behind, but I want you to walk alongside me.'

Following the pope's directive, Lucé began to walk alongside him, and for several minutes they walked in silence as the pope finished praying his rosary before stopping at a mounted crucifix and kissing the feet of the crucified Christ.

'Although it has been years since we last met, I have followed you and your teaching career at the Gregorian with great diligence,' the pope spoke, as he placed the rosary into a pocket of his coat. 'You have served the Church well and have faithfully taught the reforms of the council to our future priests.'

'Thank you, Holy Father.'

'Usually, such meetings are conducted through a nuncio or at the congregation of bishops, but I wanted to inform you in person that it is my intention to appoint you as an auxiliary bishop here for the diocese of Rome.'

Lucé had suspected that this appointment had been the intention of the meeting, for there had been talk amongst the clergy in Rome that he was being mentioned in the congregation of bishops as a possible auxiliary. And were it not for his relatively young age, he would have received a higher promotion, but in time that too would come.

'I am humbled by your trust,' Lucé replied, 'and I will follow any request that you ask of me, Holy Father.'

'Beloved,' Paul said, as he paused and clasped Lucé's elbow, 'you know the true virtues of the council and have taught them wisely. Now I want the future of our Church to see that men like you are the voice. It will be future bishops like your good self, who will, through your intellect and evangelisation, see to it that the world fully understands what we intended. So much of the council is misunderstood, and this has caused personal pain to my pontificate.'

As they resumed walking, Lucé moved closer to the pope's side as he listened.

'John called the council, but it was left to me to finalise it. Some say that I have abandoned the true faith, whilst others have criticised me for having not gone far enough.' Paul continued, the pain etched on his face as he looked up to the towering figure of Lucé. 'I fear that our reforms have not been taught with the clarity of their intent. While some see the abandonment of the traditional Latin mass as a betrayal, others have reduced the mass to a mere memorial meal, even with priests dressed as clowns on our sacred sanctuaries. Even though I am their pope, so many of my flock detest me and long for the day that my successor kneels before my final resting place within the grottos.'

'They do not detest you,' Lucé felt obliged to speak, to lift his broken spirit, 'they just fail to see truth behind the reform and direction in which you truly want to bring the church. Plus, they have been misled by so many in their cloud of misunderstanding.'

'Especially by our old friend in Tübingen. Every time I hear his name I feel a pain in my heart. That is why I cannot bring myself to utter it. It is theologians like you who need to be promoted and to take control of the argument we lost since the publication of Humanae Vitae.'

'But that decision to ban birth control was the right one to make. The line of reform had to be drawn somewhere.'

'I know it did, and I remember your support for my position at the time, but the faithful have crossed the line and are openly defying my teaching. Ever since the Tübingen professor published that book on papal infallibility, people are openly questioning every aspect of doctrine, following the primacy of their conscience whilst our church becomes more polarised with the conservative right and the liberal left. Seminaries across the world are seeing vocations declining. Priests are petitioning me in their thousands to be dispensed from their vows. Churches are seeing numbers decrease. Sacred altars are being replaced with wooden tables. Divorce amongst Catholics is increasing. Abortion services are being legalised across the world and sexual morality is being questioned like never before.' He stopped once again and looked into Lucé's eyes. 'Do you know they even called me a homosexual in the press and accused me of having a lover?'

Lucé chose to look down at the ground rather than respond to the rumour he had heard many times.

'They have persecuted me, and they will continue to do so until the day I die,' Paul uttered, his emotion clear. 'The council was meant to open the doors to Christ, but at times I wonder has the smoke of Satan himself entered the Church instead?'

The rhetorical question left them both standing in silence for a few moments as Paul turned his face to look at the clear blue sky, his frailty clear to see and a knowing that his time was drawing to its natural end.

'If we are to save the Church, we need good men like you,' he finally spoke, before searching the pockets of his coat. 'I had these made for all the bishops of the council. A few remain unused, but I would like to gift this to you, so that every day you wear it you will pray for me and remember the mission to which I have called you.'

Taking the red leather box from the pope, Lucé opened it to find inside a polished conciliary ring. The gold mitred front, engraved with a simple cross, under which stood the risen Christ with Saint Peter and Paul on either side.

'This is a most gracious gift, Holy Father,' Lucé replied as he studied the ring and noticed the miniature engraved signature of the ring's designer, *E Manfrini*. 'I will pray for you every day and I will strive to complete the mission to which you have called me.'

Paul smiled warmly. 'It is cold, will you take me back to the apartment please.'

Returning to the lift, Paul sat in the chair reserved for the pope as Lucé took the key from his trouser pocket and inserted it into the panel of the lift.

'How long have you been here?' Paul asked, as the lift began to descend.

'About an hour, Holy Father.'

'Just one hour?' Paul pondered aloud. 'I have been here for thirteen years, and they still do not trust me with that key.'

Lucé turned to him and smiled. 'This key is nothing compared to the weight of the keys you carry, Holy Father.'

Paul looked up at him intently, taken aback by his response. 'No truer word has been spoken to me in such a long time,' he said softly. 'Their weight is something this world, especially my detractors, will never fully understand.'

13.

Oliveri would love to have been walking once more through the old Rome he so intimately knew – to be breathing in the once familiar smells of the coffee shops, the bustling sidewalk cafes, restaurants and to hear the excitement of everyday conversation, and to feel the love that embraced the youth within the Eternal City. But he knew those days were gone forever. Crossing in front of Castel Saint Angelo, making his way towards the Victor Emmanuel Bridge, the city of Rome looked every part a scene from the end of times as one could imagine. The eternal darkness was broken by random fires in roadside pits that illuminated the hundreds who passed him by as they headed towards the Vatican in a vain hope for salvation.

'Do you need to take a break?'

Oliveri coughed as he rested on the bridge and gazed into the dark marbling current of the Tiber. 'A few moments, if you do not mind. It is the air. I find it hard to get a breath.'

'It will likely worsen over the coming days and weeks,' Gabriel Roth replied. 'God only knows the damage that asteroid impact made, but we can be sure that those of us who have survived are on borrowed time. We do not have far to travel.'

Oliveri knew the route well, and as Roth joined him by resting his elbows on the balustrade of the bridge, he was grateful that he was not having to make this journey on his own.

'This is where we scattered his ashes,' Roth reminisced, as his eyes ran the length of the bridge.

'Whose ashes?'

'Pope Christopher's. The lord instructed us to cremate his body in the Vatican gardens. Word came through, I presume from the Lord, that we were to scatter into the river whatever remains we had gathered. There was not much, just a few fragments of bone by the time the fire finally extinguished itself. This was the closest point to the Tiber we could find. No ceremony for the one who fooled us all.'

'You must stop calling him that,' Oliveri gently rebuked, as he stared intently at Roth. 'Whatever is happening, whoever he is, he is not the Lord. All of this, all this suffering has nothing to do with the goodness of the Lord who loves us.' Taking a deep breath, he went into an uncontrollable fit of coughing before finishing. 'He is not the one we are looking for. Instead, he is the one we need to get away from.'

The further away from the Vatican they walked, the thinner the crowds became. And as they went against the flow of people, they noticed the remarkable difference on their faces. If it were not for the darkened and poisonous skies over Rome, Oliveri would have sworn that they were faithful pilgrims, heading to the Vatican for the papal audiences and masses that brought much meaning to the lives of the people who encountered them. Each pilgrim, who passed him that night, could sense that they were close and walking the final steps of their pilgrimage. From the remaining lands of the earth, they had walked to find comfort and safety under the protection of the one they now called lord, and in whom they believed they would be saved from the suffering that no man or woman, no matter what their means could escape. The only difference from these pilgrims was that they were soiled and dishevelled but written on their faces was the same look of hope, and a surrender that they were now safe in the heart of the Church.

He wanted to reach out to them, one person at a time, and to let them know that they were heading the wrong way. To explain to them that once they fell under his spell and ate the sweet bread, they would be forever condemned. As a priest, his conscience rose within him to save their souls, but the closer he watched them, he knew they would never heed him for they were the people who had never believed in the faith. Their coming to Rome was a pilgrimage of a self-centred fear of death. Their salvation was conditioned on life in this passing world, not on the life eternal in the world to come. And for the briefest of moments, he turned to look at them as they unwittingly walked towards the sting of death, clearly hoping they would be safe in the presence of the one they believed had come to save them.

Stopping several times to allow Oliveri to catch his breath, Roth remained faithful to the ailing cardinal and the promise he made to him that he would get him safely to the Basilica of Saint Clement. The few words they managed to exchange on their journey had disturbed the peace Roth believed he had found through his position and privilege of remaining within the Vatican. Until that evening, everything that was happening to him and to other Swiss Guards, the intentions of the lord, the mysterious sweet breads, the suffering and death of the pilgrims, all these unexplained happenings were put aside in the reasoning of mind as a mystery yet to be made clear. He had no fear of death, for in the depth of his being he believed that Christ would one day return to gather the sheep who were his own. Yet, tonight was the first time that he could see, beyond the confusion of everything that was unfolding around him, that perhaps he had been following the one who was leading souls through the gates of oblivion.

The Via di San Giovanni In Laterano, with its cobbles and narrow pavements, had never appeared so deserted to Oliveri. With no pilgrims or Romans congregating outside the wine bars, a relative silence consumed the air, whilst the putrid smell of death appeared to have dispersed into what smelt to Oliveri like the burning of church incense.

Climbing down several stone steps, they arrived at the large brown doored entrance of Saint Clement's, and together they stood and listened, both aware of the silence that surrounded them for the first time in weeks. With a simple nod of his head, Oliveri gave permission for Roth to knock on the door. It took several attempts from Roth's clenched fist before a softly spoken voice was heard from the other side.

'Who is there?'

'Cardinal Oliveri, the former Secretary of State. I come here on personal business with a member of the Swiss Guards. We have been led to believe that Dom Colby could be with you.'

After a few seconds, the distinctive sound of an Iron latch could be heard as it was lifted before a large iron rod was pulled across the opening of a small wicket door. As the door opened, a young redheaded priest, dressed in the white of the Dominican order, studied them carefully. Not wishing to stand outside the gate for much longer, Oliveri raised his right hand to show his distinctive cardinal's ring.

'Eminence,' the young priest spoke, recognising the ring and then the face of Oliveri. 'Please come in.'

Stepping through the small wicket door, Oliveri, followed by Roth, entered the ancient atrium of Saint Clement's; where candles burned along the arcades that formed a cloister around the fountain that sprang forth crystal clear water.

'Would you like to drink?' The priest asked, noticing that they were intrigued by the crystal clarity of the water. 'It's not like the water that you've probably been drinking. This water's pure.'

Oliveri looked at him, seeking an explanation. Yet before he had the chance to speak, Roth had already made his way over to the fountain, and with both hands he scooped the water into his mouth with the thirst of a man on desert land. When Oliveri joined him, the purity of the water was like nothing he had ever tasted before. The cool freshness that engulfed his mouth and trickled down into his body, removed every bitter taste that had consumed him for weeks.

'We cannot explain why this water has not been contaminated,' the priest pointed out, 'nor why the air in here appears to be, well, the way it has always been. We can only believe that we, as well as a few other places around Rome, have been veiled in a cloak of Divine protection.'

'There are other places just like this?'

The priest nodded. 'Please, you must come inside.'

After taking one more drink of the water, Oliveri followed the young priest across the atrium and into the basilica, where his attention was drawn immediately towards the altar and the illuminated twelfth century Byzantine arabesque mosaic that shone like fiery gold in a furnace on the apse above the main altar. Then, lowering his eyes, Oliveri could see, positioned on the centre of the altar, with perfumed resin incense rising from two thuribles on either side, a large golden monstrance that captivated him as the white host of the Blessed Sacrament radiated like he had never seen before. In complete abandonment, with a reverence born from true belief, Oliveri dropped to his knees, and with arms outstretched, he openly called on his Lord for mercy and forgiveness.

Although Roth had joined him, by kneeling behind him, he did not have the same conviction of the aging cardinal. After a few minutes he had to rise from the uncomfortable tiled aisle, but he looked on, completely mesmerised that the cardinal never flinched nor once glanced away from the exposed eucharist onto which his whole mind, body and soul had become transfixed.

Not wanting to disturb Oliveri, the Irish priest left him and went down into the excavated ruins of Saint Clement's, where the original basilica had been converted from a home of a Roman nobleman. Through ancient catacombs he carried his candle until he reached the place where Dom Colby and the other priests were sleeping, having completed their vigil watch for that day.

Finding Dom Colby, the young priest tapped him gently on his shoulder to stir him from his sleep.

'Fr. Colby,' he gently called, repeatedly until the priest opened his eyes. 'Cardinal Oliveri is in the basilica, and he has come to speak with you. Will you come with me?'

After the confusion of being woken from a deep peaceful sleep, Dom Colby fought the stiffness in his body and got up from the makeshift camping bed that had been allocated to him, placed his white socked feet into his worn black sandals and followed him, wondering why Oliveri would want to speak with him. Throughout his tenure as a priest in the Vatican, Oliveri had never spoken one word to him. Even on the few occasions they happened to pass by one another, Oliveri would never acknowledge a priest so far below his rank as the secretary of state.

Emerging into the basilica, Dom Colby could not believe what he was seeing when he saw Oliveri kneeling in the central aisle with his arms outstretched. He looked like a mystic, transfigured before the presence of his God. Gone was the old. The cynical clerics in the Vatican had often talked about his lack of faith and his blood-thirsty ambition to become the second most senior man in the Vatican if he could not get his hands on the throne of Peter as pope. It was whispered that Oliveri had no real faith, and that God was the inconvenience of his life and the calling he had to the Church. The only ceremonies he felt worthy of his time were those led by the pope, in which he would be seen, and his place honoured by his brother cardinals. Yet, here he was tonight, transfixed on the source and the summit of his catholic faith.

For Oliveri, the presence before him burned deep into his soul as he felt the waves of grace wash over him. Never had he experienced the presence in such a way. All his ministerial life he had longed for a sign, or even a sensation that the words he spoke over the consecration meant what they said. Ever since he uttered the words during his first mass, he urged himself to believe that he had transformed the mundane objects of bread and wine into the living flesh and blood of Jesus Christ, but all he ever saw before him, resting on the linen corporal, was white unleavened bread and a chalice of cheap wine. Now, nothing else mattered except for the truth he saw radiating before him, and having found the truth he would have happily breathed his last in that moment to enter the heavenly realms of eternal life.

'Eminence!' Dom Colby spoke, as he placed a hand onto Oliveri's shoulder. 'Eminence, I believe you are looking for me?'

At first the words felt distant, but knowing they were meant for him, Oliveri turned to see Dom Colby standing beside him.

Helping the cardinal up from his knees, Dom Colby offered him the time he needed knowing that Oliveri had just experienced a spiritual encounter. For no longer was the essence of faith a quiet revelation, instead it was beginning to reveal itself in all its majesty.

'Until I entered this basilica, I had no idea why I felt the urgency to meet you,' Oliveri confessed. 'But now I know that we are meant to be present before the Lord in this moment in time.'

'I am glad that you were able to come,' Colby replied, as he turned and extended his right opened hand towards the altar. 'It is clear that you have the faith to begin to see the truth that we have professed and preached for so long.' Then turning to look deep into Oliveri's soul he asked, 'When did you last confess?'

Cardinal Oliveri of old, would have snapped at being asked such a question by a priest, but with the purest of emotions he turned to Dom Colby and replied, 'It has been so many years, that I cannot honestly recall.'

'My brother, come with me,' Dom Colby remarked, as he took hold of Oliveri's hand. 'In this spiritual warfare we need to be ready to fight the devil and his demons with a purity of heart. We will begin with your confession. And then,' he paused before turning to Roth, 'I will hear yours.'

For a significant period, Roth sat on one of the pews and watched as Cardinal Oliveri and Dom Colby stood before the Blessed Sacrament. The whole time he watched, Dom Colby listened intently as Oliveri spoke with his eyes closed and his clasped hands resting against his chest. He had never witnessed the sacrament celebrated with such dignity and the penitent freely confessing without any fear of the sins that had bound him throughout his life. When the absolution came, Oliveri stood tall like a man born again in both the spirit and the flesh, for he was a man whose burdens had been cast from him, and which would never attach themselves again.

'Will you be staying with us?' Dom Colby asked Oliveri. 'You would be more than welcome?'

'There are others living close to the Vatican that I must tend to. I came here tonight because a thought, or should I say a stirring of the Holy Spirit moved me to find you.'

'What happened?'

'This might sound outlandish,' Oliveri mused, as he recalled Mode's experience, 'but, in the light of all that is happening, it might just be the only thing that makes sense. One of the people I am with,' he leaned to Dom Colby's ear to whisper, 'the assassin I mentioned during my confession.'

Colby nodded.

'Tonight, he was convinced that he saw someone who should be dead walking close to the Vatican. The person he saw was a young priest he killed many years ago, a former papal secretary.'

'Monsignor Hasler?' Dom Colby enquired, as he watched the curiosity grow on Oliveri's face.

'How did you know?'

'Dear brother, there is so much you have yet to understand. He has been in Rome for some time. Many have seen and heard him, but only a few have heeded him,' Dom Colby explained, as a warming smile grew across his face. 'We have been expecting him and his brother to come at this late hour in time. It should come as no surprise to anyone who has studied the apocalyptic scriptures.'

In his confusion, Oliveri could only ask, 'What purpose? And who is the other one that you speak of?'

Dom Colby thought about it for a moment, before motioning Roth to approach him. 'It is best I show you in person,' he replied, 'after I hear this young man's confession. All I will tell you for now is this - Gustave Hasler has indeed been resurrected from the dead and it is his glorified body that is bearing witness to us all, because he is one of the two witnesses prophesised in the Book of Revelation. He is not far from here and when you see him, hear him and talk to him, you will have no fear even when you realise that the worst has yet to come.'

14.

'They both appear twice daily,' Dom Colby explained, as they passed the Lateran Obelisk and walked towards the basilica, 'but as you can see the numbers gathering here are much smaller than they are at the Vatican.'

'Why are so few coming?' Oliveri quizzed, estimating that the crowd numbered no more than three hundred.

'The big-ticket attraction has always been at the Vatican. Apart from the remaining faithful clergy of Rome, and they are few, the people who come here each night either dismiss what they hear and head straight to the Vatican, or else they leave the city altogether once they come to accept the truth.'

'Where do they go?'

'On the greatest spiritual journey of their lives,' Colby replied. 'The same journey you are now on.'

Walking along the paved road that led to the most important Church in Christendom where the pope's cathedra resided, Oliveri's gaze was drawn through the opened bronze doors and into the white light that emanated from inside.

'They claim to be the two witnesses foretold in revelation; the two olive trees or the two lampstands that can kneel before the living Lord,' Colby replied, as they mingled with the crowd. 'In the seminary we were taught that they would likely be Moses and Elijah, just as they had appeared at the transfiguration. Turns out God has chosen two of our own, whom He has resurrected from the dead, to reveal His final message before everything in this world comes to pass. They cannot be harmed. I didn't see it with my own eyes, but I've heard that in recent days a group of men tried to attack them, and a Divine fire of white flame emerged from them both and consumed those who tried to bring them harm.'

Oliveri did not know what to say, as a swell of anxiety rose within him the closer he came to the entrance of the basilica.

'You have nothing to worry about, for your heart is pure,' Colby replied, sensing Oliveri's trepidation as people in the crowd began to look their way. 'In these days heart speaks to heart, but for those who stand against the truth, well, the time to repent of their ways is quickly running out. In these days we must all face the consequences of our actions.'

Despite his desire to see the two witnesses with his own eyes, Oliveri felt a tense unease as he saw the faces of fellow clergy look his way and then talk amongst themselves that he had the audacity to turn up.

'Are you okay?' Colby asked, as he reached out and took hold of Oliveri's hand. 'Many still do not fully understand, and the mercy they ought to show is difficult at times to deliver when hurt and anger arise.' Then looking into Oliveri's eyes, he smiled and said, 'You are going to be alright. You were always destined to be present here this night.'

Almost immediately, the assembled crowd began to fall silent as two figures slowly emerged from the glowing light and walked out onto the steps of the archbasilica. Miraculously, an accompanying breeze of fresh and cooling air removed the toxicity around those who had gathered, and for the first time in weeks many were able to breathe in fresh air as the two witnesses invited them to sit on the steps of the Lateran.

Cautiously, and with fear and awe at what he was seeing, Oliveri approached from the back of the crowd; carefully studying the face of Gustave Hasler as he got closer to him. Mesmerised by the heavenly light that radiated from him, and the contentment that emanated from his smile, he gazed at the warmth on his face as he looked lovingly upon the pilgrims who had gathered.

With deep sadness, Oliveri's heart began to sink as he remembered that Mode had told him that he had seen

Gustave Hasler earlier that evening - or was it yesterday? For time no longer had any rhythm in the perpetual darkness that now engulfed the world. It was a feeling of sadness the likes of which Oliveri had never felt before, rooted in the knowledge that he had played a cruel part in destroying something that was so pure, beautiful and true.

To all who had gathered, Hasler greeted them with a welcoming smile, and to those who approached him he was more than happy to reach out his hand and allow them to feel the warmth of his glorified flesh.

Taking his place amongst the pilgrims, Oliveri's gaze was transfixed on Hasler for he knew he was witnessing something few had ever seen, but it was an essential element of the faith that millions had preached down through history, and billions had believed in, and that was the resurrection of the dead into a glorified state of being. Eager to hear him speak, Oliveri's attention was caught by a waving hand that was raised alongside Hasler. The moment he turned to look, he was stunned when he recognized that it was the second witness who was waving and smiling at him, was none other than Cardinal Brenard who had been killed alongside Hasler all those years ago.

In Brenard's eyes, Oliveri could see only warmth and forgiveness. They expressed a depth of love that he had never seen or felt before. The shame that swelled within him and the emotion it brought, subsided with a calmness of a heavenly peace he had longed to feel for such a long time; a peace this world had failed to give him. Then, without the need to be told, Hasler turned his attention from the others in the crowd and looked directly at Oliveri too, revealing a tender compassion that was unworldly in the truth it revealed. In that moment, Oliveri felt the shame disappear as he felt truly forgiven by them. Slowly, he allowed himself to smile back as their feelings towards him grew in warmth and affection. For Oliveri it was an experience not of this world. In that encounter, he felt like an apostle who had witnessed the resurrected Jesus, the same Jesus who had returned to love the world that had killed him so brutely.

'Brothers and sisters,' Brenard and Hasler spoke in unison, as they returned their attention to the crowd. 'Do not be afraid! Blessed is He who has returned in the name of the Most High God. Whilst the mountains crumble into the valleys, the waters return to their source and thousands fall around you, be confirmed in the faith branded on your souls that those of you who follow the right path, even though you will die, you will see the face of God and live. For our God loves the innocent of heart, and when the innocence is lost it is He alone who restores it.

'We are witnesses to the message that has been proclaimed from the ancients, for we have seen and experienced it.' Then pausing for a moment, they both looked intensely at one another as their faces radiated an unspoken joy that captivated many within the crowd. 'We have walked through the gardens of heaven; we have bathed in its miraculous waters and have eaten from the fruits of its bounty. We have seen those we once mourned as they live the eternal life they were promised. We have spoken to the prophets and the saints, and we have caressed the face of the living God as His love has anointed us with a balm of peace.

'We once lived in this world as mere mortals, vulnerable to its ways. In our brokenness we believed and through our martyrdom we were confirmed in truth.'

Oliveri expected them to look at him, but they simply carried on addressing the people. 'In our final moments, the fear of death engulfed us, but the moment we left this physical world we stood transformed before the risen Christ and were welcomed into the heavenly kingdom. For one thousand, two hundred and sixty days of this world's passing, we have lived beyond time with our Father. Whilst Christ has returned to walk amongst you, we waited for the moment to arrive when we would be sent back to this passing earth, to convince you of the Gospel truth for one last time. So that those who hear us, and who treasure their soul over the flesh, will come to taste and see that the Lord is good.

'If you are looking for an end to your suffering in this tribulation, we have nothing to offer. We can only encourage you to walk through this time of trial, knowing that the journey's end will bring you to see the kingdom you have longed for.'

'We have walked over a thousand miles to get here,' a man from within the crowd spoke up. 'Is this it? Is this all you have to offer?'

'We are offering you the gift of reassurance that the Kingdom of Heaven is very near to you,' they both continued, 'but you must remain faithful to suffering if you wish to find it.'

'We must continue suffering?'

'Suffering is the currency of the Christian way of life and the sure way to see the gates of heaven open before you. You too, all of you, will die. None of you will save your lives. If that is what you are looking for, we ask you, why? What purpose does your life now hold? Look around you. This world is passing away. No man can escape the inevitable end that is coming, but the path you choose is crucial, for you are either going to be walking towards God or walking away from him.'

'But there is hope at the Vatican!' The man argued. 'There the lord is saving people and feeding their hunger.'

'He is not the Lord. He was the one who served God before his fall. He has only one purpose and that is to take as many souls with him, as he can, into the eternal darkness of hell. He knows that his time is short. And his bread only brings death to those who eat of it. Look around you, for Rome is overflowing with the corpses of those who once believed in him.'

Reading the man's soul, they both looked at him with tenderness and compassion, as he considered the options that were laid out before him. For a moment Oliveri expected him to get up and walk away, but to his surprise the man remained and listened to them.

'The time is coming when Christ, who already walks amongst you, will reveal himself and fulfil the testimony of the prophets by judging both the living and the dead. There will be no place to hide from the verdict of your lives. Just as a natural death has brought countless generations to face the truth of their lives, so too will you, the witnesses of the end of time, experience the justice of God's mercy as well as His retribution upon those who accept or deny the pearl of great price. With no contest, the people of this world will either stand among the elect who have already been saved or be cast into oblivion.

'You are the people of the end of days. Very soon the final rage of darkness and its torment will be unleashed upon the world. It will eclipse all that you have seen to date. No one will escape, but for those who remain steadfast in faith, then they will see the dawn of eternal happiness. It is you who must decide. For those who try to save their lives will lose them, but for those who are prepared to lose their lives then they will live. In spiritual warfare there is no place for lukewarm people. As Christ himself said, be either hot or cold, for he will vomit the lukewarm from his mouth.'

As a perfumed bouquet filled the air around them, bringing many to their knees, the pilgrims pleaded with the two witnesses for more guidance as to what they should do. Oliveri barely managed to hear them speak about Jerusalem before Colby placed a hand onto his shoulder.

'Come with me,' he said, leading Oliveri away from the crowd. 'Would you like to meet with them in private?'

Getting up from the step on which he was sitting, Oliveri followed Colby into the Lateran where the sight that met him took his breath away. Rooted to the spot, he stood in stunned silence with his mouth opened in wonder and awe.

Through the bright light that engulfed the interior of the basilica, he noticed that the roof of the Lateran no longer existed. Instead, its once high vaulted ceiling now opened into the light of a heavenly realm that appeared to move. However, it soon became apparent that it was not the light that was moving, but spiritual beings that were continuously emerging through it. What appeared to be tens of thousands of winged angels; their robes whiter than snow with gold cinctures around their waists, and the locks of their hair flowing freely in the gentle breeze of their flight, emerged from the light and encircled the entirety of the basilica before coming to rest on the marbled floor. There they knelt in homage, with their wings closed behind their backs, as they gazed towards the sanctuary and the unbelievable sight that drew Oliveri's attention away from them.

On the altar, where Oliveri himself had celebrated mass many times, stood a pure white Lamb in front of a blazing golden cross. And as the angels recited angelic praises in a language Oliveri had never heard before, the enthroned Lamb turned its gaze from the vault of heaven to the angels who worshiped him. Together with the angels who knelt before the Lamb, hundreds more encircled him, reaching out their hands as they acclaimed him with songs of praise, mingling backwards and forth in a heavenly murmuration. Along with two angels standing on each side of the altar, burning incense grains into large golden thuribles, other angels walked the perimeter aisles of the basilica, carrying in their hands silver and gem encrusted bowls; from which plumes of perfumed smoke, that contained the faces of the fallen souls of the world, rose into heaven whilst they lamented in great agony.

Transfixed by the heavenly hosts that ascended and descended around him, Oliveri felt unable to pass beyond the basilica's vestibule and get closer to their heavenly presence. For they belonged to a world he had not yet attained, but for which he now longed having glimpsed a fragment of its beauty.

'Very few have seen into the meaning of the light within this building,' a voice spoke, as an arm was placed gently around Oliveri's shoulders. 'And what you see with the eyes of this world does not do justice to what is truly before you. Shalom Aleichem.'

When Oliveri heard the Hebrew blessing, he turned and looked into the loving eyes of Paul Brenard. Immediately, like a rushing wave towards the shore, his heart melted as the magnitude of his sinful past began to overwhelm him. It was a pain that pierced him deeply, and from which he struggled to escape. For a man called to live and to preach love, he had sided with a raw evil and had allowed it to consume him to the point of nearly losing his soul. With his emotions overwhelming him to the point of tears, Brenard took hold of him and brought his head to rest against his chest.

'I know you are truly sorry for what you did,' Brenard reassured him, as his right hand caressed the back of his head. 'Blessed are you, for salvation has come to your home. You have been allowed to see what is before you because you are a child of The Most High. Have no shame,' he continued, as he took Oliveri's head in both his hands to look him in the eyes, 'for I forgive you. You are my brother, and I love you!'

As Oliveri looked into Brenard's loving eyes and saw Hasler standing behind him, the remorse was so overwhelming that even the words of forgiveness could not quell the rawness he felt in the freedom of his absolution.

'We have allowed you to see beyond this world so that you will know what the truth looks like,' Brenard continued. 'Through death we have both travelled and have experienced the glorified resurrection that is promised to all. At the table of the Lord, we have eaten and have been transformed by him. There is no greater joy, and it is the reward given to all who choose to have the faith.'

'You want to know why we cannot show the people who are in Rome what you are now witnessing?' Hasler spoke, reading Oliveri's thoughts. 'The majesty of God is cloaked in the love of one another and not of the self, and that is the only way to see the face of God and live. But you must tell those whom you know what you have seen and heard and tell them this. The powers of hell will be opened for one final time, and there will be no escaping the terrors that will be unleashed. It will begin here in Rome before engulfing what remains of this passing world. You must gather those whom you love and travel to Jerusalem, for there you will see wonders never seen before and will witness the final victory over all this evil.'

'Bring nothing but the faith you profess,' Brenard added. 'Time is quickly running out and the end will come soon. Your time in Rome is over. Soon this city will fall into the hands of the one who hates us. Do not hesitate in doing what you must do. We will see you in Jerusalem.'

And with those words, Oliveri watched as Brenard and Hasler took their leave and walked across the vestibule and into the centre of the basilica as the angels parted a path for them to approach the altar so they could prostrate themselves before the Lamb.

15.

It was only after Wormwood collided with the earth, and in a hopeless attempt to numb the pain he was feeling, and no longer seeing the point of abstinence, that Walter Backhaus took the decision to drink continuously from the crates of red wine that had been shipped into the barracks of the Swiss Guards. Awakened from his sleep by the sound of pulsating music that penetrated through the walls of his bedroom, probably emanating from the officer's mess next to his living quarters, he felt the swelling of his tonsils as he swallowed; hating the life he now lived, and for a split second wishing he was no longer alive.

The once gradual awareness of death and decay now flooded his senses as the smell made him gag. It lingered everywhere from the air he breathed to the very clothes he wore and the bed sheets on which he lay. There was no escaping it except through numbing the senses with copious amounts of wine simply to get through the day. Even showering had become a routine of the past, as there was simply no point in even trying, because no amount of scrubbing could remove the smell of death that consumed the world around him.

As his young wife stirred beside him, murmuring through a dream she would never recapture, the music had a familiarity. It surfaced a faint memory from his childhood; dancing on the terrace of his parent's Alpine retreat, with the sun basking on them and the surrounding mountainside with its life-giving warmth, whilst a distant town emerged through the low-lying clouds of a new summer's morn as the world awoke in its innocence. The high-pitched voice of the British singer, and the memory of his mother dancing with him as the music played from a small transistor radio on the kitchen window ledge, brought a recognisable rhythm to his mind that, for the briefest of moments, helped him to escape from the reality of his living hell.

Stop. Spinning. Top. Dancing. Drop.

As the memory of his mother dancing lingered, with her hand raised as she stopped mid song before continuing, he saw his dad sitting on the edge of the walipini, watching them as he sipped on his morning coffee with a cigarette pinched gently between the thumb and forefinger of his right hand.

For the life of him, Backhaus could not name the song nor the woman who sang it, but he knew the tune so well that he could predict most of the words before they were sung – as someone's *baby just loves to dance*.

He had no concept of time nor day. His Tag Heuer watch read four-twenty, but he had no idea whether that was in the middle of the night or the afternoon. He knew it was pointless even wearing it, because some time ago he had forgotten to wear the watch for a few days and the automatic wind mechanism had ceased. With no way of setting it to the correct time, he simply wound it up and placed it on his wrist, for it was the only possession he owned that his mother and father had given to him; a present to honour his achievement in becoming the commander of the Swiss Guards some years previously.

He briefly thought of his parents and wondered if they were still alive. He hoped that they would have taken the decision to leave Bern and head for their mountain retreat above Simplon, as their terraced garden would have had enough food to keep them going and the stacked firewood would have lasted them for years. Then he remembered the darkness and knew that all vegetation on the earth would have died, and that only the firewood would have brought them some comfort. Once again, he considered the reality that in all probability they were already dead and that brought with it only one emotion, and that was relief because for Backhaus death was better than living in this unending nightmare.

Fumbling in the dark he felt for the lighter that sat on his bedside table and with it he lit the candle that was now his only source of light inside his home. The room was cluttered with clothes strewn everywhere, his marital bed an unkept mess and empty bottles lay where they were dropped after being consumed.

He had no recollection of how he got to bed or how his wife, who was clearly still intoxicated as she slept beside him, had spent her time before joining him. He remembered drinking with the guards after they had distributed the sweet bread and then the fight that broke out after one of the guards had knocked against an officer and spilt a glass of wine around him. Then he remembered the beatings.

In a feeble attempt to remove the dead as far away from St. Peter's as possible, he took the decision to commission young men, who were streaming into the city for their bread, to follow the direction of the guards in lifting the bodies and carrying them as far away as possible. It did not work. Even when they were denied the sweet bread until they assisted the guards, the young men simply attacked the weaker pilgrims and the poor, and stole what bread they had to satisfy their desires. Not even beatings from his guards could coerce the men to follow their orders, and in their frustration the beatings became more extreme as the bodies piled higher and the mounds crept closer to the walls of the Vatican.

His role as a guard was at one time ceremonial, respectful and despite being a trained soldier it was exercised with a genuine heart of love for pilgrims, the clergy and for the greater good of the Holy See. Now, one wrong look or word from a pilgrim was met with the most wicked lashing of violence, and the more he delivered it the more he enjoyed the feeling of inflicting pain onto people who were weaker. He had been trained to kill but had never killed until recently, and he loved the power that it gave him. His first murder was that of a young Italian man, probably in his late teens whom he had caught stealing sweet bread from a child. When he challenged the young man, the teen gobbed a mouthful of spit into his face. Backhaus's response was to punch the teen right on the nose until he fell to the ground and kept repeatedly punching him on the face, not even stopping as the skin on his knuckles broke with the injuries he was inflicting. Only when it became apparent, from the expressionless look in the young man's eyes that he had died, did Backhaus finally cease. No remorse or regret troubled his conscience, for this was now the way of the world and the role he was prepared to play.

The sudden silence, that came from the cessation of the music, made him listen even more intently in the way only silence can. He heard distant voices, but could not make out their words. Then hearing a door opening, he realised that it was the main door to his residence. Standing up, he grabbed his dishevelled uniform and clothed his nakedness before someone knocked on his bedroom door.

'Just a moment,' he insisted, as he hastily fastened the brown belt around his waist.

'You have been summoned to the mess room,' came the reply.

As a soldier he had been summoned and ordered his whole life, but as he tied the laces of his boots, he realised that as the commander of the Swiss Guards he now did the summoning and that only one person had the authority to call him.

'Come back to sleep,' his wife groaned, as her outstretched hand tried to find him in the bed.

He chose to ignore her, not out of loathing as he still loved her, but simply because he knew there would be no point as she was still drunk and would forget him once he had left the room.

Choosing to lift his white plumed helmet, out of respect for the lord, he left the room and accompanied the young guard out of his house and towards the mess hall. The pain in his head throbbed with every pulsating beat of his heart, and he wished for nothing more than to be able to place his mouth around the nozzle of one of the many water fountains within the state and drink to his contentment, but the water was too polluted to quench any thirst he had. It was clear to see that the young guard was worse for wear as he had to steady himself against the wall as he stumbled from the effects of the wine he had consumed. A few months ago, he would have been disciplined and expelled from the guards, but as Backhaus reminded himself with his all too familiar saying – *this was the new norm*.

Upon entering the barracks, he noticed through the open door of the officer's mess that some of his guards were struggling to stand. Walking towards them, he felt disgusted at how unkept they looked and how far their standards of appearance had fallen, but the truth was that his position of rank held no respect amongst them and at any moment one of them could challenge him, end his life and take his position from him. Up until now he knew he had been fortunate, but it was a perilous road that he had to walk each day, and control was no longer in his hands.

Approaching the door he saw the clutter of wine glasses, some half-filled but most empty, strewn around the once immaculate room. Brass plaques along with framed pictures and medals of honour, which once adorned the walls, had been knocked out of position and some had smashed to the floor with no care for the sentiment attached to their history.

No one turned to look his way, instead they stood looking ahead out of a sense of duty, their once perfect stand to attention faltering with staggered steps, as they swayed in a desperate attempt to hold a uniformed rank for the one who now had the real power.

'Commander!' Lucifer spoke with controlled dignity, as Backhaus entered the room. 'I am glad that we managed to find you,' he continued, before he turned to look at the men, 'maybe I need to reduce the ration of daily wine that is being provided. Afterall, the purpose of the wine is to ease the sting, not to inebriate basic functions.'

Backhaus and his men knew better than to reply as Lucifer stood watching them all, his eyes revealing his displeasure and a glimpse of the anger that consumed him from within.

'An issue has arisen, and I have come to seek your assistance in dealing with it,' he continued, as he brought an opened bottle of wine to his nose before removing it with disgust. 'There are two men who are, right now, leading souls away from me. I simply cannot allow this to continue and therefore need to put a stop to it with immediate effect. They are defiling my name on the streets of Rome, and many have heeded their cries and are no longer listening to my voice. I need them silenced to complete my mission, and to bring as many souls with me as I can.'

The guards remained silent as none of them knew to whom he was referring. Backhaus however had an inkling and stepping further into the room he genuflected in front of his lord before he dared to speak.

'My lord we are at your service. Are these two men the ones who are speaking at the basilica of St. John Lateran?'

Lucifer fixed his gaze intently on Backhaus, and without speaking he simply nodded.

'I have heard that they are two men of God,' he continued. 'I have not seen them with my own eyes, but I have heard the rumours.'

'Enlighten me,' Lucifer replied, as he took a deep breath and his skin radiated even more brightly.

'Well…' Backhaus stumbled, raising his eyes from the ground to look at the feet of the one he believed to be the lord, 'it is claimed that they have been resurrected from the dead. Two men who once walked these sacred grounds.'

'They are evil men, not men of truth,' Lucifer interjected, placing his right hand on top of Backhaus's head as he continued to kneel before him. 'That is why they need silenced.'

'Forgive me lord, but can evil resurrect the dead?'

Lucifer tightened his grip, almost digging into the scalp of Backhaus, tempted to crush his skull and to end his life before the guards he commanded. Restraining himself, he urged the commander to his feet and looked convincingly into his eyes.

'Walter,' he said almost in a whisper, 'I need you to fix this for me. Take a group of your men and go and destroy this evil that is standing opposed to me. The souls of many are at stake and we need to ensure that they find their way home to me. For I am the true way, and soon the world will see me in all my glory. What you have all witnessed now is but a glimpse of what is to come, and it will come soon.'

With his lies woven into an element of truth, for he knew that his power was restrained until the appointed time, Lucifer acted warmly towards the commander and the men who had faithfully stood by him, their minds clouded in a mist of confusion.

'I will deal with it,' Backhaus replied, before being embraced by Lucifer. 'I will always serve you faithfully.'

'When you return to me your reward will be great,' Lucifer whispered into his ear, before turning to the other guards. 'You are my disciples, and you will be fed with the food from the finest wheat and drink from the purest vines. In this time of war, in a time when confusion and fear have taken their hold on those who remain, I need men of honour who will stand by me and fight for me to the death. Will you take up your swords and follow me?'

In unison the guards cried out a resounding *yes*!

'Then let me see!' he demanded, before each one of the guards went to the armoury and returned with a ceremonial sword in their hands. 'Let me see!'

Raising their swords above their heads, they stood as best they could to show their loyalty to the one, they believed, would lead them to eternal happiness.

Then raising his left hand, Lucifer reached out and a light emanated from him before it touched the sword of each man, turning it into a burning flame.

'I am the light that will guide your way,' he explained, as the guards stood awestruck as the swords burned in their hands. 'Go in my name and take heart, for this world cannot overcome me.'

16.

His Fourth Pope.

Thursday 28th September 1978.

Since his consecration as an auxiliary bishop of Rome, Bishop Vittorio Lucé found that his international prominence as a theologian saw him called to lecture across the world. As he awoke in the presidential suite of the Los Angeles Conrad, he sensed a difference. Although his powers had been limited until his appointed time, he knew that something had happened, something that would change everything for him.

The previous pope, Pope Paul, to whom he served as an auxiliary, was delighted to see that he was in such demand. Known as the *'Council Bishop'*, he had the freedom to do what he believed was necessary to promote the reforms and to publicly challenge any descent from fellow bishops or theologians. From the moment his bestselling book, *'The Council Understood'* was published, he had been inundated with engagements to speak to diocesan clergy, congregations, and at mass public events across the world. For the past two years he travelled, lectured, wrote and promoted himself as a humble servant of the Church.

In all that time he continued to avoid celebrating the sacraments in public. From his days as a theology lecturer, he only appeared in the Gregorian lecture hall, tutor meetings and official public gatherings when it was necessary. He was left to pray and to offer the mass in private in the little oratory he had created at his home close to the Piazza Navona, yet in truth he did neither. Instead, he preferred the company of darkness and his demons.

Since the beginning of time, he had known truth but had despised it. Even in his recent earthly incarnation, with his memories at times distant and remote, he knew more than all the knowledge of human history combined. From the scriptures he read through the words and saw the reality that he had once known. Through the eyes of those he met, he read into their very souls. Yet, it was agreed that until the appointed time he could take any form and roam the world, but just like he did with Job, he could not harm nor take life away – at least not for now.

At seven o'clock the door to his suite was knocked, and after opening the door, he led the Turkish barber into the bathroom where he sat, and in complete silence he allowed the barber to shave him.

It was only after his shave was complete, that a second knock of the morning came to the door. Wrapped in only a dressing gown, he tipped the barber and led him back to the door, and upon opening it he saw the young priest from Los Angeles, who had been appointed to escort him to all his engagements throughout his stay.

'Good morning, Fr. Corbon,' Lucé greeted him with a warm smile, as he stepped aside to allow the barber to leave, and for the priest to enter. 'Coffee?'

Corbon could only stare at him, with a bereft look on his face. And the moment Lucé looked deep into his eyes he knew what he had come to tell him. And although it was a surprise, it came as no shock. Still, he managed to stop himself from smiling and continued to play the role of the gentle bishop.

'If you would take a seat,' Lucé continued, 'I would like to pour some coffee before you begin, because you clearly have something important you need to say.'

'It's sad news, I'm afraid,' Corbon finally blurted out. But, before he had a chance to continue, Lucé brought a finger to his own lips and insisted that the priest remained quiet.

'Coffee first,' Lucé whispered. 'It was a late night, and I am jetlagged. If there is something that you need to tell me, please allow me to have my coffee.'

Out of reverence to a superior, Corbon walked over to the leather suite of furniture to sit and watch as the bishop poured two cups of coffee from the decanter which had been left by the maid.

'I can tell from the aroma, that American coffee will not be as good as the coffee back in Italy,' Lucé said, as he handed a cup to Corbon before taking a seat opposite him and sipping the coffee. 'I knew I was right.' Lucé commented, as the bitter taste made him screw up his face. 'Now, what is it that you want to tell me?'

'The pope has died,' Corbon spoke, as tears filled his eyes. A slight trembling in his hand forced him to set the cup onto the table beside him.

Lucé laughed. 'I know that. He was buried last month.'

Corbon shook his head. 'The new pope. I'm talking about the new pope.'

Lucé leaned forward and allowed a look of concern to creep across his face.

'Pope John Paul?' Lucé asked.

As tears flowed, Corbon nodded.

'How?'

'They still don't know. He was discovered this morning by his secretary. He died during the night.'

As he witnessed the priest's love for his pope, Lucé felt a slight admiration for the young man, but he also felt sickened that such love could be expressed towards anyone, let alone a person one had never met.

Immediately, Lucé recalled a dinner he recently had with Cardinal Ehard from Switzerland, who confided in him, even though he was breaking the seal of the conclave, that the young Polish cardinal had come a very close second. And so, Lucé knew that it would not be long before the Pole would reside in Rome.

'You must contact the Cardinal's office here in Los Angeles and cancel all of my public and speaking engagements,' Lucé finally uttered, as he rose from the chair. 'I need to get back to Rome.'

17.

Believing he was armed with a sword of truth, Walter Backhaus selected twelve guards, the soberest he could find, to escort him the two-mile journey across Rome to the John Lateran Basilica.

Mesmerised by the swords that they gripped tightly in their hands, none of the guards in the mess noticed Lucifer depart from them. By the time any of them remembered that he was in their presence and turned to look for him, they discovered that he was gone, and they instinctively looked to Backhaus for instruction.

Strangely, no heat emanated from the swords. Yet, each blade had a blueish hue due to the intense flame that consumed them, but which did not scorch or destroy them. The incandescent light, however, was something not to be taken lightly, for although there was no heat, this unearthly flame left no doubt of its broiling intensity and ability to destroy anything that it encountered. If ever a sobering moment was needed for the Swiss Guards, this was it.

Leaving their barracks, Backhaus led his men through the side streets of the Vatican towards the gate of Saint Anne; the flames from their swords illuminating the buildings around them and guiding the path before them. Fascinated by what they were seeing, their fellow guards who were manning the official entrance to the state, stood aside as Backhaus led the march out onto the streets of Rome.

Into the thronging masses that had descended into Rome, the people parted at the sight of the guards as they approached. The unending clamour and commotion that had gripped the atmosphere in front of St Peter's Square, quickly died away as the pilgrims watched on in a mixture of astonishment and trepidation at the sight of the guards as they marched away from the Vatican and into the darkness of the eternal city. No pilgrim stood in their way. No pilgrim dared to challenge them. With an air of unspoken authority, everyone knew to step aside and to allow the guards to pass unhindered, for their mission was appointed by an authority never seen by humankind.

Down the Via della Conciliazione they marched on, the crowds thinning the further from the Vatican they went. The glass from the obelisk-shaped lamp holders of the avenue, now reflected the light from the swords they carried and briefly illuminated the buildings on either side.

For Backhaus it was a mission like no other, and in his heart he felt a deep sense of duty to complete this task for the lord. If souls were at stake, then he was determined to do everything within his power to ensure that few as possible were lost. Despite the toxicity in the air and the alcohol they had consumed, they managed a good and steady march to the Lateran; such was their resolve to please the one to whom they owed everything.

Past the colosseum they sought the shorter route through narrowing streets, approaching the abandoned Scala Sancta before turning right onto the cobbled piazza of the basilica where a small crowd had gathered outside the main entrance.

Ordering his guards to halt, Backhaus took a few moments to allow himself and his men, as best they could, to catch their breath before they proceeded.

Anything but inconspicuous, the people who had gathered turned to look their way. At first it was the bright illumination that caught their attention, before astonishment took hold when they realised that the light was emanating from the swords that the Swiss Guards held in their hands.

'Slowly!' Backhaus insisted, as he started to lead his guards towards the crowd. 'We are here to protect them from what is inside the basilica. No harm should come to the people.'

Instinctively, the people backed away in fright from the guards and despite Backhaus' reassurance that they had nothing to fear, they grouped tightly together and made their way up the steps to the opened doors. But once they reached the top, they found that they could advance no further as an invisible force, hidden by the light inside the basilica, prevented them from entering as it sealed the entrance shut. Realising their predicament, some of the crowd began to scream whilst others fled; neither group wishing to be caught up in the middle of something they knew was about to unfold.

'You need to disperse from this place,' Backhaus ordered the people. 'This is not the place for you. Go to the Vatican, and there you will be looked after. I promise, you have nothing to fear from us.'

With fearful hesitation the people slipped away from the basilica and ran off into the night, as the guards held their position at the old bronze doors that once hung on the ancient Roman Senate. The supernatural light that appeared to shine much more brightly than the light from within the Vatican, brought a swelling sensation of great nervousness to Backhaus when he realised that he could only go so far. It was as if an invisible wall was blocking his access to the basilica. He considered sending some men to scout the perimeter for another way in, but he knew there would be no point as the basilica and the curial offices that were attached to it were fortress like.

He touched the light with his hand, but felt the force push him back. Then he tried to press forward, but again there was no success. Then a thought crossed his mind, and he decided to give it a go. Lifting his flaming sword, he let it fall and found that it cut through the light with no difficulty. For the briefest of moments, he could see past it and into the basilica where the sight almost took his breath away. Yet, the moment he withdrew his sword, the light sealed itself shut to protect all that it shielded.

Once the other guards saw what had happened, they too lifted their swords and cut through the light; each slash briefly revealing the glory that was within. Yet, each time they made a cut it quickly closed over and it became apparent that they could not succeed. But with no other way to gain access, and with no other means to break through, they foolishly continued to use their swords in the vain hope that they would overcome the light.

'You cannot bring any harm to us,' voices with commanding authority spoke in unison from inside the light. 'We have the protection of the just one, He who was and who is. You have no place here and should take your leave. You have been warned.'

Initially startled, the guards stopped and listened for the voices to speak again. When nothing happened, they lifted their swords and with desperation they once again tried to cut their way through the light.

'You have no place here,' the voices insisted. 'Place down your weapons, for you attack what you evidently do not understand.'

This time the guards, clearly exhausted, ceased what they were doing and turned to Backhaus for direction under his command. Backhaus, although sensing the defeat, refused to give up. Unable to think of another way to complete the mission and with frustration that was beginning to boil into a humiliation in front of his men, he imprudently lifted his sword one more time and attacked the light. This time the light fought back.

With a surge of energy greater than any power he had experienced in his life, Backhaus felt the light expand with such an explosion of force that he and his men were lifted off their feet and thrown into the air and away from the entrance to the basilica.

Finding themselves on the grass lawns, some one hundred feet from the entrance, stunned with the pain of the blast and from landing on the ground, most of the guards struggled to get back on their feet as Backhaus, winded and his anger growing by the second, turned and faced the entrance. This time the light parted and two men emerged from within, and without fear or trepidation they walked across the piazza towards Backhaus and his men.

'We do not understand why you have come to attack us with your swords,' they spoke with authority as they neared them. 'We have come to lead men to the truth and to prepare the way for the one who will return to judge each soul by the measure of its worth.'

'He is already here,' Backhaus spoke, clutching his sword tightly in his right hand. 'It is he whom we serve!'

The two witnesses shook their heads. 'You risk losing your souls for all eternity as you have chosen the wrong path. We serve Christ – the Way the Truth and the Life. You are serving the fallen one – the one who condemns everyone who believes in him. The price already paid for you cannot be sold or exchanged. So please seek the path that leads to truth by laying down your swords and seeking the forgiveness of the one who truly loves you.'

Backhaus struggled to steady his nerve as he tried to breathe deeply. Still gripping his sword he looked at the two men, both of whom he had known from the past before everything in the world had imploded into chaos. He considered for the briefest of moments that he could indeed be on the wrong path, but when he remembered the extent his lord was prepared to go to feed the people that came to Rome, and the hope he gave them, Backhaus was convinced that the two men before him were the real enemy.

'Death can come to us no more, for we have been resurrected and glorified for eternity,' they both spoke, as they watched the guards gather around their commander. 'We have the authority to take life from those who seek us harm. There is no other way but the truth we profess. Stand against it and you will lose everything because of this choice that you make.'

Standing just feet from them, Backhaus took a deep breath and lifting his sword high he urged his men to attack and kill them both. It was the last act of his life, and his soul perished in that moment never to encounter the joy for which it was created.

The last thing Backhaus saw, but which he would never remember, was the two men raising their right hands and opening their mouths, and he believed they were screaming with fear.

To those who watched from the darkness of Rome, what they saw were the guards destroyed by a cloud of fire that came from the hands of the two witnesses, as their mouths extinguished their earthly breaths. Such was their power it was over in the briefest of moments. And as the fire consumed the bodies of the Swiss Guards, the two witnesses returned to the sanctuary they had created for the end of times.

18.

'We need to leave today!' Oliveri said, as he sat at the kitchen table with Mode, Lincoln and Gabriel Roth.

'And how are we going to get there?' Lincoln asked, noticing that Mode was not questioning the cardinal nor the stranger who now sat at their table. 'It's not as if there's flights departing from Fiumicino to Tel Aviv.'

'There is a group about to leave from Rome,' Oliveri explained, hoping to convince them both. 'To answer your question, I do not know how this will all work out. But I believe we need to be with that group when it leaves because things are about to get a lot worse. The time to decide is now.'

Oliveri felt a glimmer of hope when he noticed that Mode was gently nodding in either agreement or understanding, but it was Jane who looked doubtful.

'You have nothing to be afraid about Jane,' Oliveri reassured. 'After what I have seen I know that this is the right decision. All it requires from us is a little faith.'

'We aren't even prepared,' she remonstrated, as she looked around at their surroundings. 'What should we bring?'

'Nothing! Oliveri replied. 'God will provide.'

'So, you want us to leave what security, food and medicine we have here to walk into the unknown?' she questioned.

'Jane, there is no security in what we have. Soon all of this will be taken,' he tried to reason. 'There is only one thing that matters now, and that is the soul that is being called back from this time and place. This is what it is all about. This is what it has always been about.'

Mode tapped the table with the fingers of his left hand before placing his right hand onto Jane's shoulder. 'I'm going with the cardinal, and I want you to come too.'

'Are you serious Dave? This is madness!' she quizzed, as she grabbed hold of his hand. 'What you have going here is a good thing, not perfect but ... together we can continue to wait it out.'

'And wait for what?' Dave replied. 'There's nothing to wait for. It's all quickly disappearing. Having seen what I've seen and having listened to the cardinal, I want, just for once in my life, to do the right thing and to walk the right path and to live in the truth.'

Having known him since he was a graduate, Jane Lincoln had never heard Dave Mode speak with such conviction.

'Okay, but let's wait a little longer,' she suggested, before turning to influence Oliveri. 'Let's work together and get what supplies and medicines we need and consider our options more carefully. And if, after a few days we still feel...' her words tailed off when she saw Oliveri shake his head in disagreement.

'You are looking for distractions,' he spoke, before his lips gave a sympathetic smile. 'I am sure you never thought that the actions of your past would return to challenge you, but today they have. Dave, Gabriel and I have seen and experienced something you have yet to see. Our decision is made, and I plead with you to trust us. Come and see these resurrected men, in whose death you too played your part, and then you will understand that they desire only one thing and that is to save you. In true love there is no envy, hatred or resentment, only the desire to do the right thing for the betterment of others. Having passed through death and into eternal life, they have been made perfect and pure. Allow yourself this opportunity so you can best make the decision for yourself, but time is against us.'

Mode stood up at the table and nodded in agreement with the cardinal, whilst Lincoln remained seated, afraid and confused at what they were asking from her.

'What should we bring?' Mode asked.

Oliveri looked around the apartment and considered his words carefully. 'Nothing!' he finally replied. 'We travel with no purse or haversack.'

'But I've gold and money here, surely that would be needed?'

Oliveri shook his head. 'Soon it will have more value to the dogs on the streets. This is how we show our faith in Christ, by completely abandoning everything and trusting in him alone. Just like he did when he became man and was born in a wooden crib and died on a wooden cross, carrying with him nothing but trust in the love of his Father.'

Reluctantly, Jane Lincoln went with them that night, but deep down she believed that they would be returning to the apartment and following her plan, except this time she hoped it would be for as long as possible. Not once did she really believe that they would be leaving Rome for good.

When they arrived at the steps of the Lateran Basilica, a large crowd had gathered and were standing before the illuminated door. Oliveri knew some of the people gathered, and after embracing each one he knew and speaking a few words with them, he urged Mode and Lincoln to follow him closer to the door. Sensing Lincoln's fear, Mode tightly gripped her hand as he walked with her through the crowd. Having met Hasler he no longer felt afraid, but his past deeds still pained him, and he felt some trepidation in coming face to face with Brenard. In the end, just as he had expected deep down, his encounter with Brenard was filled with openness and love.

'Blessed are you for the path you have chosen to walk,' Brenard said, as he embraced Dave Mode for the first time and then whispered into his ear. 'Heaven rejoices for the son who was lost and has returned. His love for you is overwhelming and when you see Him, you will find the peace you have been looking for your entire life.'

Holding Mode close to him, Brenard turned his gaze to Jane Lincoln. He knew who she was and the role she had played, but all of that was insignificant to the beauty of her soul which he could see, like a delicate aura around her body. He looked lovingly at her and smiled reassuringly as he could see the fear written large in her eyes. Then, still holding Mode close to his chest, he reached out his hand and invited Lincoln to come close. Hesitantly, she stepped forward and took hold of his hand as painful sobs came forth like a cleansing ointment of healing as she surrendered to him and allowed him to embrace her too.

As she was held, she felt the warmth of his body radiate into her and the beautiful smell of his presence eliminated the harsh reality of death and decay; a smell like a mixture of frankincense and cloves from an ancient anointing oil. Breathing him in, her mind was filled with memories of her past, and as each one came to mind, she felt her heart cry out for mercy as it sought forgiveness for the wrongs she had committed, especially for the lives she had taken or had ordered to be taken. Like the freeing of a prisoner from a cell of despair, she let the past go and clung to the healing she felt grow within her. In that moment, every reservation and hesitation was dispelled, and she felt determined to walk with them and to discover the truth for herself. For this was a peace like no other she had experienced, and it was a peace she wanted to cling to forever.

Like one emerging from a long daze, she had no idea how long she had been held by him, but it felt like a lifetime lived again before she could look up and see Brenard's loving face smile upon her.

'You need not fear,' he replied, as he spoke to her heart. 'The price of your salvation has been paid, and now you must go and claim it. Fear not any illness, for you have been made a new creation and He will guide you every step of the way.'

They numbered just over one thousand people that night; amongst them were Dom Colby and the others who had now abandoned Saint Clement's, and many of the pilgrims who had heard the two witnesses and had come to believe them with their hearts. Not a single person carried anything with them, except the clothes they wore and their coats to shelter them along the way.

'When Moses led the chosen people out of Egypt,' the two witnesses spoke to those who had gathered, 'his guide was a pillar of cloud by day and a pillar of fire by night. To each of you He will give an even greater sign, for you now dwell in the shade of the Most High and under His wings you will find the refuge you desire. So do not fear the terror of the night nor the arrows that will fly by day. Thousands will fall around you, but upon you no evil shall fall, for He has commanded His angels to keep you in His ways. He will save you in this time of distress so that you will live to see and share in His glory.'

In that moment, the light around the entrance of the basilica parted and before all who had gathered a host of angels emerged, and into the darkness of the night they flew above the heads of the faithful remnant. Hundreds of Divine spirits hovered all around them, protecting them with an angelic fortification as they beckoned the faithful to follow them away from the basilica and to begin their journey out of Rome.

Together Oliveri, Mode, Lincoln and Roth walked in the middle of the chosen, mesmerized by the heavenly array that surrounded them on all sides; the wings of the angels fluttering a fresh breeze towards their faces as they smiled upon them with a knowing expectation of what was to come. The smell and decay of Rome was no longer present amongst them, and the air they breathed was now pure and renewing. Not once did they stop as they climbed a narrow pathway up the Monte Mario, only occasionally glimpsing back to see the city that was disappearing below them whilst others, like Oliveri kept walking and praying, ignoring the terrifying screams that punctuated the endless darkness.

Only when they reached the top of the hill did they stop as the angels allowed some time for them to rest. From a clear stream, each of the chosen took a drink of cool and untarnished water, before settling down to get some sleep. It was only then that Oliveri could bring himself to look upon the city he had loved since the moment he first walked its streets as a young seminarian. Now that the darkness had engulfed it, the only real light he could see, apart from small flickering flames of fires lit throughout the city, was the light coming from St Peter's Square and the majestic dome of Michaelangelo.

No morning came when the faithful remnant stood to continue along their way. And as they were about to disappear over the brow of the hill, Oliveri and the others turned to take one last look. Turning his gaze away from it for the final time, Oliveri knew that Rome was lost forevermore. Then taking another step forward, his heart became set on seeing Jerusalem.

19.

There was a time when Patrick Lennon would have taken this opportunity to broadcast himself live from Saint Peter's Square to his followers on YouTube. But since the attacks against America, his social-media platform of choice had collapsed and his voice, which he had painstakingly crafted to build up a following of three and a half million subscribers, had fallen silent.

What started off as a small channel documenting historical ruins of the ancient Celtic church, which he broadcasted from a boxroom in his Dublin home, quickly became an internet sensation when he discovered that his videos had more views when he criticized Rome and the pope, and allowed conspiracy theorists to appear on his channel to talk about freemasons, the Saint Galan mafia, the antichrist and usurpers to the throne of Saint Peter. Whilst his following was loud, many dismissed him as a crackpot, and he was accused by the hierarchy of creating scandalous division.

Rome was the place he wanted to be, and long before events against the United States unfolded, he had sold his home in Ireland and had moved to the city; publicly funded through various online sites by those who had donated to his cause and who were happy to watch him grow in notoriety. Now he had nothing, for what small fortune he had gathered over the years had vapourised with the collapse of the worldwide banking system. He was just like the others as he stood in the middle of thousands of desperate pilgrims as they waited to see the one whom they believed was their true lord. With his devoted wife by his side and his young son tightly clutching his hand, he stood on the steps that led up to the main vestibule door of Saint Peter's; armed Swiss guards preventing them from entering the basilica as pilgrims pushed and swelled in number behind them.

With no concept of time anymore, Lennon had no idea how long he and his family had been there, but it felt like days with no sleep and little food apart from the sweet bread, and their clothes were caked in filth. Where they had hoped for peace, they had experienced pain and suffering as people around them attacked and cursed one another, showing no respect for the dead who fell beside them nor the sick who begged for mercy. It was a living hell, and his wife and son continually cried in their misery and despair, finally doubting him and his wisdom for having brought them to this forsaken place and demanding to know what he believed was going to happen next.

They had witnessed the lord address the pilgrims many times, but they could not count the exact number as the memory of being in his presence merged into a confusion that lacked any clarity. Lennon believed that they needed to be there and close to him, for the reality of wandering amongst the dead in the streets of Rome was unthinkable. Therefore, they stayed with hope, waiting for something but not knowing what that was going to be, fighting for survival in the middle of the mayhem that surrounded them. Yet, despite their apprehensions and feelings of insecurity, the one thing Lennon and his wife agreed upon, without a shadow of doubt, was that they were witnessing the end of times. The only mistake they had made, was they really believed that they were following the lord who would save them.

Existing in the chaos that had engulfed the Vatican and the surrounding streets, the level of noise only became evident to Lennon when it quickly died away, as the pilgrims ceased their wailing and their ferocious screams as they became captivated with the sight that was beginning to unfold above them. Like a knife cutting through the web of night, a streak of light appeared before it began to widen, flooding the earth with light and forcing the pilgrims to shield their eyes and to look away.

In doing so, they were prevented from seeing the white light of heaven as the thin veil between this world and the next was parted, whilst the angels of the heavenly realm held open the entrance to allow one of their own to pass through.

Lennon wanted to look up into the light, but his eyes could not bear the pain as it was more blinding than looking directly into the sun. But as the veil was closed by the angels, the brightness quickly dimmed, however, the darkness did not fully return to the city as a new light had appeared. Then, as he looked behind him, Lennon could see with his own eyes that it was emanating from the middle of Saint Peter's Square, and as his eyes slowly adjusted, he could not believe what he was seeing.

On top of the rubble that was once the great granite obelisk, that had stood as a testimony to the entire history of Christian civilisation and that had witnessed the martyrdom of Saint Peter himself, there stood a spiritual being that no human eye had seen but of whom every human being knew by name. Standing with a flaming sword by his side, he stood facing the basilica as the pilgrims looked on with total wonder and awe. Towering above them, he rose to a height of twelve feet, with his muscular physique adorned with an armour of pure gold, as his long fair hair moved in the breeze caused by the white feathered wings that moved gracefully on his back. Even though the people could feel his gaze look upon them, no one could see his face, as the light that emanated from it concealed his true nature from them, for he was the one who could look upon the face of God and live.

Instinctively, Lennon knew who he was, for he had read about his description from books on antiquity and prophecy, and holding his family ever closer to him, he watched on as the spiritual being descended from the rubble and began walking towards the basilica. With dread, the pilgrims parted way before him, as he walked with an authority that had been bestowed upon him from Being itself. And as he walked past the Lennons and up into the basilica, Patrick Lennon began to wonder if he had made a mistake in bringing his family to this place.

Where the high altar had once stood, above the tomb of Saint Peter, Lucifer sat enthroned as his demons encircled the dome above him and along the ceiling of the nave. The arrival of his visitor came as no surprise as he watched him enter the basilica, for he knew that he too had a role to play in this final test that would determine the hearts of all men and women.

Walking towards the throne of lies, the spiritual being looked around him at the demons he knew by name and had once truly loved until their rebellion against the One who had created them. Now he felt nothing but disgust for them, and in this realm of time, into which he rarely sat foot, he knew that soon he would be casting them all into the flames of their hell for all eternity.

'Ah, the one who is like God has finally arrived,' Lucifer spoke, as his demons screamed and shrieked at the presence that had appeared before them. 'What do you want, Michael?'

The Archangel Michael chose not to reply as he stopped in the middle of the nave and looked around him at the destroyed interior of the greatest church in Christendom. It was not its physical destruction that angered him, for the basilica was merely an attempt by humanity to glorify God in the only way they knew how, but it was the intent behind the destruction and the insult towards God by the demons that angered him.

'It has been so long, Michael,' Lucifer continued to speak, 'but then, you do not have to live in this forsaken context of time and physical boundaries - unlike myself, who has been forced to wait and watch as the time of this creation has slowly ticked by, second by agonising second.'

'You will not have to wait much longer before you, like everyone, is freed from this creation of time and place,' Michael finally spoke. 'Your destiny is waiting for you and your legions, but it is a place where you will be no more.'

Lucifer sneered as he rose from his chair, extended his wings, and leapt from the sanctuary to face Michael who used to stand beside him before the rebellion was defeated. Feet from him, Lucifer looked upon Michael with revulsion as he saw him wear the heavenly armour that he himself once wore and hold the flaming sword of truth that he once possessed. For it was he, Lucifer, who had led the angels in heaven and who had the privilege to look upon the face of God. Where love once reigned with purity and where he once led heaven with loyalty, Lucifer forever cursed the moment human beings came into existence when they were born through the pure love of God's Being.

'How many have I won?' Lucifer asked, as he allowed himself to smile at the thought.

'Even I do not know that number,' Michael replied, 'but the final judgement will come soon enough, when Christ will cast his gaze upon both the living and the dead.'

'Him?' Lucifer scoffed. 'The Nazarene who loved so much that He lowered himself to become one of them, only to die on a cross in a pit of dirt! Such indignity for the Word.'

'This is why you will lose, and those who follow you will die too,' Michael spoke, as he gripped the sword of truth even more tightly. 'Now sentence is being passed on this world and soon you, the prince of this world will be overthrown, and under my heel you will be pressed into hell.'

Lucifer pondered his response for a few moments as he turned and looked up at his legion, knowing that soon it would all come to pass and his destruction secured, for it was always going to be the price he would have to pay for losing the battle he had begun. It brought him no fear, for such was the insufferable languishing of time on this earth for a heavenly being such as himself, that he too wanted it all to end and to take with him the souls he had won.

'Before we enter into this final phase,' Lucifer said, as he walked back to his throne of lies, 'would you satisfy my curiosity by telling me where you hid that body?'

The question, and the desperation behind it, made Michael laugh for the first time since seeing Lucifer, for he realised that for over five thousand years the not knowing of the location had been a painful torture. It had been the last battle they had fought each other over, for God had commanded Michael to protect and seal the remains of Moses from the people of Israel lest they worshipped his remains instead of honouring the promise of His covenant. Revealing the location now would have made little difference to this ordained time and what was unfolding, but it humoured Michael to keep the location to himself knowing the annoyance it was causing Lucifer. The truth was that in a simple grave, in a valley of Moab, the prophet lay in rest until his resurrection on the last day.

'How I longed to find that body,' Lucifer mused, knowing that Michael was never going to give up the location even now, 'I could have changed things, maybe in my favour.'

'Nothing would ever change things in your favour,' Michael replied. 'Even when the Word Incarnate died on the cross on Calvary, and you rejoiced at the death and in his anguish, the power of love dispelled the darkness, even of death, and restored him to life eternal and thus it has destroyed you.'

'Here we go!' Lucifer said mockingly, as he took his seat on the throne. 'Blah… blah… blah! When Jesus died on the cross my power died with him. Blah… blah… blah! And when he rose the price of sin, which was death was destroyed once and for all. Blah… blah… blah!'

As the demons roared with laughter and spat insults into Michael's face, the Archangel would not permit them to glimpse the anger he felt over their insults towards the one he loved and for whom he would gladly lay down his very existence and place in heaven. Soon, he would have his day with them all, and then they would face the true power of God's wrath, for there was no chance of them being forgiven for the wrong they had done and the rebellion they had caused.

Ignoring them, Michael raised his left hand and from it emerged a white flame that slowly drifted towards Lucifer before it divided itself into seven smaller flames. This was the purpose behind his arrival that day, for this was the last chance the souls of the world would have to seek forgiveness from the One who loved them but from whom they had turned. Not since God allowed Lucifer to attack His beloved prophet Job, had such a test been allowed to descend upon the earth, but it was a chastisement that was required, for it was now the only way in which the people would see that they needed to fall on their faces and to beg God for His Mercy in light of the wrongs they had done.

Until Christ himself walked the earth and was subjected to the most heinous of torture and ultimately his crucifixion, no human being had suffered as much as the prophet Job. Michael remembered the test well. His wealth and substantial livestock had been taken from him and slaughtered, many of his servants and children had been killed, and his home, his health and his way of life had been crushed, yet not once did he curse God. Nor did he ever lose his trust in his creator.

Unlike Job, this test was never destined to be recorded or remembered. For there would be no surviving its wrath. For those who had already chosen the path of truth and who were headed to Israel, their protection was already guaranteed at the hands of the Hosts of Heaven. No harm would ever touch them; such was the promise granted to them for seeing the truth. But, for those who remained, the greatest trial was about to be unleashed upon them and the final chance permitted for their souls to repent. These were the children who had not listened, who had not heeded and who had not lived in accordance with the will of the One who had created them. Time and time again they had been warned to turn from their ways and to embrace the truth in their hearts and not some warped notion of the truth they had formed. Death was about to come for them, the gateway into the eternal, and the final test that waited them was built on the back of Job's suffering; would they praise God and ask for His mercy, or would they curse His name?

Lucifer was surprised at what he saw Michael do, and he felt tricked that it was unfolding in this way. As the balls of flame settled before him, bringing into existence the seven bowls that contained the means of the final chastisement, he always believed that they would be poured upon the earth from heaven itself.

'Let there be no doubt that you cannot go beyond the limits of what is contained in these bowls,' Michael said, as he watched Lucifer gaze upon them with great anticipation. 'This permission has been granted to you, just as it has been foretold. You and your demons will have the freedom to roam this world and to test those who remain, but your time is limited and once the final bowl is emptied you will be defeated along with your demons and those you win over.'

For Lucifer, Job had been his toughest adversary; such was his loyalty to God. Against him he had used every means at his disposal to break his spirit and to get him to doubt God's love for him and to whisper a curse against His name. He had sent evil men to steal and to kill. He had used lightning and wind to destroy, and sickness to inflict so much pain and suffering. His calculated timing had been perfect, as one disaster followed another to overwhelm him and yet he could not break him. In the end Lucifer walked away realising that God's love could not be bought with protection and an abundance of blessings in this world. Instead, it came from something he no longer possessed, and that was an inherited awareness of God's Love in one's life; something to desire with all one's heart.

'Do not take too long,' Michael said, as he stretched out his wings and took one final look at the legion of demons who had been waiting for this moment to begin. 'Do what you must do and do it quickly.'

Allowing himself to levitate a few feet above the floor, Michael turned towards the door of the basilica and headed out into the square where the pilgrims screamed with terror at his angelic presence. As he rose above them, he knew that many of them were to be lost forever, but he remained hopeful that those who had the wisdom of heart would see through the test and repent to save their souls. Then, in the same way he descended, he ascended back through the veil. And as it opened the people shielded their eyes from the blinding light before the darkness returned.

'Who was that?' Kerry Lennon asked her husband, as conversations of confusion and panic grew amongst the people that surrounded her.

'The Archangel Michael,' he replied, as he drew both her and their son close to him. 'Do you remember when you asked me how this all ends?'

She nodded fearfully.

'Whatever happens,' he carefully explained to them both, 'We must never allow our hearts to lose hope in God. For I think we are about to be tested in a way no one has ever been tested before.'

20.

Pope Number 5.

Thursday, 15th October 1992.

Cardinal Vittorio Lucé sat looking at the three brown dumas files that sat next to his chair on the mahogany table. On each file, his secretary had meticulously penned the names of the chosen three that Lucé had discerned worthy of the new appointment. Yet, one file was clearly larger than the other two and that was the file of Archbishop Ryan Flynn, from the somewhat insignificant Archdiocese of Alton, Illinois.

The other two, slender files. contained the names of two holy men. Men he had no doubt would serve the Church faithfully if appointed to the new role. Both were without blemish and had no whiff of scandal attached to their names. The first was a Jesuit theologian, from Washington, a priest called Fr. Richard Wells, and he was being openly talked about as a possible successor to the recently deceased cardinal of his home archdiocese. The second name was that of the bishop of the diocese of Quincy, Ralph Zeglen, a media favourite, and a rising star of the Church in America with his popular television station *The Way Productions*, and a great vocal advocate of the teachings of the Holy Father. It was a name Lucé knew the Holy Father was aware of, and Zeglen was the main threat to getting his choice through to succeed as the new archbishop of Washington D.C.

Lifting Archbishop Ryan Flynn's file, he opened it and studied the face on the photograph that was attached to the inside cover; the pious Flynn, with his piercing eyes, looked back at him intently. They were the eyes he had seen in the flesh many times when he encountered him in Rome and during conferences in Saint Gallen, Switzerland. The eyes belonged to a man with intent and ambition to climb the ladder of power within the Church. Flynn was a force to be reckoned with. His name was well known in America and whispered with wagging tongues of rumour amongst the clergy across the States. Rumours of homosexuality were synonymous with his name. Stories of a beach-house hideaway in North Carolina were rumoured, even to congregations within the curia in Rome. And as he flicked through his file, Lucé saw the list of accusations along with a legal settlement that Flynn had paid out to an alleged victim, a seminarian from his own diocese. His activities were so notorious, that he was referred to as Uncle Flynn, even amongst the prelates in the Vatican curia. It was a scandalous secret that everyone knew, but Uncle Flynn was a man that could not be challenged. Cardinal Lucé knew that Flynn's financial backers from across the United States and the world, had given him a power and an influence that reached beyond his own archdiocese. Hundreds of millions of dollars had been raised by this one man, all in the name of charitable donations, from big businesses and the organisations of various papal knights to illegal crime organisations and those with masonic connections. Flynn was the man with the power in America, and Flynn was the man he wanted to see appointed as the new Archbishop of Washington D.C., and soon after to be elevated to the Sacred College. Lucé knew that Flynn would be forever in his gratitude for such an appointment, and he would be a sure backer within the college once his time would come.

Right on schedule, as a distant clock chimed in the noon hour, the door he had sat facing opened, and the Polish secretary Lawnizcak appeared and invited him into the small private study of Pope John Paul II. Adjusting his pectoral cross and zucchetto, Lucé lifted the folders and walked into the room and as was custom, he walked to the side of the pope's desk, genuflected, and kissed the gold crucifix ring on the trembling hand of a pope whose health was deteriorating.

'Please,' Pope John Paul invited him, with a gesture of his hand, to sit on the chair that sat adjacent to his desk. 'The See of Washington! I take it we are ready to appoint?'

'I believe so, Holiness,' Lucé replied, as he sat the folders on his lap in the expectant hope that the pope would not ask to see them. We have reduced the list down to three names, and with your assent the announcement will be made.'

'Is Ralph Zeglen on the list?' The pope asked, gazing down at the folders that rested under Lucé's hands.

'Yes.'

'A wonderful man. Filled with the Spirit of God in the age we live,' the pope looked at Lucé. 'Would you agree?'

'Absolutely,' Lucé replied, with an agreeable smile. 'He certainly is not afraid to call people onto the rooftops to proclaim the gospel. Do you watch any of his shows?'

Pope John Paul shook his head. 'No. But I know of him from my travels to America. I met him,' he continued before pointing to a series of books behind him, 'and he gave me his complete works. I have yet to start reading them. Hopefully, when I next visit Castel Gandolfo, I will find a little more time for some leisurely reading. Do you think he would be a suitable appointment?'

Lucé thoughtfully nodded his head. 'He would be a popular choice for the laity,' he explained, before pausing to collect his thoughts. 'My only advice to you would be that his prominence in evangelisation could dwindle if he were appointed to a prominent diocese like Washington. Would he be able to manage both? Or could his network suffer because of such an appointment?' Lucé paused to open Zeglen's file. 'As prefect for the congregation of bishops, it would be remiss of me not to point out the missionary success of Ryan Zeglen's role, not only within America but also across the global church. It might be best to leave him where he is, and perhaps to allow him to continue with what he is doing. Have you heard that he is working on a documentary series of your life in Poland?'

The pope remained silent as he watched Lucé scan the file.

'From what I am aware, his production company are negotiating the rights with other world broadcasting companies,' Lucé looked up at the pope. 'I don't think he is best suited for a role in Washington, especially when such an appointment requires a man of great diplomacy.'

Pope John Paul pondered what Lucé had to say before asking him for the name of the second candidate.

'That would be the Jesuit theologian, Fr. Richard Wells, the head of moral theology at the Catholic University of America. He is the preferred choice of the clergy of the Washington diocese.'

Lifting a pen from his desk, Pope John Paul wrote down the two names he had been given so far. 'I am not one for allowing the clergy to have their way in such appointments,' he finally spoke, setting his pen down onto the notepad. 'Tell me about him.'

'He's forty-five and ...'

'Too young,' the pope interjected, 'and too inexperienced. He could be in that position for thirty or more years.'

'Yes, Holy Father,' Lucé replied, wishing he could point out the irony that the pope had been ordained the archbishop of Krakow in his late thirties. 'The last name is Archbishop Ryan Flynn.'

The very mention of the name stopped the pope in his tracks. 'Thee, Ryan Flynn?'

'I believe there is only one, Your Holiness.'

For a few moments the pope sat back in his chair and stared quizzically at Lucé. 'You do know that there have been allegations, serious allegations, made against him?'

'Allegations that are founded on nothing of substance but vicious rumours against a faithful son of the Church.'

'The prefect of the Congregation for the Doctrine of the Faith does not see it in the same light.'

'I know,' Lucé replied, 'I have his documents of concern in this file.'

'Has Ryan Flynn not settled financially out of court against such allegations?'

'There was one occasion, and it was against a seminarian because it was deemed best to prevent scandal from emerging in a public court, as it also involved a major sex abuse scandal in the seminary in which he was studying. In claims of damages against the seminary, the seminarian had to sign a non-disclosure agreement and under oath legally testify that Ryan Flynn was not the perpetrator of his abuse. Ryan Flynn was acting in his capacity as a bishop when this settlement was agreed, and that was over ten years ago. What the Congregation of the Doctrine of the Faith has brought to your attention is baseless rumour and calumny.'

'That is a serious accusation to make, Eminence.'

'I can only but advise, Your Holiness. I have been in this role for over ten years, and in that time, I have made it my moral duty to vet every priest consecrated a bishop, and to thoroughly investigate their past and present. Rumours surrounding Ryan Flynn are from a small minority of people who are seeking to destroy this good and holy man. Many bishops in the United States applaud him for his faithfulness to Mother Church, his fundraising for religious charities and for his no-nonsense orthodoxy when it comes to Church teaching considering the wave of relativism that is sweeping across the western world. He is outspoken on the sanctity of marriage, the ravages of abortion and has taken a strong public line against the calls for women's ordination and the abolition of clerical celibacy. Furthermore, he has been fiercely opposed to the schismatic Society of Pius XII sect and sedevacantist groups who are growing in the States. Such faithfulness to the Church, and you, the successor of Peter, brings with it much hostility and anger against the truth he proclaims.'

'You talk of scandal, surely such an appointment would cause a scandal in and of itself, would it not?'

'I do not think it would,' Lucé replied, without hesitation. 'In fact, it would show his detractors that Rome has full faith in this son of the church. I know him personally, and he is a true man of God and a faithful disciple of Christ and to you his vicar on earth.'

Pope John Paul lifted his trembling right hand and rested it against his temple as he closed his eyes, entering into deep thought and prayer.

'The communists did the same,' John Paul finally spoke, as he slowly opened his eyes. 'They accused many priests and bishops behind the iron curtain of the most heinous of crimes from perversion to child molestation.' He turned to look at Lucé. 'None of it was true. It was pure propaganda aimed at destroying the beauty of the Church in its moral fight against their evil.' He paused for a moment, as his left hand took hold of his right hand to control the tremor. 'Some were imprisoned, and some shed their blood as martyrs. The old saying is true, that behind every catholic priest there is a demon waiting for his downfall.'

Lucé smiled.

'Could the same be happening in the west?'

'Yes, Holy Father,' he reassured him. 'It is happening to a good bishop like Ryan Flynn. It is his appointment these people fear the most, and yet I must advise you that he is the right man to take on this responsibility in leading the American church. He is also, if I might add, highly respected by the President of the United States for his conservative principles, his diplomatic connections and charitable fundraising. America needs a leader like him for this dark time and place.'

'You really do believe in him,' the pope replied, as he studied Lucé's face.

'Yes, I do. And furthermore, if I had even the slightest concern then I would not have let his name reach your ears.'

The pope considered Lucé's response for a moment as he continued to control his tremor. 'The last time we spoke you had appointed your six-hundredth bishop since I asked you, or rather you asked me, for this specific secretariate role. It has made me wonder why this role meant more to you, after all, you are a theologian, and I did offer you the chance to head the Congregation for the Doctrine of the Faith which you politely declined. Remind me again why you wanted to lead the congregation of bishops?'

'Well,' Lucé pondered for a moment. 'I am convinced of our mission since the council issued its reforms. You yourself were one of the council fathers, and I was nominated by Pope John to become a theological advisor. Despite the careful direction in which the council's decisions led our church, many have misunderstood it. On both sides of the argument, they have failed to see the core elements of truth; the conservatives believing it has destroyed the church, while liberals believe that the reforms did not go far enough. Despite my theological background, I believed that in overseeing the appointment of new bishops, ensuring that they are orthodox and with hearts set on God and close to Rome, that I could serve the church more faithfully by ensuring that we are appointing men who will take the Church into the next generation. Men who share your vision for a new evangelisation of the world. I believed, and I still do, that this is the best way for me to serve the church and to ensure that the teachings of the council are taught and implemented in dioceses across the world by men of good faith and theological understanding. And, where needed, not to be afraid to correct errant bishops through the authority that my curial office gives me.'

'That you have,' the pope uttered, as he slowly nodded his head in agreement. 'You have advised me well over the years, and I trust and respect your counsel. But I must take time to reflect and pray on the appointment of Ryan Flynn.'

'Of course, Holy Father.'

'This appointment is to one of the most influential positions within the Church.'

Lucé shifted ever so slightly in his chair so that he could lean closer to the pope. 'May I offer one more reason why Ryan Flynn should be considered for this appointment.'

The pope invited him to continue with a gentle wave of his left hand.

'Ryan Flynn has raised, to date, over two hundred million U.S. dollars for charitable works, and he has ensured that this money has been spent in assisting the evangelisation of peoples in poorer parts of the world. A prominent role in Washington D.C. would see his connections grow and would financially benefit poorer dioceses and their bishops in their roles, especially financially assisting bishops and dioceses that are emerging from Soviet oppression.'

'I will be honest with you,' the pope replied, as he lifted his fountain pen and added Ryan Flynn's name to his list. 'I am inclined to approve his appointment, but I still want time to pray about it. Unless something, or someone changes my mind over the coming week, then I will approve your recommendation.'

Less than a week later, Cardinal Lucé sat alone in the Valitori restaurant not far from the Vatican, where he regularly had a Tuesday evening meal. As the waiter poured him a single glass of house Barbera, he smiled knowing that he had gotten his man appointed. Before leaving the Vatican, he personally rang the Apostolic Nuncio of the United States, to instruct him to inform Archbishop Ryan Flynn that the Holy Father was translating him to the episcopal see of Washington D.C. He brought the glass to his lips and sipped the wine.

After a simple starter of pastina soup, he celebrated the appointment by ordering a main of Bucatini all'Amatriciana. Just as he had finished his meal, he felt his brother cardinal approach from behind.

'Cardinal Ratzinger,' he spoke, before his eyes even noticed him. 'Feel free to join me.'

'Eminence,' Ratzinger replied, as he stood alongside him, declining his offer. 'I had an audience with the Holy Father yesterday, and he informed me that you had personally recommended that Ryan Flynn should be appointed as the new Archbishop of Washington.'

'Yes,' Lucé confirmed, as he looked up at Ratzinger.

'I have strongly advised the Holy Father that he should not appoint such a man. You have read the information that I provided your office?'

'Yes.'

'Information that raises serious concerns and should be considered very carefully!'

'And I did.'

'The Church does not need to face the risk of such an appointment.'

'Too late,' Lucé confirmed, with a wry smile. 'As we speak, Ryan Flynn is being informed of his new appointment and being reassured of the Holy Father's full faith and confidence in him.'

Ratzinger's face could not hide the shock of what Lucé had confirmed. He could only stare at him in complete disbelief.

'We all have our roles to play, Joseph,' Lucé continued, as he sat down his napkin and rose from the table. 'You stick to correcting the heretics and I to appointing the future bishops of the Church. Now, if you will excuse me, I need to leave.'

And as he left the restaurant and a bewildered Cardinal Ratzinger behind him, Lucé knew that the next step on his own path to the papacy had been secured.

21.

The legion of demons wailed and screamed with delight as they watched Michael depart and their master rise from his throne to examine the seven bowls that burned on the rubble of what was once Bernini's baldacchino. For this was indeed the moment they had been promised, and like muzzled dogs straining on the leash for what seemed like an eternity, they were finally about to be set free to destroy as many souls as possible, before facing their fate.

The heavenly light could be seen within the bowls as the white flames burned but did not consume. Weaving his hand in and out of each bowl, he took delight in the tools that were now at his disposal. He knew he would never win over all the souls that remained, but he was determined to bring about the ruination of as many as possible. Many would quickly succumb to their trials and in their wokeness curse their creator without any attempt to fight the good fight. These were the low hanging fruit that he never took much interest in, for they were too easy to prey upon and no enjoyment could be found in them. Nor did he waste his energy in those who resisted him and time after time returned to their God, for such was their desire for that love that he struggled to penetrate their hearts. No, for him there was only one fight worth fighting for and that was for the souls of the indifferent. These souls swayed like shafts of wheat in a summer breeze, occasionally pondering God and turning to Him whilst finding too much enjoyment in the ways of this world, in the passions of their flesh and in the desire for comfortability in this life. It was these souls that he desired above all others, for they had the eternal truth within their grasp without realising it, and with one test they would easily toss it away and reject the true destiny of their souls. Winning these souls brought him the greatest pleasure and now he wished to capture as many as he could, for this was now his last roll of the dice.

He knew Michael was right, and that there would be no escaping his fate nor a chance of redemption. That was one more reason why he hated humanity, for in this place and time he knew that Christ had died for them and that his blood on Calvary was enough to atone for the sins they had committed. All these humans had to do was to accept it, to trust in it, and the kingdom from which he had been expelled would be forever theirs.

On the Friday he stood close by and watched the flesh being flayed from the back of Christ, he remembered the feeling that it was all happening too easily. His creator who had become man, in what was a miracle unlike any other, simply surrendered himself and allowed his creation to torment him, to mock him and finally to crucify him.

From the moment Christ was conceived within the Virgin, Lucifer wanted to destroy him by crushing the fruit of that womb. But the limits of his power meant that he could only watch on from afar. Day after day he followed him, watched him grow as he led the chosen people into the truth, despising him each day as his loathing grew greater. Yet, when his appointed time was granted to him, and he was finally allowed to unleash his wrath against the Christ through the viciousness of the Roman guards, he was determined that the Son of God would fall and finally be destroyed.

No one had ever been whipped like he was that day. By the time they had finished, his flesh hung from his bones as the agony consumed him, yet he did not cry out for their mercy. Even when they swapped the throne room of heaven for a wooden stump, clothed him with a tattered cloak and adorned him with a crown of thorns, before slapping and punching him, and even spitting into his face, he did not for one moment resent them. And when they drove the nails into his hands and feet and pinned him to the cross, with his body agonised with nerve pain and cramps, he forgave them for what they had done.

Then for a fleeting moment, when Christ was still alive on the cross, Lucifer thought he had won the victory when he heard him cry out to his Father to ask Him why He had forsaken him. Amidst the crowds who watched on, Lucifer absorbed himself into that moment and with disbelief thought he had conquered him, but with one final breath the Son looked up and offered everything to the One he loved and into His hands he commended his Spirit.

In that moment Lucifer realised he had been defeated, for as the earth shook and the veil of the temple was torn apart for all to see into the empty Holy of Holies, the price of a new covenant had been secured by the cross. For everyone who accepted its price their eternity in the kingdom was forever secured. No matter what he did, Lucifer could not break Christ and in the end, death could not destroy him.

The resurrection came as no surprise. For three days he sat and watched the tomb from a distance, as the Roman soldiers fell asleep before the angels of the Lord rolled away the stone and the light of heaven emerged from the darkness as the resurrected Son stepped forth into the world.

From that moment, billions of souls had been won and billions had been lost. The battle had raged, and many had fallen but many more had held firm in their belief that their Creator loved them no matter what. Now this was his final opportunity to condemn the creation he loathed with every fibre of his being, and as he had promised his demons, they would take with them as many souls as they could for this would be their only victory.

'Our time has come,' Lucifer addressed the wailing lament of the demons, as they fought each other to get as close to him as they were allowed. 'Soon, those who remain will see the prince of darkness in all my glory, for there will be nowhere to hide. You will torment every living soul. Hurt them with a pain so great that they will spit into the face of God as a price for death. Under every rock you will search, across every plain you will chase and through every home you will hunt and bring them down into the bowels of this forsaken earth. No one is to be spared. Everyone without the protection of God is ours for the taking. We need not hide our faces anymore, let us reap what we have sown.'

With their eyes burning a flaming red, the demons continued to scream and gnash their teeth as their expectations grew with the knowing that they would now have their time to ravish the earth. Across one another they scrambled as they descended the walls of the basilica, and with bated breath they waited for their lord to give them the right to proceed.

Looking into the seven bowls, Lucifer judged each one carefully and pondered the consequences of pouring out each one upon the earth. He considered unleashing them all at once, to cause the greatest pain and suffering upon those who had survived thus far, but in the end he decided to release their wrath one by one and to watch the suffering grow greater by the second.

This would be his final act of rebellion against the powers of heaven and with it he knew it would complete the rejection of everything God stood for and had promised. From the moment he walked through the garden in Eden, until now, he could not accept what God had created and the Love that had brought it into being.

From the seven bowls, he chose the one in the middle for he knew this would cause the greatest suffering and from which many would beg for the mercy of death and even oblivion of their souls just to escape from its torment. Looking to his demons for their approval, he smiled when they jeered him on as their expectancy grew. Then with his right foot he kicked the bowl down into the nave of the basilica where it toppled over, and its contents spilled out.

Returning to his throne, he raised his left hand for his demons to fall silent and together they watched on as the fire from within the bowl turned to a fine smoke that slowly crept across the floor and towards the door of the basilica and out towards the pilgrims.

Still restraining his demons from leaving the basilica, Lucifer listened as the pilgrims fell silent, no doubt able to see the smoke as it spread out amongst them. Then summoning two pairs of demons, he instructed them to lift two more bowls and told them where to pour them. And then, it happened.

It was one scream that pierced through the darkness. A scream of despair as the first bowl of wrath took hold. Lucifer's smile widened as the demons edged closer to the door, and one by one the screams of the pilgrims grew and filled the darkness with a suffering never experienced before.

22.

Patrick Lennon noticed the fine smoke emerge from the basilica, and like a low hanging fog it descended the stone steps and covered the lower half of his legs. Initially the pilgrims watched on in silence as the mysterious smoke spread across the square, but then some reached down to feel it, which his wife did and claimed that it felt warm to the touch. Around him most people were bemused at the sight, but Patrick felt his heart pounding in his chest with a fearful knowing that this was more sinister than innocent.

Like stage fog, it eventually appeared to have run out as the last of it emerged from the basilica, but it did not stop moving and spreading through the people as it headed towards the city of Rome. Eventually, as it moved on, Patrick noticed that it began to thin out and as he turned to move, he felt something crunch under his feet, as if he were standing on shells of some kind.

Through the darkness it was hard to see, but his interest was caught by a man who had produced a lighter from his pocket to have a closer look. That was when Patrick, and those around him, noticed that the cobblestones of the square had been covered in what looked like a dusting of small white grains of rice. This dusting was even on his shoes and lower trousers, and every time he moved, he felt the grains being crushed under his feet.

'What is it daddy?' his son asked, feeling the urge to reach down and touch it.

'Don't!' Patrick insisted, grabbing his son's wrist, and pulling him back up from the ground.

He was just about to explain that he did not know what the grains were, when the piercing scream of a woman or a child punctuated the silence of the pilgrims. Looking in the direction from where it came, the scream was quickly followed by another and then another and then another. They were screams, the like of which he had never heard before in his life. Screams filled with pain and fear that could not be silenced.

He immediately lifted his son into his arms as he saw the pilgrims stamp on the ground as the panic and screams drew closer to his family.

'Whatever happens here,' he said, as his wife clung to him and their son, 'Don't lose your faith. Remember that God is with us!'

Then kissing her for one last time, he drew his son closer and whispered that he loved him into his ear and to keep loving God even through what was to come. And as he spoke those words, he noticed that the man beside him screamed out in agony, dropping his lighter to the ground to reveal that what had initially looked like rice were in fact larva that were now moving on the ground and splitting open with small parasitic flies emerging from within them and taking flight.

What little peace he had in this life lasted for less than a second longer, before he felt the first bite of a parasite as one flew up and bit into the flesh of his right arm as he held his son. The scalding pain was impossible to stifle, and Patrick found himself screaming out as his son looked into his eyes with the terror that had possessed him. He heard his wife scream, but he could not take his eyes of the child he loved, even when a second bite took hold on his neck, a third on his leg and a fourth on the right side of his face. Each time the pain became more excruciating as the parasites began to swarm around him, and then the inevitable happened as his boy began to scream with the pain.

The parasites attacked relentlessly, biting and nipping at whatever flesh they could find, swarming around the pilgrims and out into the city of Rome where the screams continued to grow as the agony quickly spread. Yet, despite his own pain, Patrick was determined not to let his boy go, but the pain for the child was too much, and in the end it was he who fought and wriggled free from his father's arms, to stand on his own and to swat away the parasites and to scratch at their bites in the hope of some relief - but none came.

It was his wife that he first noticed removing her clothing, before he became aware that others around them were doing the same, and soon he felt the urge to do it too as the parasites were becoming trapped under his clothing and causing him the most pain. Stripping as quickly as he could, Patrick felt them fly into his mouth as they swarmed around his face, and with every breath he took he felt them crawl into his nasal cavity. Soon he had to close his eyelids as he felt them attack his eyes, along with every inch of flesh from the soles of his feet to the crown of his head.

Naked, the pilgrims cried out in agony as they scratched at the bites and prayed for mercy from the wrath that had engulfed them. The parasites from hell, laced the hair of every man, woman and child. They crawled across every part of their flesh, sinking their barbed mouths and injecting their poisonous venom into the people repeatedly. Through mouths, noses and ears they found entry and began to eat away at the flesh from within, all the time multiplying in number and growing in the ferociousness of their attack.

Patrick Lennon could taste the blood in his mouth as he gnawed on his tongue to deal with his agony. Soon, he could no longer see as the pain from the bites in his eyes was so excruciating that they had completely closed over. He reached out for his family, but he was not sure if the flesh he was touching belonged to them or to some other unfortunate soul. And every time he opened his mouth to cry out, the parasites swarmed in. No matter what he did he could not stop himself from being attacked or bitten. Now completely naked he felt himself fall to the ground, unable to withstand it anymore and soon his cries and the cries of pilgrims grew to a tiny whimper as they lay motionless and endured their sufferings.

He had no idea how long he had laid there, nor for how long the parasites had ceased attacking. But he did become aware that they had stopped, and that the screams of the people had quietened. Every inch of his body was in agony and the level of the pain was something he believed he could never have endured. Yet, there was no respite, despite the absence of the parasites, for the damage of their attack could be felt with every movement he made and breath he took.

Lying where he fell, he at first wondered if he was imagining the sensation of something moving behind his eyes, as if something was burrowing up into his brain. But he knew the parasites had entered his body, and he realised that this was how it would end for him. His whole life and that of his family, had been brought to this moment and to this level of suffering.

Why? He found himself questioning. *Why would He allow this to happen?*

Bringing his right hand up to his chest, his body did not feel the same with all the boils that now covered his skin and the festering rash that drove him to scratch at his flesh in the hope of some relief. He prayed for death to come. He begged God to relieve him from his suffering. Yet, through his pain he remembered what he had read regarding the final test, and despite his suffering he mouthed words that no one would ever hear, *save us Lord.*

For the demon Tyzarian, he watched from the entrance of the basilica as the people languished in their torment, taking great delight in the screams that came from the depths of true despair. It was the moment he and his brother demons had been waiting for, and now he was desperate to be set free.

'Take pleasure if you must in their suffering,' Lucifer addressed his legion, as he walked from his throne of lies towards the entrance, 'but always remember that it is their souls that we wish to harvest for an eternal damnation. End the suffering of those who curse Him, but to those who resist do with them what you will.'

Tyzarian, along with his fellow demons eagerly turned to look upon their master. The moment Lucifer gave a nod of his head, they charged from the entrance of the basilica to torture the living. Whilst some flew off into the darkness of the night to find their prey across the earth, Tyzarian remained close as his eye was upon one man.

Finding the deputy commander of the Swiss Guards, Egger Meier, slumped against the façade of Saint Peter's, Tyzarian crawled on top of him and began to press open his eyelids for the deputy commander to see him.

'Egger! Egger!' he called out his name, stirring him into a form of lucidity. 'Wake up Egger!' he commanded, as he pressed a pointed fingernail into a boil on his chest; causing it to burst and the pain to bring a groan to Meier's lips.

Egger Meier became aware that someone or something was on top of him, holding open his eyelids. But he could not make out who or what it was, as tapered larvae swam across the cornea of his eyes, preventing him from seeing clearly.

'Are you in pain?' Tyzarian asked, bursting more boils to keep the deputy commander awake. 'What do you think of your God now? He has caused all of this. What a waste of a life you have lived.'

Driving his finger deep into an infected wound, Tyzarian felt Meier squirm with the agony.

'I can take all this suffering from you,' Tyzarian whispered into his ear as agonising screams, caused by the suffering inflicted from his fellow demons, once again began to fill the air. 'Would you like it to end?'

Egger Meier managed a muffled yes through his exhaustion, as Tyzarian continued to inflict more pain upon him.

'God has allowed all this to happen, where is His love for you now? Do you still love Him?'

He brought his ear close to Meier's mouth to listen carefully.

'Egger! Egger!' he called out again, as he gripped his wrists as tightly as he could. 'Do you still love Him?'

As the agony engulfed him, Egger Meier felt the final emotion of his life well up within him with such clarity. And it was one simple thought that came from his heart, and he knew that a loving God could not be real for why would love allow this to happen?

'Do you still love Him?'

With his final testimony, Meier managed to say, 'No.'

In that moment, Tyzarian sank his nails into Egger Meier's wrists and cut up through his flesh, feeling his life-giving blood ooze from his body. Tyzarian had won his prize and left the deputy commander to die.

Crawling over the corpses who had succumbed to the parasites, he found his next living victim and turning him onto his back, Tyzarian realised that it was Patrick Lennon, and his presence and the fact that his fate now belonged to him brought him even greater excitement than having dealt with Egger Meier.

'Patrick! Patrick!' he called out his name, forcing open his eyelids to look into his eyes. 'Wake up Patrick!'

As he felt himself awaken into a semiconsciousness, Lennon once again felt the excruciating pain and then the weight of something sitting on top of his chest. In a moment of clarity, he could sense that it was a form of pure evil, but no matter what he did he simply did not have the strength to throw it off.

Tyzarian felt Patrick Lennon fight against him, but he knew the man did not have the strength to do it. In recent years, he had fought them bravely by standing openly against them, siding openly with God and warning people that these days would come. No matter what suffering came his way, from losing his job to being humiliated on social media, Lennon publicly offered it all up to the Lord and taunted Lucifer and his demons to do their worst; convinced he was on the side of goodness and righteousness.

Prophet like, Lennon had foretold every detail of what the world should expect. He had pinpointed the corruption within the Church. He had foretold of the wars and famines, and in doing so had converted the souls of many who embraced the suffering that came with the knowing that it would all quickly pass and give way to the eternal happiness of heaven.

Oh, what Tyzarian would give to steal the soul of Patrick Lennon in these final moments of his life, and as he brought his face close to Lennon he could smell and taste the fear coming from him. Slowly, he repeated the agony he had inflicted upon Backhaus and allowed Lennon to experience the pain before he spoke to offer him a chance to end it all. But the more pain he inflicted the more Lennon kept repeating, *'Blessed be the name of the Lord.'*

No matter how much agony he inflicted, Tyzarian could not break his spirit to access his soul. With frustration he tore at his flesh and screamed into his face that God had abandoned him and that there was no hope for him except through death at his hands; a merciful death that would end it all.

Then Tyzarian glimpsed the lifeless body of the young boy who lay next to Patrick, and the woman whose hand the boy held tightly. Realising that they were the remains of the man's beloved wife and child, Tyzarian immediately stopped what he was doing. Then lifting himself off Lennon's chest he lay beside him, and began to comfort him, caressing his face and hair as he held him close.

'Patrick, I feel so sorry for you,' Tyzarian whispered into his ear, as he watched him gasp for breath. 'Look at what He has done to you!'

But Lennon, hearing the words, continued to pray silently into his heart so that the demon could not hear him. *Blessed be the name of the Lord!*

'Your poor wife and son,' he continued, as he ran a finger over Lennon's lips. 'He killed them!'

The words grieved Lennon, but they came as no surprise for he knew that this moment would come.

'How cruel is He, to take something so beautiful and so perfect away from you? What you had was love. Tell me, how can you still believe that God is Love when He does this to His creation?'

Thoughts came and then faded as he prayed in his heart for their souls, commending them into the loving arms of God, convinced in the sure hope that their suffering and death would give birth to eternal life and happiness.

'You are a good man Patrick,' Tyzarian continued, restraining his impatience at the faith he was still witnessing. 'You did not deserve this, nor did your beautiful wife and son.'

For several hours Tyzarian lay with him, whispering into his ear thoughts of doubt and consolation in the hope of winning his soul. Although he could not read his heart, he knew that throughout the torment, Patrick Lennon continued to praise God with every remaining fibre of his being.

In his torment, Patrick Lennon glimpsed a light. It was a light that grew and drew him closer to where he knew he belonged. Soon the pain appeared to be no more, and the words of the demon could no longer be heard. With his heart, mind and soul he kept blessing the name of the Lord, until he heard a familiar voice call out the name he loved to hear - 'Daddy!'

Tyzarian knew he had failed as he watched the soul of Patrick Lennon pass from this life, and despite his suffering the man had died with a knowing smile.

23.

The demons, Farchara and Gyrena rose high into the sky above the Tyrrhenian Sea. With the second bowl of wrath clutched firmly in their hands they were mesmerised by the marbling light that burned within. Through the darkness, they carefully carried the bowl as far away from the shores of Italy as they could, until its weight became too much to bear.

The honour they felt in being the ones chosen by their lord, for the privilege of pouring out the contents of the bowl upon the earth, reached fever pitch when they screamed with excitement as they looked each other in the eyes and slowly turned the bowl, allowing the light to pour out.

Like a liquid flame, the marbled white and blue fire decanted from the bowl and fell thousands of feet from the sky into the sea below, where the waters failed to quench it as it sank deep into the water, before the light faded from view. At first, Farchara and Gyrena looked at one another in complete confusion as they believed that they had somehow failed in their mission, and for a moment considered the consequences of returning to Rome and having to explain their error. But they both knew that they had done everything as they had been told to do, and therefore the contents of the bowl should not have failed. Slowly descending towards the surface of the sea, they both watched intently around the area where the flame had disappeared and then they both saw it happen. Initially, the light reappeared like an underwater explosion before the foulest odour rose into the air; a thousand times worse than the stench of death and hell combined. They quickly rose high again, delighted that they had succeeded in their mission. Their screams filled the air as the second wrath came upon the earth.

From a balcony on the fourth floor of the Liliana hotel in Andora, on the Italian Riviera, Elio Zuccolo smoked a cigarette and wondered what the strange light, that he had just seen fall from the sky, was. *Had he just imagined it?* He thought. In a world that had been completely turned upside down, and in which each day was one of fight for survival, he stubbed out his smoke and returned inside the room where his elderly mother slept on the double bed.

They had been visiting her brother in Turin when the asteroid hit. Thankfully, they were not at home when the subsequent tsunami ripped their coastline apart, taking with it thousands of people along with their family home and their livelihood, which was a small waterfront bar for the tourists who flocked to the beautiful beaches. Upon returning to the devastation, they found that the hotel offered them the only reasonable shelter as all the rooms above the third floor were undamaged. Along with a few other families, Elio Zuccolo and his mother made the hotel their new home and sharing what little food the hotel had left in its stores, they all bunkered down and waited for a future that lacked any real hope.

From his business storage facility, which was outside the main town, and therefore undamaged by the disaster, Elio Zuccolo had enough wine and cigarettes to last himself and his mother a lifetime, and packets of crisps and nuts to last them many months. Trading his neighbours for votive candles that they had sourced from the abandoned local church, his days were spent sitting by a small light, eating whatever food he could find and drinking wine and smoking the cigarettes. Smoking had been a habit he had given up for over ten years after his father had died of lung cancer, but knowing that life was now limited he took up the habit again. Now it was the only comfort he had.

Not sure how many glasses of wine he had drunk that day, as time no longer had any bearing on the living, he allowed himself to open another bottle. It was reaching for the corkscrew that he first heard the high-pitched buzz of what sounded like a mosquito that had entered the room. More interested in opening the wine he did not give it a second thought, opting to close the balcony door after he had poured himself a glass. But that idea quickly changed when his mother awoke from her sleep with an agonising scream that made him jump with fright, causing the sharp point of the corkscrew to slice across the top of his left hand.

'Mammina!' he called out, as he rushed to her side. 'What is the matter?'

The old woman could only cry with the pain as she wriggled on the bed.

'Do you want me to help you up?' he suggested, not knowing what to do.

From nowhere, a parasite bit him as he felt the sting on the side of his neck, and the pain felt like someone was pressing the point of a soldering iron into his flesh. As he cursed aloud in agony, he heard his mother scream out for a second time, and then more screams could be heard from others who were living in the hotel. Immediately he got up and quickly went across the room to slide the balcony door close to stop any more of the parasites from entering. In the dimly lit room, he could not see whatever it was that had bitten him, but he could hear it buzzing, before it would stop and either his mother would scream, or he would be the one battling with the pain of a new bite. Then the buzzing would start again.

Upon hearing voices in the corridor, he took the decision to help his mother up from her bed and together they left their room and closed the door behind them.

'Were you bitten too Elio?' a female neighbour, whose name he did not know asked.

'Yes,' he replied, rubbing at his neck and the side of his face, where he felt swelling from the bites. 'My mother too. What the hell is going on?'

As the corridor filled with residents and they struggled to find adequate light from their supply of little candles, they were all given a brief period of respite before they all heard the high-pitched buzz of not one but two or more of the parasites. Again, the screams could be heard as the biting continued.

Unable to remain where they were, one family tried to go back into their room, but they found that they had only opened the door to a swarm of the parasites that now flew out into the corridor. With no other option, they all descended the stairs and made their way through the dirt and the muck that had settled in the hotel, being forced each step of the way by the swarm that chased them. It reminded Elio of the time as a teenager when out with a group of friends they got an old rag, wrapped it around a stick and set it alight to burn down a hornets' nest they had discovered on the walled bank of a little tributary that flowed along the edge of town. Elio was the brave one that day, the one who approached the hive, and he was the one the hornets attacked. No matter how far away he ran they followed him and stung him, and still attached to their sting they buzzed all over his body until he jumped into the water. That was when he had the idea.

'We need to get to the sea!' he shouted, 'They cannot sting us when we are in the water.'

There was no time for any discussion as he quickly lifted his mother into his arms, and without even looking to see if any of the others were following, he ran from the hotel and across the road towards the beach. Despite being repeatedly bitten and the screams coming from his mother, Elio did not stop as he bore the pain through gritted teeth and continued to carry her across to the beach and into the sea where they could no longer be bitten. Many within the hotel had followed him, and in the water they all remained submerged up to their necks; some bobbing up and down in the water to stop their faces and heads from being bitten, whilst others continuously splashed water above their heads to keep the parasites from approaching.

Elio Zuccolo knew that this could not last forever, but like everyone else who was in the water, he was glad of the relief he now experienced from the bites of whatever it was that was swarming around their heads and the entire town of Andora. He remained close to his mother, splashing water above her head as well as his own, and each time he asked her if she was alright, she did not reply, instead she prayed out loud to the Madonna and her Son to save them and to protect them.

Her words of prayer did not surprise Elio, for his mother was a woman of immense faith, and her belief in God came as easily to her as breathing in air. Her religion he inherited through his birth, but it was a faith in which he could not believe. As he watched the people around him fight for their lives in the sea, he knew that this was yet another battle imposed upon them, and he cursed God in his heart for the suffering he and the others were having to endure.

It was when he went to lift his hand to splash the water, that he felt the back of it hit something fleshy. Initially, he thought he had hit is mother or another residence, but when he turned to his right to look, he saw no one nearby him, but instead he saw a dead fish floating to the surface, before another one did too. As confusion and panic began to spread through the people, it became harder for them to splash at the water as every creature that once lived in the sea began to surface.

Once more the biting resumed and the people in the water had no choice but to hold their breaths and completely submerge themselves below the surface for as long as they could. Then, resurfacing they would gasp for air before going back under, each time risking the attack of the swarm who were becoming more aggressive. Each gulp of air was a lottery, and Elio could have sworn that some of the parasites had entered his mouth.

Each occasion he came up to the surface, he had to break through a mass of dead sea life, and as he gasped for air and looked around for his mother, he was bitten repeatedly. Stifling the need to scream under the water, he realised that he could not find her, and he began to panic. Each time he surfaced, he looked for her, but it was impossible. Soon every inch of his face was bitten, and he found that he could no longer open his eyes.

Not one person who entered the sea lasted more than thirty minutes. Elio Zuccolo, just like his mother and neighbours, succumbed to the swarm's attacks and exhaustion, and without being aware of it happening, he drowned in the sea that was once part of his way of life in Andora.

Within hours of the bowl being poured into the Tyrrhenian Sea, every living creature of the world's deep that had survived the impact of Wormwood and the worldwide Tsunami, was dead and now their remains floated in a thick mass on the surface of the waters. Slowly, the temperatures rose, and the seas and oceans began to boil, and everything that had died in the waters was boiled into a toxic mess. Nowhere on earth could escape the smell that followed, and for the first time since the dawn of creation nothing lived in the depths.

24.

Hazarath and Waywallah, the demons charged with pouring out the third bowl carried it beyond the Alps and into France, where they accessed the bowels of the earth by carrying the bowl down into the Gouffre Mirolda cave entrance and deep into the Lucien Bouclier cave network. With their way illuminated by the flaming light of the bowl they carried, it helped them to find the fresh water source that was over a mile below the surface of the earth. Then, with no hesitation knowing what the consequences would be of their actions, they poured the bowl into the water, were the light fell into its depths before turning blood red.

Ten years after being ordained a diocesan priest, Fr. Luke Harris sought permission from his bishop to live as a hermit. His initial three-year period of leave had lasted for fifteen years, and he now knew that his life would soon end at his highland hermitage.

High above the Scottish hamlet of Glenfinnan, along a remote path that was inaccessible to vehicles and off the beaten path for ramblers, he purchased an old croft with the money he had saved over the years from his priestly stipends and had converted the croft into his off grid hermitage where he spent his days; praying his liturgy of the hours and offering mass in his little oratory, painting Byzantine icons to pay for his living and manually working his land to grow whatever food he could to support his contemplative way of life.

With no television, radio or internet, he lived a life cut off from the world. It was a way of life that enabled him to pray for the world whilst living apart from it and each day growing closer in union with the creator in whose Being and light he wanted to bathe. When necessity required, he would leave his hermitage in the hidden glen and walk down into Glenfinnan, where he had an arrangement with a local farmer to borrow a car to drive to Fort William, to stock up on supplies and to attend to other mundane affairs.

He became aware of the nuclear attacks upon America and the Islamic States during one of his visits to town, where the local shop keeper who knew about him and his ministry had told him about what had happened. He knew then that the world was ending, but he did not fear and simply took his supplies and returned to his way of life in the hermitage to pray, garden and create his icons. Unable to post anymore and with the collapse of the banking world, his trips became less frequent as he found that the resources in the town were becoming fewer and more expensive. With staples of flour and rice purchased with what little money he had left, he accepted the kindness of the catholic farmer who brought him eggs, milk and butter to his hermitage every week, and occasionally the odd piece of meat from a slaughtered farm animal or a fish caught by one of his sons from Loch Shiel.

Then one day the world turned dark, and the light never appeared again. Alone he lived for weeks, but when the farmer did not come to visit him, he finally left his hermitage and walked down into the hamlet, only to discover that everything had been completely devastated, including the farmhouse that had been turned to rubble and the little car that had been crushed by a fallen tree. With no one alive he returned to the hermitage and entered his little oratory and prayed his office. He had no awareness of the Tsunami that had destroyed the hamlet and the surrounding towns, for he had no way of even knowing about Wormwood. But he knew that he was now alone, and that this was his calling, and so he prayed and entered deeper into his soul.

He continued with his simple way of life and was thankful that he lived high above the hamlet and that his hermitage, designed to exist off-grid, had its own electrical power supply from two small wind turbines that allowed him to still have some electrical light and supplied power to two electrical heaters, a small stove and a box chest freezer in which he still had food to last him for many months.

Permitting himself one meal a day, he was content in his way of life, and because the darkness meant that he had no need to work his land anymore, he used the time to read the books from his hermitage library, focusing on the writings of Chesterton and the classics of Saint Augustine. In this rhythm he found that his internal joy grew greater, as Christ had become his complete focus and every distraction of the world had been removed from him. Like the early desert fathers, his mind and heart felt completely at one with the God he searched for with his whole mind, body, heart and soul.

In his solitude, he knew that following his horarium was of the greatest importance, and with the chiming mantel clock that he believed was the heartbeat of his hermitage and the wall calendar which he had drawn by hand, he knew the exact date and time in which he was living, give or take a few minutes. So, on Wednesday 1st of November, at six o'clock in the morning, he arose, and if his calculations were right, he knew that the day was the feast of All Saints and the beginning of the month in which the deceased souls were remembered and prayed for.

In a small room inside his hermitage was the little chapel he had built by hand and whose walls were adorned with his byzantine icons. Striking a match, he lit the candles on the altar and brought the religious artwork to life as the light reflected off the gold leaf borders of each icon. Vesting in his white robes for the solemnity, he offered up his mass for the suffering of the world and the people who remained, and for the repose of the souls who had departed this life. Elevating the host and the chalice, he wept as the realisation hit him that he would be forced into a passion and death of his own, but he surrendered that fear to God and allowed himself to unite more with the Christ who was physically present on the altar before him in the Blessed Sacrament.

After his morning prayer and mass, he allowed himself to drink some tea, and as was his custom he went into his little larder and lifted one of the bottles of water he had stored, filled the kettle to boil it and headed outside to walk over to the mountain spring that was the fresh water source for his hermitage. Ever since the nuclear attacks, he made sure that every spare bottle was used and that water was amply stored, used efficiently and replenished daily from the spring. Thankfully, he never had an issue with his water supply, and his storing of it had simply become a daily routine that got him out of the hermitage for a few minutes. Unbeknownst to him, his water source which came from somewhere deep inside his neighbouring mountain had until that day remained pure and untarnished. But as he neared the flowing spring, which had been welled into an old Belfast sink by some previous inhabitant of the croft, he noticed that it sounded different as the water did not appear to be flowing the way it had always done. Taking a small torch from his pocket, he flashed the light towards the spring, and his heart sank when he saw that the water ran like thick blood.

Getting closer to inspect it, he smelt a horrible odour and lifting a broken branch from the path, as he was hesitant to use his own finger, he placed it under the red liquid, and it coated the branch like thick red paint. Taken aback, he turned off the light, and realising that his water supply had been ruined, he returned to his hermitage and worked out that he now had enough water to last him three weeks at most. Like any man he felt an initial surge of panic well within him as he rotated the bottles and rationed them in his head to see if he could make them last longer, and then he hoped that the well would run clear, and that his way of life would return to normal. But as the hours moved on, and as the reality of his situation became more clearer, his heart and mind began to settle, and he surrendered everything into the hands of the Father he knew loved him and who was about to call him home.

Clearing the small table in his kitchen, he took the largest panel of linden wood he had in his store, onto which he had some months ago attached a fine linen cloth across the surface that had been soaked in sturgeon glue and allowed to dry. Securing it to the easel, he decided to create the last icon of his life. No one would ever see it, but through writing it he would spend what little time he had contemplating the loving face of Christ his saviour.

With a razored knife, he carefully sharpened the edge of his pencil before taking many hours to carefully draw the outline of his spiritual vision of Christ; focusing on the detail of the face and the right hand that was raised in the gift of a blessing. Each day he slept, woke, prayed, offered his mass, painted the icon and focused his mind on the death that he would soon have to pass through to see the face of the living God.

It was a few days later that he first noticed the smell, and stepping outside to investigate it he felt sick at how strong and putrid it was. Closing the doors tight, he began to burn liturgical incense inside his hermitage to mask the odour. Soon, once he was consumed with writing his icon, the odour troubled him no more. And on the eve of the following Sunday, he mixed some titanium white pigment and with the finest brush he carefully painted a pure white line around the inside of Christ's halo and then touched the edge of his eyes to bring them both to life.

To celebrate finishing the icon, he fetched from a kitchen cupboard a bottle of Il Poeta Barolo and poured himself a glass before putting on a CD of Mozart's Don Giovanni. Then taking a seat in his armchair, he gazed upon the face of Christ, enjoyed his wine and listened to his favourite opera.

It was a perfect end for Fr. Luke as he sat back in his chair, his mind so lost in both the music and the icon that, as he sipped on the wine, he did not even hear the arrival of the high-pitched buzz.

25.

Lucifer's demons were filled with desperation to be given the freedom to roam the world again, and to hunt down the souls of those who were still living. But he had ordered them back to allow the fourth bowl to be poured upon the world, knowing that the parasites were multiplying and spreading, that the seas had died and were boiling, and that all fresh water in the world had been made undrinkable.

As suffering compounded suffering, he waited and held his time to allow the thirst to dry the throats of those across the world who remained. No longer would they be able to curse out loud in their agony, but from now on they could only do so from the depths of their hearts. Around Rome no one had survived, and he knew that across Europe most people had already perished or were perishing from the lack of water or at the hands of the parasites.

As a gift to the world, he went to the balcony of Saint Peter's Basilica for what he knew would be the last time. In the darkness of all that had surrounded him, he breathed in the stench of decay and the rancid air that was becoming more polluted by the second as the seas continued to boil.

Holding the fourth bowl in his hands, he looked up into the darkness and with great delight he threw the bowl high into the sky, where it appeared to break through the darkness. As the light emerged for the first time in months, Lucifer felt the need to cover his own eyes as the dust clouds and pollution dissipated and the noon day sun shone once more upon the earth. And as his eyes adjusted to the blinding light, the sun revealed the nakedness and death that covered the square and the surrounding streets of Rome, and Lucifer knew that his tally of the harvest had been considerable.

No matter what Emilie Pedersen did to seal up the drafts in her home, the smell from the deep waters of Geirangerfjord had managed to permeate its insulated walls, and had caused her and her two girls nothing but suffering as the nauseating odours and gases made them sick with vomiting and diarrhoea, which in recent days was made even greater as the fresh water being pumped into their home was running blood red and had become undrinkable. Knowing for sure that her husband, who had set off to fish in the fjord with his brother, was most certainly dead, she lay on her kitchen floor, unable to move except to watch as her children lay dying close to her. In the agonising moments of her final hours, she begged for death to come, for it was now the only way she knew that their suffering would end.

Semiconscious, she felt some hope when she first saw the glimmer of light flow through the gap in the curtains and rest across the kitchen floor. *Is it all over?* She pondered, as she tried to lift her head to look. *Is someone here to help?* She considered, unable to find the strength to call out. But no one came as the light remained.

Fixed in its place, the noon day sun was initially welcomed by millions who were still surviving and clinging to desperate hope, but it quickly became clear that the darkness of the earth was better than the power of the sun. For as the hours passed by, the heat of the earth began to rise and soon it became too much for those who lingered on the cusp of death. With nothing to quench their thirst the heat intensified, until it became a scorching torture from which there was no escape. With no dusk to cool the earth, it baked in the unrelenting rays.

In the open, millions could not escape as they burned in the heat, and for those shaded indoors it also became impossible to live as the temperatures rose and like ovens their homes quickly became their tombs.

In the intensity, fires broke out and began to consume the lands of the world. Across the oceans the waters continued to boil, and the stench became even more putrid. And in the fresh rivers and wells of the world, the red blood thickened and hardened as the life-giving source of this world dried up into a fine red dust.

Emilie Pederson did not hear the buzz of any parasitic flies as they finally arrived at her home, but she did feel the sting of their bites. There was no escaping from the pain that they inflicted upon her, but she had no strength left to cry out, let alone try to protect herself. All she could do was to lie there on the floor as bite after bite tore at her flesh, until her eyes could no longer see her daughters that lay beside her.

This was her fate, and somewhere, lost deep within her, there was an unfathomable sadness that this was how her existence would come to an end. With no dignity and without burial, she and her daughters would die alone like so many others. Occasionally, a thought broke through the pain and her fears, and it brought with it a hope. Indifferent her entire life to faith, a proclaimed atheist who had scorned any notion of faith and reason, she found herself pondering for the first time ever that it was possible that there could be something more than this. It was borne from a desire that this was not the end, and that she would see the smiles on her daughters' faces and hold them close once more to her breast. When she thought of her husband Halvor and what must have happened to him, she again found herself hoping that once more he would hold her, kiss her and reassure her that she was safe.

If there was a God, she asked Him to save her soul if she had a soul, and to protect her husband and their children who were on the same journey. With this being her only hope, she clung to it in the final moments of her life.

26.

Pope Number 6.

Sunday, 10th July 2005.

Cardinal Lucé had convinced everyone that he had family in Rome. Truth was, he had no one and no one cared to investigate his background. With a relentless web of lies, his story changed for whoever wanted to listen. No one version of his life ever matched another – such was his cunning deceit.

From the moment the gates of Hades had been opened for the final battle, he knew how it would end. The cross had tricked him, and for over two thousand years, he cursed the God he once loved, not able to comprehend how he did not see calvary coming. Trapped within himself, he planned the path he would take. It was a plan to bring as many as he could away from the Nazarene, and to bring them deep into the pit of his hell.

From the moment he was set free to test the world, and to bring about the end of days, he knew that it was through the Church and the vow of obedience that he would bring many souls away from their destiny and to see them destroyed. No one saw him coming, no one cared of his past, and no one saw the truth that was masked behind the veneer of piety. He had emerged from the depths and had taken possession of human form; namely that of a young Roman boy who had emerged from the aftermath of the second world war. Presenting himself to the Church, he was taken by the hand and led to its heights. Biding his time was the hardest discipline of all, but throughout his time in Rome he saw the destruction he had caused by imploding the Church from within.

Upon the death of Pope John Paul II, he had, along with other officials within the curia, to tender his resignation. Since the election of the new pope, all the officials had been reappointed except for himself. Instead, he had to sit back and watch as an Indian prelate replaced him in the congregation he had controlled for twenty years. He did not care, and nor did he mind. Nothing could stop the events that were set in motion.

As he was driven to Castel Gandolfo to meet with Pope Benedict, Lucé knew that he was never going to be appointed to any significant role. The sole purpose of the audience was to inform him of that very fact. And so, it had to be, because this was the time in which he would begin to open deep wounds within the Church; wounds so putrid that they would cause the faithful such scandal that many would turn and walk away.

Driven up the hill towards the pope's summer retreat, he had no fear nor regret. This meeting was merely a motion that would spark a chain of events. Without thought nor consideration, he exited the car and followed the pope's secretary into the private residence, preferring not to even engage in small talk.

Even when the pope entered the room, he refused to genuflect and to venerate his fisherman's ring. Instead, he stood with his hands clasped at his waist and slowly looked the German pontiff up and down with a sign of great disdain. Pope Benedict, who was initially shocked by the lack of respect from one of his cardinals, asked his secretary to leave them alone.

'Cardinal Lucé,' Benedict finally spoke, once the door to the library had been closed, 'thank you for coming. Please, have a seat.'

Lucé deliberately chose not to speak.

Benedict, clearly unnerved, walked towards a chair, but instead of sitting down he unconsciously found himself moving to stand behind it.

'I can see that you are clearly annoyed with my decision not to reappoint you to your former curial post,' he said, the nervousness clear to hear in his voice. 'Is that what this is?'

Lucé, turning slowly to face him, continued to remain silent.

The silence and the defiance, panicked Benedict to such an extent that he contemplated calling his security detail to have Lucé removed from the library. Instead, he found himself speaking in defence of his decision.

'Are you here to find out why?' he asked, his voice slightly raised. 'Are you not going to speak?'

Lucé continued to give no response, and his intense stare faded to a vacant look.

'Very well,' Benedict said, stepping out from behind the chair to walk across the room to stand behind his desk. 'I had hoped for some discussion today so that we as brothers could find a way to move forward, but your intransigence is self-evident. I was going to use the word petulance, but I would not want to offend.'

Lucé smirked at his pitiful sight.

'How dare you! I am your superior, the Bishop of Rome and you come in here with an attitude so contemptuous that I...' he sighed, knowing from Lucé's eyes that he was not troubled in any way. 'It would be best for both of us if we end this audience. I have made my decision. It is my intention not to appoint you to any curial position or diocesan post. You will still retain the title of cardinal with all its rights and privileges, but I want you to enter early retirement. That is how you will best serve the Church. Dedicate the remaining years of your life to prayer and penance.'

With a slight turn of his head, Lucé gave a quizzical look and uttered one word, 'Penance?'

'Yes, penance! Surely, you can see the harm you have done to the Church? Can you not?'

Lucé frowned and shook his head.

'I have prayed for years trying to discern you. I can only come to one of two conclusions, and they are that you have acted with malicious intent or that you are completely incompetent. To give you the benefit of doubt, I have convinced myself of the latter, but within my soul something cries out that I am wrong. I suppose the truth is too hard to face, but it is now my duty to protect the faithful from someone like you and begin to unravel the damage you have caused.'

Lucé let out a single laugh, before walking towards the desk and finally taking a seat. Then crossing his legs in an act of defiance, he gestured with his left hand for the pope to continue.

'I do not know how you did it,' Benedict continued, preferring to stand behind his desk, 'but ever since you were ordained, your fingerprints can be found on everything that has gone wrong with the Church since you got involved in the council. I tried to warn my predecessor to distance himself from you, but he would not hear of it. You have appointed bishops, some of whom are now in the college of cardinals, who are mired in scandal and corruption, and who are destroying the Church from within.'

'Such as?'

'You know what I am talking about!' Benedict replied, in a raised voice. 'You attended the conclave. One of your questionable appointees was nearly elected pope. Thank God, we were spared from such a pontificate.'

'It was close,' Lucé replied, with a knowing grin.

'Ryan Flynn,' Benedict uttered with disdain, quickly moving the conversation on. 'You were warned! You had the evidence and still you ignored it. Now he is facing trial in the United States for the abuse and rape of former seminarians and serving priests. Every day, more accusations are emerging of so-called gay mafias active within the Church, his connection to organised crime and masonic membership. His scandal has ripped apart the Church in America. Conservative Catholics are demanding that bishops he ordained, or was closely associated with, should be immediately suspended, for they are claiming that he is part of some conspiratorial antichristian network that has infiltrated the hierarchy of the Church.'

'And what are you going to do about it, now you are pope?'

'I do not even know who you really are. The history that is written within your Vatican file is different from the stories people have told me of your past. It is as if I am dealing with a man who has lived multiple lives. Even now when people talk about you they reveal something unknown, and facts that simply could not be true.' Benedict steadied himself as best he could as the sense of unease grew within him. 'I think it would be best if you left here immediately, for I feel uncomfortable in your presence.'

Lucé rose to his feet. 'Thankfully, you and I will never meet again,' he replied, as he buttoned his coat. 'You have my word that I will not speak publicly out against you, nor the Church. In return, you will not come after me in any way, and you will not speak of me. It is hard to imagine that we were once friends, but it has become clear to see that we are on different paths in this world.'

As he gazed into Lucé's blue eyes, Benedict, for the briefest of moments, felt a fear touch the essence of his being. Restricted by the confines of this world, he could not see that around him the spirits of over a thousand demons, implored their master to set them free so that they could set upon the Vicar of Christ and show him where their power truly rested. Hundreds at any one-time screamed obscenities into his face while others spat and vomited upon him. But their time had not yet come, and although Benedict felt an uncomfortable presence within the room, he could not see nor hear it and therefore would never understand what was happening to him in that moment in time.

'You will never summon me again like you did today,' Lucé continued, with a hatred so deep for the pope that he wished the appointed time was now so that he could have his way, if even for the briefest of moments. 'I have business of my own to attend, and I intend to go about it my way without hinderance or interference. Good day, Joseph!'

Minutes later, Pope Benedict stood at a window and watched the black BMW drive Cardinal Lucé back to Rome. Soon, any anger within him died away to a quiet resolve to have nothing more to do with his rogue cardinal, and to simply watch him from a safe distance to see if he kept his word.

Once back in his apartment in Rome, Lucé unlocked the door to his study and switching on the lights he gave a suppressed laugh as his eyes slowly scanned the hundreds of files that rested on the shelves that covered all four walls. Files he had gathered daily for years and which he knew he would need for this moment. Each file contained both a secret and the evidence to prove the truth behind the secret. Secrets of the Vatican bank, the private lives of prelates and cardinals sympathetic to Benedict, homosexual sex scandals and blackmail within the Vatican clergy, financial corruption with organised crime, agendas of the St. Gallen mafia, masonic and illuminati membership, ritual satanism and most importantly of all, evidence that the Church had covered up the reporting of child sexual abuse for decades.

It was enough to bring the Vatican crashing down around Benedict. Lucé knew that no pope could survive such revelations. He longed for the day when he could leak the documents one by one, but that day was still a few years into the future. For now, he was prepared to simply fall silent, to be alone in the company of darkness and his demons that feared him.

27.

For seventy-two hours the sun, with the intensity of a mid-summer's day, remained stationary in the sky as the earth scorched, wildfires raged, and the air thickened with smoke. For those who had managed to survive, some relief came on the third day when even the parasites succumbed to the heat and choked in the thick smoke. Yet, with no fresh running water and with the seas and oceans heating and evaporating, the toxic air made it almost impossible for any human to survive or to catch a breath in the acrid fumes. Hundreds of millions had died since the first bowl was poured upon the earth, and tens of millions more wished they too were gone.

The three days had been a long time for Lucifer and his demons, as they could only wait and allow the temperatures to rise, but the fourth bowl provided them with little enjoyment. In fact, they had become bored, and the demons pressed Lucifer to push ahead and to pour out the remaining bowls. Although many had died, Lucifer felt cheated that the bowls proved to be somewhat of an anticlimax. For millennia he had waited for this moment with great anticipation, dreaming of the pain and the suffering that he would be able to inflict upon the creation of God. Yet, once they were dead and their fates sealed, he felt nothing but disappointment. Across the globe which he had been allowed to manipulate and destroy, he sensed the end quickly approaching and that his time would soon be over.

The suffering the world had endured had been greater than anyone had predicted, or any prophecy had foretold. The beautiful way of life that people had, was within a generation transformed into one of hatred towards their fellow human beings. Once allowed to reign across the globe to rise to his power, his lies and deceit made it almost too easy. Like playing a game of chess against an amateur, it soon lost all enjoyment and had become boring. For him there would be no second chance and this was his lot.

This creation of humanity wanted with all its heart to see the face of God, and to live an eternity within His presence. They had thought and pondered what heaven would be like. Countless books had been written on the belief, billions of sermons preached since the time of Christ and an infinite number of thoughts and prayers offered in the hope that they would be counted amongst the faithful who would get to see it for themselves. Lucifer, who had seen the face of God and who once lived in the wonder of His love and being, stood looking upon the remaining bowls, as a jealous anger welled within him, because for those who had died with faith he knew where they now were, and in truth he knew that it was beautiful. Cast from the presence never to return, his sin of pride and those of the demons who followed him, meant that there would be no redemption nor a saviour to pay the price of his sin. The moment he rejected the presence of his creator, was the moment he shunned His love. But these mere mortals, with their divinely created souls had never seen His face nor had they experienced His presence. In this time and place of creation, their purity was tested, their Saviour's blood had been poured out for them to absolve the sins of their hearts and of their flesh, and in the end when death came the greatest blessing was waiting for them. Unlike him, humanity had its saviour. Oh, how he hated them. Oh, how he hated himself.

Once when he was alone in the world, shortly after the Nazarene had ascended back to the Father, he took himself off to make sense of what had happened over those three days in Jerusalem. In a remote valley, on the western edge of an island the world would one day call Ireland, he hid himself from his legions and gathered his thoughts. With no one to talk to or share his confusion, he roamed the valley for many years, trapped within his anger and his hatred. But one day a thought crossed his mind that made him stop, a thought so terrifying that he never considered it again.

Sitting on a rock close to the shores of a freshwater lough, and as his mind was filled with thoughts of revenge, he asked himself the question that if God extended the hand of forgiveness to him would he reach out and accept it? If all could be forgiven and his place and position reinstated in the kingdom of heaven, could he fall on bended knee and plead for the mercy of God and the Word who had been made flesh?

Lucifer knew that he was beyond forgiveness and that he had been cast from the Divine presence forever, but the question intrigued him for many years. When he served God and led the heavenly angels, he was at one time happy and lived in His divine presence, wanting for nothing except the need to gaze upon the Beatific Vision. But it was the force of divine love to bring into being a new creation, made in His image that had souls connected to Him, able to love and create new life, and who had an exalted place above the angels, that brought Lucifer to stand opposed to the One he once adored. So how could he even accept the possibility that he would walk back into heaven on bended knee? He had pondered the possibility for a long time before accepting that forgiveness would never be open to him. He never considered it again, and instead left that valley and with his demons targeted the believers of the world one by one, causing wars and famines across the globe, and promising themselves that they would never stop as long as there was one soul left on the face of the earth that they could tempt to doubt God's love.

Still in control, Lucifer walked from his throne of lies, lifted the fifth bowl and walked to the entrance of the basilica and poured it upon the earth. Immediately, the liquid fire ran out but it never touched the ground, instead it rose high into the sunlight sky where it turned black and spread across the light of the sun, and once again the earth was darkened.

Those who were barely alive initially took comfort in the fact that the sunlight had disappeared, and as the darkness came, they hoped for some relief. But that did not arrive. Instead, they found themselves trapped in a darkness that was so thick that they could not see beyond a few feet. All the time the fires continued to rage around them and the smoke, which was now trapped beneath the blanket of darkness, continued to build up and to choke them without any mercy.

'There are two bowls left,' Lucifer addressed his demons. 'I know what is in the first of the two-remaining bowls, but I do not know what will be poured upon the earth in the last bowl.'

Each demon remained silent, as their angers grew and their thirst for souls became greater.

'We have already been cast from The Presence,' he continued, as he walked amongst them. 'There is no hope for us, and there never was. Our expulsion was our defeat, but we still have a small window of time to test those who remain before we are extinguished forever.'

His demons moaned with rage at the fate that awaited them.

'When this bowl is poured, you will have the freedom to go wherever you want and to harm whoever you wish. This will be the last opportunity for you and for me to bring with us as many as we can. Once this tribulation is over, we will meet in Armageddon for the final time. Do not be disappointed, prevent as many as you can from entering the Kingdom that has been promised to them.'

Lifting the sixth bowl, he poured it into the middle of the basilica where it hovered in the air and burned brightly, as it slowly moved its way towards the seventh bowl, above which it rested.

Turning to his legion, Lucifer gave them the command to, 'Go!'

With the screams of hell, they fled from the basilica to hunt down those who remained.

28.

Leaving the basilica, they fled into the smoky darkness that had engulfed the earth; their demonic screams filling the city of Rome as their unleashed desires overran what they had to control for so long. No one was to be spared and no one saved, for this was the time of darkness and the light of hope had no place.

Frustration quickly set in for the demons as they found no one alive in Rome. Through each apartment and home they entered, searching for signs of life but all they encountered was death. Now that they had the opportunity to torment the living, the demons felt cheated as they looked upon the remains of the righteous and unrighteous as they lay side by side, indistinguishable in the rawness of earthly decay.

With the souls of the virtuous already in the arms of God, where no torment would ever touch them, the demons sought out those who had somehow managed to survive, and when they found them they made no distinction between the compassionate and the indifferent, those content with the blessings of life alongside those who had lived with covetousness in their hearts, the virtuous and the impure, those who sought wisdom against those who pursued natural inclinations, the truthful alongside the deceivers, saints of sincerity with the folks of hypocrisy, the self-controlled along with those who had self-indulged, men and women of humility side by side with people of pride, those once filled with love next to the selfish, the meek and humble of heart with the ones consumed with anger, the grateful with the unthankful, the gentle with the harsh, the forgiving with those who had rejected, those who had endured in their search for God with those who had given up and trusted in themselves alone, those who gave with those who took, people of compassion with people of indifference and the faithful with those who had presumed that they knew the way.

On the ancient road from Rome to Brindisi, along the Appian Way, a group of demons found their first group of living humans who had hidden inside the catacombs of Saint Sebastian. Deep in its tunnel network, several hundred people had taken refuge, and although the catacombs had afforded them some relief from the horrors above ground, many had already succumbed to death and those who had survived were close to it. The demons were unsure if those still living could hear their anger and see their hatred as they shook them to awaken them, because most of them remained unresponsive and did not seem to fear the terror that had come for them. With no satisfaction, the demons at least could satisfy their thirst for blood by using their blackened fingernails to slit the throats of the living and to watch their life-giving blood flow onto the hallowed ground that had witnessed the martyrdom of others many centuries ago.

As the people of the world held their breath in anticipation for Wormwood's impact, some came together to fight for their own survival. A group of billionaires, with a lucky contingent of people willing to serve them, had purchased the Queen Victoria cruise liner from Cunard, and setting sail into the sheltered coves of the Adriatic Sea, they had survived the initial impact and subsequent tsunami but now they were struggling to survive as their rations ran low. With the ship able to provide its own power they were able to keep it cool and sealed shut from the parasites. However, they had fallen into a false sense of security because when the demons spotted the ship, secured in a drydock close to Dubrovnik, they immediately descended to attack.

The first to see them was the crew on the ship's bridge. Terrified, they were helpless as they watched on whilst the demons used their fingernails to cut through the windows of the wheelhouse to access the ship. The sight of their blackened flesh and flaming red eyes, along with their demonic screams, was enough to paralyse the crew with fear as they slumped before the demons and with outstretched arms vainly attempted to defend themselves from the inevitable. No questions were asked or confessions sought, for once they entered the ship, the demons slit the throats of the living and hunted those who tried to hide from them. No matter who they were or where they hid on the ship, it made no difference as the demons hunted them down and killed them. Amid terrifying screams for mercy, the demons went from deck to deck and cabin to cabin, taking the lives of the living whether they were the richest or the poorest, for in death all souls were priceless and worth heaven and hell fighting over.

Deep in the salt mines near Krakow, thousands had managed to survive but now found that the lack of drinking water was going to lead to their deaths. Not willing to venture back up and into the world, they had accepted their fate with complete resignation and sat back and waited for their deaths to arrive. At first the large bang that filled the mines came as a surprise, but when the demonic screams filled the wooden stairwell as the demons flooded down into the caves, the people instinctively knew that their end was coming sooner and in a manner that they had not expected.

As fathers and mothers held their children, as people crawled and clung to the priests inside the church and as children cried with a fear of the living nightmare that was unfolding outside of their dreams, the demons terrorised them all with death as their lives were taken, and the people were helpless to defend themselves. For the priests who stood firm, the demons had reserved their greatest torment as the bones of their sacred hands were crushed before their blood flowed from their necks.

Deep in a crypt of Saint Michael's Golden-Domed Monastery in Kiev, the monks had taken refuge and had sealed themselves in from what was unfolding across the city. With enough bottled water to last them many weeks, they had remained in a state of prayer and fasting, offering the sacramental rite of their divine liturgy for the souls of the departed and for those who had managed to survive. It was the banging that first alerted the monks to the fact that something had arrived at their hiding place. As the crypt was also a secure treasury, the reinforced door afforded them some time as the demons thumped and kicked from the other side. Steadying themselves in faith, the monks stood together in the middle of the crypt, clutching their pectoral crosses as they waited. For a brief moment there was a glimmer of hope as the banging ceased, but in the candlelit crypt the monks saw the walls move as the demons clawed their way through the earth to gain access to them. And as they broke through, the wind that followed extinguished what light there was and the crypt was plunged into darkness. Through agonising cries and with pleas to the Divine for His mercy, the monks were stripped of their robes before their flesh was ripped from their bones; each cry an offering of delight to the blood thirst of the demons who did what they could to cause them great suffering in their final agony.

On the outskirts of Brussels, in the largest nuclear bunker ever built, European commissioners and their families, members of parliament and their staff thought they were safe. With enough food and water to last many years, and with wind turbines above the ground powering their electrical supply, they were content to live out each day following a strict routine of sleep, a little work, a good daily meal, and a lot of time engaging in pursuits to occupy the mind from reading to gaming, to watching movies to playing boardgames with one another. Above ground the military, who had sworn oaths to protect them as their final line of defence, lay dead. Protected by blast doors and the lead-lined reinforced concrete wall of the bunker, the elite were indifferent to the suffering of their people. Their aim was simple, and that was to bunker it out until they could reemerge and rebuild a new world in the aftermath of what had happened.

Their first realisation that something was wrong was when the bunker was plunged into complete darkness.

Initially, they were unfazed as temporary blackouts were common and a fully charged emergency backup lighting system always kicked in within minutes. But when that failed, they began to wonder when they heard clawing at the earth around them. With only torches illuminating their underground world, they could only wait as the demons burrowed into their protected space to torment those who believed that they were safe and untouchable. This was what the demons had hoped for as these people were fully alive and completely overwhelmed with the fear of what was unfolding around them and the knowing their end in this world had arrived.

High above Madrid, sealed within the Torre de Cristal skyscraper, a group of bankers had, since the outbreak of the parasites, sealed themselves into a conference room where they shaded as best they could behind the closed curtains and drank from the water coolers they had within their offices. Unable to escape the scorching heatwave, they found themselves completely spent of all energy and now were left hopeless as even their water supply had run dry. With no emotion left, they simply drifted in and out of consciousness as they waited for the inevitable to arrive. Only a few of them saw the red flaming eyes of the demons as they peered through the windows, having scaled the exterior of the building. The break in the room's vacuum as the glass panels of the walls were smashed, stirred a few to glimpse the horror of the demons as they gained access to the building. However, they were too far gone to express any real fear, and their blood simply flowed from their bodies without even a whimper.

In the sewage tunnels of Helsinki, people had fled for refuge from the onslaught that had engulfed the world. In the end their hideaway echoed with the screams of horror as the demons accessed the tunnels and tormented and killed those who in a desperate hope for survival had opted to live in the bowels of the modern world. In their darkness they heard the thumps, and the splashing sounds of the dying as they fell into the rivers of sewage.

On the south island of New Zealand, in the mountains north of Alexandra, at the Siloam House of Prayer, a group of interdenominational Christians had gathered to face the end in a spirit of praise and worship. From a holy well they had bottled their water, and with firepits surrounding their building they had managed to keep the parasites from getting close. But with the heat and the toxic air engulfing the world, they all knew that it was only a matter of time before their Lord would call them home. Despite their fervent hope, none of them could have imagined how it could truly end for them all. Their pastor had reassured them that upon their last breath they would awaken to look into the eyes of Jesus, the saviour who would bring complete peace to their souls and quench all pain and suffering of this world. What none of them had anticipated was how harrowing their end would be. In their prayer room, they were gathered by candlelight when the demons arrived. Yet despite their natural fear, the Christians did not yield to the terror, nor did they abandon their hope. Instead, they praised the name of Jesus until their throats were cut, and even then His name pulsed with every final heartbeat of their being as they entered their final reward.

The terror of the demons lasted for three days as they crossed what remained of the world to seek out the living. From every palace to condo, from farm stead to home place and from shepherds' huts to makeshift camps, they found those who had survived and took from them their lives in this world. Like the Angel of Death, there was no escaping the destiny that awaited everyone. People ran but they could not hide. They sought their own escape but in the end they were delivered into the hands of evil.

For those whose protection was guaranteed until the final day, the demons could not touch them. As these bands of people continued along their way to Jerusalem, they were encircled by the angels of heaven and were blissfully unaware of what was happening around them. And as the demons spat their fury at the angels and cursed the Archangel Michael who stood at the veil between this world and watched what was taking place, they finally came to the realisation that it was over as no one remained alive. Soon, they all fell silent.

As a grand silence filled the earth, Lucifer realised that he had been cheated. With no one left to torment, he wondered what was in the seventh and final bowl. As the demons returned to him in frustration, realising that there was no one left to harm, it dawned on him that this moment could be his actual end.

For days he sat on his throne in fear as he stared into the possibility of the fire that burned within the bowl, pondering the consequences of what it might contain for him and his legion. This final unknowing morphed into weeks and before him many months passed by until the flame grew weaker and began to burn itself out. Then, with the last flicker of light a stillness, like the one that existed upon the calming of creation's chaos, fell upon the earth.

As if the hand of God swept across the sky, the darkness dissolved, and the light of a gentle sun rose again in the east, as the winds dispelled the toxic air that had gathered. And almost immediately, the remains of the dead dissolved into the ground as new life sprung forth. Then, as a new dawn emerged, a voice from the sky which Lucifer recognised, spoke with authority. 'It is accomplished!'

29.

His Seventh Pope.

Thursday, 14th March 2013.

The morning following the conclave in which Pope Francis was elected, Cardinal Lucé stood in the Sala del Concistorio, and along with his brother cardinals he applauded as the new pope entered. Although he had been instrumental in securing the votes this time in favour of the Argentinian, Lucé had chosen to remain in the background the previous evening, and to allow the glory to be focused entirely on Francis.

Lucé knew that the Argentinian was determined on bringing about major change and reform, and he had promised to stop the pantomime that had gripped the Vatican under the previous pope as scandal after scandal broke within the Church. There had been no way of controlling it, and only the sudden resignation of Pope Benedict meant that a new man could take the helm and steer the Church into much calmer seas.

'This is all your fault,' Francis said, his right index finger wagging as he walked towards Lucé. 'I am going to need you close by my side.'

Lucé's face pulled a warm smile, and he reached out and hugged the new pope, whispering into his left ear, 'Whatever you need my friend. I will always have your back.'

Then for the briefest of moments, they stood holding each other's arms and looked with warm contentment into each other's face. Both knowing where this relationship had to go if the new pontificate had any chance of succeeding.

'My brothers,' Francis finally spoke from the papal throne as the cardinals took their seats in the hall. 'At the last conclave, eight years ago, I just about managed to make it back home to Argentina.'

Most cardinals laughed, knowing that he had come a close second in the ballots, while the cardinals who had firmly backed Pope Benedict, sat with dispassionate self-control, and feared where this new papacy would lead the Church.

'This time the Lord has called me to remain in Rome and to shepherd his Church. Yes me, His unworthy servant and pastor. I do not know how long He intends my pontificate to last, whether it be long or short, that is for Him to decide. However, there can be no denying the fact that the barque of Peter is being flooded with wave after wave of scandals that are an affront to the face of Christ. We cannot endure much more, or this Church will become so crippled that we will be left drifting with no direction and with no promise. Make no mistake, I intend to save that from happening. I intend to make this a Church of the poor and suffering and to direct it into the waters that Jesus is calling us to sail. These waters will become uncomfortable for some of you, but these are the waters that will bring true renewal, much needed healing and from there we will be able to clearly hear and discern the calling of God.

'I say that some of you will become uncomfortable, and when you become aware of this you should pray that you will be able to embrace the reform of charity that is coming our way. Like Jesus himself, the Church exists to comfort the disturbed but also to disturb the comfortable. For too long, some of you have lived like princes, feasting on the donations of the poor. No more. From now on, you will be expected to lead by example. No more palaces, no more flash limousines, no more fine wining and dining. Instead, you will open your homes and your hearts to the poor. You will walk humbly amongst your people until you become at one with them. And you will feed the hungry before you put food into your own mouths.

'There will be no more toleration of scandalous behaviour. Ordination will no longer be a free meal ticket for life. Those who commit the most criminal of acts by preying on children and the vulnerable, they will be fast-tracked to laicisation, for they have no role to play within the church and I am sick of watching such men become a mortgage for life upon the faithful.

'My brothers, the Holy Spirit has guided you to elect me. This is the way he is desiring the church to be restored. Make no mistake, I am old, but I intend to act very swiftly in bringing about the reforms that are needed, and no one, especially within the Roman Curia will be able to stand in my way. I will not tolerate disobedience. Furthermore, I do not fear attacks from any side, because experience has taught me that the more one is attacked, the freer one becomes.'

Moments after Pope Francis concluded his words, Cardinal Lucé was the first to rise to his feet and show his full support by applauding. Soon, every single cardinal, most of them freely but some out of a great unease, stood and joined him in showing their solidarity with the new pontiff.

For the next hour the cardinals mingled in the room with Francis, acknowledging him one by one by venerating his simple silver ring, and speaking to him with words of warmth, prayer and encouragement in a desire to be recognised by his favour.

Later that morning, Cardinal Lucé was summoned to the hotel room in Santa Martha where the new pope was still residing, amid growing rumours that he was not going to move into the papal apartment.

'Vittorio,' Francis greeted him, as he entered the small bedroom before inviting him to sit down in one of the two armchairs that sat next to the window. 'Thank you for coming, but I thought it best that my first meeting should be with you, after all you have paid a great price under Benedict's pontificate because of your loyal support for me. If it were not for you, I would never have been elected yesterday. To me, that is a sign that God's will has been at work throughout this, and that he has used you as his instrument.'

Lucé lowered his head in an act of humility.

'Therefore, I want you to remain close to me. You will be left in the shadows no more because I want to appoint you to the most important post within the curia, the Secretariate of State. Will you serve me?'

'I will do whatever you ask of me, Holy Father,' he replied, with a warm smile.

'I meant what I said to your brother cardinals,' Francis continued, as he lifted a piece of paper from the edge of the desk beside him and handed it over to Lucé. 'A list of reforms that I intend to at least explore and begin a conversation around. However, it is my intention to see most of what is on that list achieved through major reform of the Church.'

As he carefully read through the list, Lucé feigned an agreeable smile. He already knew what Francis was planning, but as he read, he felt the demons around him fly with wild abandonment as they saw what Francis had planned.

'Can you work for me in implementing these reforms?' Francis asked, when Lucé finally made eye contact.

'I have no hesitation,' he replied, in his manner of fact way.

'I want to shake up the college of cardinals by appointing bishops and priests, and no longer appoint metropolitan archbishops who believe it is their entitlement simply because they shepherd dioceses where the red hat has usually gone to. I want to appoint men who will carry on my vision when they come to elect my successor.'

'That would send a very clear message to the church, Holy Father.'

'I also want to open a conversation around our gay brothers and sisters and their relationships. For they have not only been excluded from the Church, but they have also been deeply wounded by it. They are after all, baptised sons and daughters of God. They should have a place at our table, without feeling they have dirty hands that need to be washed in public. The same goes to those who, through no fault of their own, find themselves divorced and now in second marriages which brings them the fullness of love and joy, but is overshadowed with a feeling of condemnation.'

'It is a debate that will rock the Church,' Lucé replied, 'but I concur, it is a position that we need to change, and I will help you to navigate your way through what will be unchartered waters.'

'As for the Vatican Bank, well…' Francis sighed, as he rolled his eyes and raised his arms in despair, 'I have no experience of banking, but it is clear to see that it needs cleaned out from within. There should be no place in the Vatican bank for corruption, money laundering, property and financial irregularities, and trading in shares that are opposed to the teachings of Christ.'

Lucé nodded in agreement.

'It is also my intention to reopen the debate around the role of women within the Church. We are too male orientated. Why should catholic mothers, sisters and daughters not have a greater role within our institutions and in our sacramental rites?' Francis stopped abruptly and raised an eyebrow to see if Lucé agreed.

'We all know that one day this will come to be,' he counselled. 'Therefore, we need to begin the conversation at the synodal level. My own personal view is, if we can have married permanent deacons, then why can we not have women deacons like they did in the early Church?'

'Exactly,' Francis replied, as he leaned forward in his chair. 'And on that point, we will need to look at optional celibacy. We can no longer bury our heads in the sand whilst vocations continue to fall around us. There are too many good married men who would make excellent priests.'

Lucé pulled another agreeing smile.

'We will also have to look at ways to humble the Church in poverty and to eradicate luxurious living by the clergy as a matter of priority.'

For over an hour Francis continued to talk through his vision with his new secretary of state.

By the end of the day, it had been announced that the Eminent Cardinal Vittorio Lucé had been appointed to serve in the most prestigious role within the curia. As for Lucé himself, he graced the corridors of the Vatican with great humility for all to see. He gave up his evenings to feed the poor on the streets of Rome and he lived simply in a small apartment within the Vatican. For twelve years he served his pontiff with great diligence. In that time the debates were had and divisions within the church were widened, but little reform came to pass. Yet, there was for him one important success, and that was by the time Pope Francis had died after a short respiratory illness, the college of cardinals had been filled with men who lived the spirit of Francis in poverty and charity, and each one of them looked to Cardinal Lucé as the true successor to the Great Pope Francis.

30.

Fifteen months later.

It was a journey just short of fourteen-thousand kilometres, and it took them four-hundred and fifty days to complete, as they walked from Rome to Jerusalem; walking to the north-west of Italy and through the Balkans towards Greece, progressing through Turkey and crossing at the ruins of Istanbul, then entering Syria they made their way through the ancient Holy Land towards the city where it had all begun.

It was a journey of complete abandonment and trust, as the initial steps for Oliveri, Mode, Lincoln and others who left Rome back on that night were one of physical and emotional pain that gave way to a thirst for their newfound faith and life, as they lived their encounters with one another and shared the discoveries that came with each new step. In the first few weeks many of the remnant talked and confessed their past experiences to one another, making sense of the new way of life they now found themselves living, until each man, woman and child within the group became quieter and found themselves listening more and becoming the fullness of what they were created to be, and that was to know that they were loved.

Each day they walked for many hours and went for nothing. Under the radiant light of the angels, their every need was provided. Shielded from the horrors that were unfolding in the final stages of the tribulation, they were fed manna from the hands of the angels and drank crystal clear water from endless springs. After a few days they were handed their white robes to wear, and with no sandals or shoes on their feet, they walked each step of the journey as if they were walking through the gentle grass of a sweet summer's day. Walking past vineyards and through farmlands they journeyed, as vines and fruit trees miraculously bore fruit for them to eat, as the honey from hives and the milk of herds was fed to them when they came to rest at the end of each day.

Not once did the angels speak to them, but they dutifully guarded them and led them along the way. But whenever one looked up, the angels would acknowledge their presence with a warming smile as they moved in and around the faithful remnant as they continued along the ancient way to Jerusalem.

For Oliveri, the journey into his true self deepened with each day of his pilgrimage, and for the first time in his life he was able to fill the God shaped hole that had existed within his heart. For all his life his ministry to others masked the infinite abyss that existed within him. But with no distractions to hinder him anymore, and facing the gravity of his situation and the natural poverty he now lived, he was able to embrace his own feeble and mortal condition, and instead of overwhelming him it brought him to a place of great peace for he knew that despite his microscopic place in the great cosmos, God was literally moving heaven and earth for him to experience just how important he was in His sight.

A journey that started with strangers, soon changed into one of close relationships and fraternal love that grew deeper by the day. Initially he remained close to his companions, and often sought out the company of Dom Colby, but as the days turned into weeks and then months, a natural rhythm grew as people opened their hearts to one another. Soon, people began to mingle as they walked along the way, wanting to get to know each other, to question, to listen and to reassure. For hours Oliveri found himself talking to people he did not know as they would join and walk alongside him. And when the initial fear of their situation gave way, and they surrendered themselves into the care of the angels, the warmth of each soul shone brightly in the light of each living being. Through experiencing such love, the remnant wondered why it had taken this to happen for them to realise that the people of the world could always have had this purity with one another as it already existed within the heart of everyone.

For Oliveri, the biggest change he could see was in the life of Dave Mode, and each day was a new wonder as Mode found his true calling in assisting all he could, talking and laughing with anyone who wanted to walk alongside him. And at the end of each day, Mode was never happier or content than in serving the other faithful and ensuring that each one of them had what they needed before he would feed and nourish himself.

Occasionally, and usually during the silent moments of their pilgrimage, the remnant would remember that beyond themselves there was a world that did not have the peace and protection they were experiencing. Often, glimpsing past the light of the angels, they would see the turmoil that had been brought upon the world. Yet, through this chaos, the greatest moment of their pilgrimage was when they arrived at the ancient city of Istanbul, and amid the ruins they walked between what remained of the Blue Mosque and the Hagia Sophia. Under the watchful eyes of Christ the Pantocrator, whose glorious colours reflected the light of the angels, they gazed upon the figure in his golden and blue robes as he appeared to bless them from a history that had passed forever.

'Do you think we'll get to see the real thing, in Jerusalem?' Mode asked as he stood alongside Oliveri, as they both admired one of the greatest art works of the Christian world.

'It will be beyond all imagination,' Oliveri replied, as he draped an arm around Mode and brought him close, with a love so great. 'In my youth I wanted nothing more than to see him in the flesh,' Oliveri continued, as they both gazed up at the Pantocrator, 'but in adult life I loved the power of the church more and the gospel less, how insane was that? So yes, I believe that we will, for he has promised us that he will return and walk amongst us at the end of time. How privileged are we that we walk as the chosen to see the end of time give birth to the eternal promise of heaven?'

'I cannot wait,' Mode replied, as he stretched out a hand with the desire to touch the glorious image. 'Even though I cannot see him in the flesh, I can already feel him alive in everyone that I talk and listen to, and if that is what is giving me this great peace within my heart, how much more wonderful will it be to see him and to touch him in the flesh?'

Oliveri could see the light reflect off the joy that came from the tears that filled Mode's eyes, and like a father to his son he gently pulled his head towards him and kissed him tenderly on the forehead. 'You are right, he is already here in spirit. But, how much more joy will we experience when we see him face to face in Jerusalem!'

Jane Lincoln reminded them both each day that she was glad they did not listen to her by remaining in Rome. The sheer wonder of the miracle in which they were living, including the full restoration of her health, was all she could talk about with great joy and the fact that someone like her, with a history so dark and cruel, could be forgiven and allowed to walk alongside others of great purity and depth of goodness. In moments of genuine humility, she would often stare up at the angels only to find herself completely mesmerised and overwhelmed at the wonder that was unfolding around her, and then looking at the people and realising how blessed she was, she would simply sit and quietly give thanks within her heart to the Love that had consumed her.

Along the way their numbers grew as other groups of people, guided by more hosts of heavenly angels, merged with them. From all directions the faithful remnant came, and with great joy they journeyed together towards their final destination.

The remnant collectively realised that their pilgrimage was ending when they first saw the light emerge beyond the horizon; far more radiant than the dawning of a new day. No one needed to inform them that it was Jerusalem, because it burned deep within their hearts that this was so. Eager to get there as soon as possible, they found it amusing that the angels continued with their routine of stopping and feeding them, whereas the faithful wanted nothing more than to hurry to see what it would be like. But the wisdom of the angels brought a greater sense of anticipation, knowing that in rest they would dream and grow in the wonder of it all.

When they finally walked over the brow of Mount Herzl, Oliveri was humoured when he realised that nothing had really changed in the city. In his own imagination he had envisaged the city to be destroyed and rebuilt into something no living eye had seen, nor mind imagined. Yet, the sand-coloured stones of the buildings reflected brightly in the light that surrounded the city, and the green trees of the olives and vines spread everywhere as the city sounded vibrant and alive. But it was on top of the walled ruins of the Temple Mount that the landscape was different. He was not sure if the Al Aqsa Mosque or the newly built third temple were still standing, because the whole mount had been consumed by a mesmerising light that radiated across the city, into which the angels flew and reemerged, and into which no human being could see or draw near.

The sight captivated each faithful member of the remnant as they sat on the hill and watched on, wondering with endless possibilities as to what the light veiled. No doubt it was a heavenly realm to which they were not yet invited to approach, but the wonder of it enthralled them for many days until they realised that the angels who had guided them from Rome and the other cities had already departed from them and were submerged within the light.

No one knew for how long they had been sitting on the hill and gazing at the wonder of the sight before them, but it was finally hunger that drew them to want to enter the city and that was when they noticed the flaming ring of fire that encircled Jerusalem. Not sure how to pass through it, it was a woman known as Gretna who was brave enough and had the faith to not fear it and to simply walk towards it. And as the others watched on, the flame parted before her and she was permitted entry to Jerusalem.

Together, Oliveri, Mode, Lincoln, Colby and Roth held hands as they too walked towards the flame. And as they did, it parted right before them and allowed them to walk through; its heat soothing them as they saw the Damascus gate lit up before them with its protective doors plated in sheets of pure gold. Walking down the steps that led up to the gate, they smiled with great anticipation as they took the final steps of their pilgrimage and walked into the city.

Inside the walls the people had gathered in their thousands, finding places to rest as they ate from street tables laden with food and drank wine from the finest of vines. Each street was vibrant with love and laughter, as strangers became sisters and brothers, and the people consumed one another with a tender love that the world had never seen before. It was if all the world's nationalities had merged into a city of equality, with no one greater or less than the person next to them, and everything they needed was provided for them.

Almost in a trance, Oliveri and the others spent days walking the ancient city and exploring the side streets and sites that told the story of the greatest love ever told. Time and time again, they would meet complete strangers and begin talking, and with a feeling greater than falling in love, they would sit for hours and become consumed by the strangers who quickly became their friends.

In what Oliveri had known as the Baka district of the city, they were led by an angel and shown into a home where they could live. In this apartment the five of them settled and found that it was furnished to cater for their every need, and that the kitchen was filled with all the food that their hearts desired. But they spent little time there except to sleep at the end of each day. Instead, they met in the cafés and restaurants where everything was free, and the people mingled and served one another. And the whole time they were there, the fascination remained as to what the light on top of the Temple Mount kept hidden.

Several times each day, everyone found themselves drawn close to it, but they could only go so far before they knew that they could go no further. For the remnant were encouraged to gaze in wonder at what they saw, but the time for the revealing had not yet arrived and the faithful knew and respected this, because in that city it was simply enough to live close to it knowing that they now had nothing to fear from the world.

Over many weeks, other groups of the faithful remnant would arrive on Mount Herzl and they all followed the same pattern of sitting and looking on in awe and wonder, before passing through the protective ring of flame and the Damascus gate and finding their place within the city. And there they spent their days, all one hundred and forty-four thousand souls as they basked in the love of God and for one another.

31.

Pope Number Eight.
Sixteen days following the death of Francis.

Within minutes of white smoke emerging from the Sistine Chapel, the Campanone bell, followed by the other five bells of Saint Peter's Basilica, began to toll in announcement that a new pope had been elected.

With the cardinals still locked in conclave, the accompanying staff of the electors gathered in the hall, adjacent to the central balcony of Saint Peter's, from where the new pope would soon be announced to the world. Whilst Vatican staff made the final preparations, of placing the massive red banner that contained the coat of arms of the late Pope Francis over the balcony, those who had permission to accompany the cardinals as their personal secretaries and confessors, gathered in anticipation; each one wondering if their man had been elected.

As Monsignor Gustave Hasler took his place along with his fellow priests, he was growing rather tired of their speculative chatter that his man would be elected. After all, Cardinal Lucé had dismissed the possibility himself, and reminded him that the man who enters conclave the favourite emerges a cardinal. Hasler was convinced that the Spirit would have descended upon another man, one close to Francis but not known to the public. His own choice would have been the newly appointed protodeacon of the college, Cardinal Guarducci, or the eminent theologian, Cardinal Oliveri. His man had become too old, and the division caused by Francis required a man with enough energy to unite and to heal the open divisions that had emerged during his papacy.

Twenty minutes later, Hasler watched as Cardinal Guarducci walked towards the library balcony; still wearing his red pontificals, he talked to the deputy master of ceremonies before he prepared to make his announcement to Rome and the world.

As the curtains onto the balcony were opened, blinding artificial light flooded into the hall as the crowds that had gathered in the early evening cheered. The moment they had been waiting for had now arrived.

As Cardinal Guarducci stepped onto the balcony and disappeared into the light, the curtains were closed behind him. Inside the hall, everyone felt the anticipation of the mighty silence that fell across the people who had gathered in the square as they waited expectantly.

'Annuntio vobis gaudium magnum,' Guarducci's voice announced to the world. 'Habemus Papam!'

The people in the square erupted into an enormous cheer that lasted for several moments before a second mighty silence emerged from them.

'Eminentissimum ac Reverendissimum Dominum, Dominum Vittorio.'

Hasler expected the silence to remain amongst the people, but as that name was announced, everyone in the hall looked to him, for there was only one Vittorio in the conclave. Suddenly, he felt a rush of foreboding, as he realised in that moment that his life had changed too.

'Sanctae Romanae Ecclesiae,' Guarducci continued, 'Cardinalem Lucé.'

This time the cheer that emerged from the people was like a wave of thunder.

Hasler closed his eyes and prayed for the strength he would need, and to avoid looking at those within the hall who were clapping for him just as much as they were for the new pope.

'Qui sibi,' Guarducci spoke into the cheering thunder, before pausing to allow the faithful to fall silent for one last time. 'Qui sibi nomen imposuit, Clemens.'

With his formal duty complete, Guarducci left the balcony to return to the Sistine Chapel. As the bells began tolling again and the people in the square celebrated the election, he walked solemnly between the assembled clergy, his eyes darting from side to side until they met with Gustave Hasler's, and only then did he allow himself to smile at him.

Hasler found himself so shocked that he could not bring himself to return the smile. Every moment now became surreal. And as those gathered came to congratulate him on the success of his cardinal's election, Hasler found himself unable to speak let alone hear what they were saying.

As the anticipation from the faithful grew, the first sign that the new pope was about to emerge was when the Swiss Guards marched through the hall and formed a guard of honour. Moments later, a sea of scarlet walked across the hall, with each cardinal smiling that a man had been chosen.

And as he looked on, Hasler spotted the white zucchetto at the rear of the procession draw closer, as he eagerly found himself watching for the first glimpse of his superior who had just been elected.

The moment he first saw him dressed in white, Hasler felt the hairs on his arms stand up as Cardinal Lucé was no more. Instead, he found himself gazing upon Pope Clement XV. And as he took it all in, he was drawn back to reality as the new pope walked towards him. Hasler genuflected and reached for the pope's hand, but Clement refused to let him venerate his ring as he grabbed Hasler by the shoulders and urged him to rise to his feet.

'My dear son,' Clement spoke, as his lips pulled a smile. 'It looks like my prediction was wrong. I can only do this with you by my side. I want you to journey with me through this mission which God has called me.'

As he looked into the pope's piercing blue eyes, Hasler found himself utter, 'Yes.'

Hasler could not remember how it happened, but those assembled later told him that Clement insisted that his secretary, the new papal secretary, would stand behind him on the library balcony. And as Hasler watched the new pope address Rome and the world, little did he know, nor the people who had gathered to witness the historic event, that

Satan had taken control of the most important office within the Christian world.

32.

As a priest, Oliveri had seen the faith come alive in young people and converts, who always embraced it and lived it with true devotion, acceptance and without question. His rise through the ranks of the hierarchy meant that he had removed himself from such engagement with people, and instead focused on governance and became entangled within the clerical power struggles that saw many a good man crushed by their fellow brothers as they found themselves unwittingly becoming the rungs on the clerical ladder.

Yet, he had never seen a conversion in his life like he had seen in Dave Mode, and as he lay on his bed thinking about him and what he had once been, Oliveri found himself smiling and thanking God for the change within Mode's heart. The sceptic would argue that his conversion was made easy by the sight of heavenly hosts and the miracles they were witnessing in Jerusalem, but Oliveri knew that Mode's heart had converted on the darkest of days and that his faith was genuine and rooted in the depths of his soul.

For many weeks Oliveri had walked with Mode through the streets of the city, visiting the great sites of Christendom and Judaism, retracing the steps of Christ and reliving the scriptures that they had carried with him. With no sellers pushing their wares upon tourists, pickpockets or builders clambering over scaffolding, these daily walks with Mode had become precious to Oliveri who had come to love him like the son he had never had. And each morning they would both set forth together and explore the city, have a little lunch and then return to spend the evening in the company of the others; both friends and strangers as they gazed upon the light and the angels that hovered about the Temple Mount.

Sitting on the edge of his bed, Oliveri was amazed at how youthful he felt inside his body. Although he saw an old man each time he shaved in the mirror, he had no aches or pains, and found that his levels of energy were on a par with Dave Mode's. The first time he had taken Mode to walk the Via Dolorosa and to visit the Church of the Holy Sepulchre, Oliveri believed he would pay a high price for climbing the ruins of calvary and bending to enter the shrines along the way. In the end, he felt nothing but the desire to walk it again and to see and do more.

Walking down into the kitchen, Oliveri met the others who were clearly waiting for him before they began to eat their breakfast.

'You've got to taste this,' Mode said with great enthusiasm, as he handed the cardinal a glass of freshly squeezed orange juice. 'I discovered it on a new stall this morning.'

Oliveri took the glass and brought it to his lips.

'Isn't it amazing?'

The fresh taste of the sweet orange juice brought a smile to Oliveri's face as he joined the others at the table for a breakfast of croissants with cheese, some of the juice and coffee. At the table they ate and joked, mainly at Mode's expense of wearing down the cobbled streets of Jerusalem with his morning runs and newfound hobby of discovering the food stalls that had been placed along the streets for the faithful to sustain themselves and to enjoy. Throughout his clerical life, breakfast for Oliveri consisted of dining alone with a transistor radio broadcasting the morning news, while he read the paper, drank bitter coffee and ate buttered bread with jam. But now he looked forward to nothing more than to eat with people he had grown to love, to share in their laughter and to listen with true empathy and interest as they shared experiences from their past or revelations of their new selves from their heart.

After breakfast, the others set off and left Mode and Oliveri to what they had nicknamed *their ramblings*. With two bottles of water, they both left their home and set off on what Oliveri had promised Mode was one of the most important and beautiful sights in the Holy Land and yet it was a sight few pilgrims ever ventured to see. They had no map or guide to take them through the streets, and like everyone else in the city they walked with a familiarity as if they knew exactly where they needed to go, as if they had lived a thousand years within its streets.

The journey that morning had excited Mode, especially when the cardinal had told him that the place they were going to visit was the site of the greatest miracle of Jesus's life. The cardinal refused to give any more detail as to what the miracle was, and this intrigued Mode even more because he sensed from the cardinal that this place was indeed particularly important to him.

As they headed back towards the Mount of Olives, Oliveri did at one point express a concern that they might not be able to get to the site if the ring of fire cut off the town of Al Eizariya, which was next to the ancient city, but they soon discovered that the ring of fire was just beyond it.

'This is much easier than the last time I was here,' Oliveri explained, as they walked out of the old city. 'In the old days you had to be searched by Israeli border guards as you were entering Palestinian territory. I do not know where the checkpoint used to be, but it put a lot of people off coming this far. That was sad, because the Muslim people here were so welcoming to any Christian pilgrim who came to visit. I suppose it had to do with their own sense of duty to pilgrimage and to welcoming strangers.' Oliveri, continued as they began to climb a set of steep steps. 'The last time I was here, there was a lone souvenir stall outside the entrance that our tour guide had told us about and had promised that not only would we find a bargain, but that we would find some of the most beautiful hand-crafted rosaries and icons that you would find anywhere in Jerusalem. The seller, when he noticed the gold ring on my hand, and after enquiring if I was a bishop, but only to be told by a fellow pilgrim that I was a cardinal, gifted me a beautiful icon of the place we are about to enter. He would accept nothing for it, and for years it hung beside my desk in the Vatican as a memory to this prominent place in the life of Christ.'

And with those words Oliveri pointed to an old doorway that led to a twisting stone staircase that descended into complete darkness. Like all the shrines of Jerusalem, it was ancient and surrounded with mystery and intrigue, but the simplicity of what he saw stumped even Mode.

'What happened here?'

Taking the scriptures from the backpack he was carrying, Oliveri turned to the gospel of John, chapter eleven and handed it over to Mode to read aloud.

Standing at the entrance, and looking deep into the darkness, Oliveri listened as Mode retold the story of Jesus coming to this very spot in the town they once called Bethany, but which was now named after its most famous son, Lazarus whom Christ had loved and whom Christ had raised from the dead.

'And this is where it happened?' Mode asked having read the passage, a little unimpressed as he investigated the entrance.

Oliveri was a little surprised as he watched Mode gaze into the entrance with a look of puzzlement on his face as he tried to make sense of what he was seeing.

'What are you thinking about?'

'It doesn't make sense!' Mode replied, as he stepped closer to the entrance to have a better look. 'How could Lazarus have climbed those steps if he was wrapped in a burial shroud?'

Oliveri laughed, for it was a rational question that even he asked when he first saw the place.

'This is not the entrance to the tomb,' Oliveri explained, as he fumbled with his hand above the inner lintel to find the light switch to turn on the fluorescent lights along the steps. 'Over the last two thousand years they have built on top of the sight, but the original tomb and the entrance is down here. Come and see.'

Carefully, they walked down the steps, which had become smooth with hundreds of years of countless pilgrims having walked up and down them, to see the place where the impossible had been made possible and the dead had been brought back to life.

'This was what triggered the plans to have him executed,' Oliveri explained, as he led the way down. 'From the moment Lazarus was raised from the dead, Jesus was a power that had to either be recognised or destroyed. The leaders of the day chose the latter and had him crucified.'

'And how do we know that this is the actual place?' Mode asked, carefully watching each footstep he took.

'Because it has not changed in two thousand years, and the people in this area have revered this tomb because their ancestors personally knew Lazarus and his two sisters. That is why it has never been lost or destroyed. They were real people and what happened here was one of the greatest moments in human history. And this is where Jesus would have stood!'

Reaching the bottom of the stairs, Oliveri stood back to allow Mode to see the entrance into the chamber. With a single light burning above them, Mode cautiously looked down and into a rectangular hole in the ground that led into a chamber that was lit from the inside.

And as he looked in, Mode felt the hairs on his arms stand on edge as he felt a cool breeze flow up from the entrance as he hunkered down to get a better look.

'It feels cold in there!' Mode said.

'Even on the warmest of days it is always cool in there,' Oliveri replied. 'Would you like to go in?'

'You are joking?' Mode quizzed, as he looked back at him. 'It would be hard for even a child to fit in there.'

'There's a way of doing it,' Oliveri replied, as he signalled for Mode to move aside. 'But I want you to ask yourself one question when you go in there, what part of you would you like to leave behind in this tomb? That is a question I ask myself each time I come here.'

Then standing above the entrance, Oliveri took off his backpack, turned and began to descend backwards, going down the four steps and lowering his upper body so he could easily enter the chamber. Eager to see inside it for himself, Mode did the same and feeling his head touch the stone beam of the entrance he backed himself into the tomb before he was able to stand up.

In a stone vaulted cave, with burial niches in the walls, Mode stood alongside Oliveri and took it all in; from the temporary wooden floor to the glass panel that covered a chamber that looked like a grave into which any human would be laid to rest. And in the corner, a red vigil lamp flickered as the wick consumed the olive oil that fed it, and that made Mode think of what the place would be like without the electric light, for he could sense that something had happened in here, something remarkable.

Together they stood, and with no tourists to rush them, Oliveri slowly reread the gospel passage as they pictured with great vividness the resurrection of a man people knew had been dead for days and considered what it must have felt for Lazarus himself to awaken within this very tomb and to hear his name being called out from beyond the realm of death. Emotions so powerful that it made Jesus weep. Mode had so many questions to ask, and as they flooded his mind the tomb itself became more alive to him and more tangible than any other site he had visited in Jerusalem. He was just about to ask the cardinal what had happened to Lazarus after he was brought back to life, when the lights went out for a moment, leaving only the vigil lamp burning before the lights came back on again.

'Hello!' A man called out from the street entrance to the tomb. 'Is there someone down there?'

Oliveri sighed deeply that their time together had been disturbed by the arrival of someone else who had come to visit the tomb, but as he went to the entrance to give back his reply, he knew that they had been both blessed with the time they had already been given together.

'We can come back another time,' Oliveri said to Mode, as he smiled with surrender. 'But before we go, remember what I told you to think about?'

'I don't understand what you are getting at?' Mode replied, as he could hear someone descend the twisted steps down to the tomb. 'What do I need to do?'

'It is a spiritual exercise,' Oliveri replied, getting flustered that the spiritual moment he had planned for Mode was being ruined by someone they did not know. 'We all have things in our lives, especially in our past that we would like to leave behind, and there is no better place to leave it than in this tomb and like Lazarus to step forth into a new way of life.'

Mode tried to make sense of what the cardinal was saying but knowing that someone was right outside the tomb he felt as if he did not have the freedom nor the time to contemplate what the cardinal was asking of him. Yet, it was something he really wanted to experience, but it was becoming clear to them both that this was not the time. 'Can we come back tomorrow and do it?'

Oliveri smiled once more and nodded, but in his heart he felt saddened that the moment of the first visit to the tomb had been ruined for Mode and what he had planned for him to experience.

Sensing the cardinal's disappointment, Mode reached out and stopped the cardinal from leaving.

'I'm sorry, but could we have a few more minutes alone?' Mode asked the stranger who was standing above the inner entrance to the chamber.

'Please, take as long as you need,' came the reply.

Bowing his head, Mode spoke into the depths of his soul to seek what it was that he needed to leave behind in the tomb. Once again, the memories of his past actions and faces of the people he had killed came back to him, and although he had confessed his wrongs and had been told many times that he had been forgiven, he could not allow himself to let it all go and feel that forgiveness deep within his soul. He understood that that was what he needed to leave behind, in the hope he could exit the tomb and for the first time since his conversion feel that he was worthy of God's forgiveness. And that is what he prayed for in the depths of his heart, for God to allow him to feel that worthiness and to leave the baggage of his guilt behind him.

Opening his eyes he saw Oliveri looking at him, his fatherly smile much warmer than it had ever been. 'Are you ready to leave?'

'Yes,' Mode replied, as he walked towards the steps. 'But, we must come back another time!'

When the cardinal gave his nod of approval, Mode leaned forward and went under the stone beam and began to climb the four steps out of the chamber.

Immediately, the stranger on the other side spoke to him with great authority.

'David, come forth!'

And as he looked up, Mode saw the stranger extend his right hand and just as he was about to grab hold, Mode saw a light radiate from within the wound on the wrist that a nail had made.

33.

There was a moment of grace, born through a sudden stillness, that forewarned Oliveri that the atmosphere within the chamber had changed. Afraid to disturb the stillness and to interrupt what was taking place above the entrance, he slowly edged forward to listen to what was being said. Although he could hear two voices conversing, they were muffled and incomprehensible. He could see the back of Mode's heels as he stood just at the top of the four steps and the feet of the stranger who stood opposite him, which had a slight golden haze radiate from them.

Notwithstanding the conversation that was taking place above the chamber, an engulfing silence enveloped Oliveri as he stood alone and watched, wondering what was happening. The harder he tried to listen, the greater the silence appeared to consume him until he felt something flutter deep within his being and he found himself asking the question, *could it be him?*

The terrifying reality became so overwhelming that it forced him away from the entrance and back to the far corner where the vigil lamp was burning, as he contemplated the possibility that standing just feet from him was the physical presence of the one he had spent his life searching for; the one he proclaimed and the one whom he had many times ignored, forgotten and questioned. In recent days there had been rumours of Christ appearing to small groups of the faithful in Jerusalem, and although he had listened to the testimonies with great interest, Oliveri believed that the fallen like him, who had caused great harm to the faith, would never have been chosen to have such an encounter. But here he was, just feet away from an experience that Dave Mode was having right now.

Throughout his ministry he had often used the line in many sermons that upon taking our last breath in this life we will awaken to see the loving face of Christ in the next. Never once did he think that that encounter would take place in this life, and he had often doubted some of the sermons he had preached, but here he was in the tomb of Lazarus convinced that Christ was on the other side. The feelings he was experiencing were beyond surreal, and he knew all he could do was wait – wait for him to be called forth.

Realising that he could do nothing else was the moment he stopped worrying and allowed himself to simply be. In taking a deep breath, he steadied his nerve and looked around him and realised that not only was he in the tomb, but he was also standing in the place of Lazarus and just like him he was waiting for the unknown.

If his instincts were correct, he found himself trusting that the encounter would be one of love, yet he knew that his betrayal had been great, and he feared some form of judgement against himself and his actions. Although he had confessed to everything that he had done to undermine the Church and the faith, he closed his eyes and spoke to the Lord in his heart, expressing his fears and begging for his mercy. In his mind the accusations of unworthiness rebounded against the wisdom that he had nothing to fear for the forgiveness he had received was real and genuine. And then he thought about what he had said to Mode, about leaving something behind in the tomb and realised that in his own case he needed to leave everything behind that had stopped him from knowing the truth, following Christ and feeling the love of God in his life. In those moments he knew that everything had to be let go so he could feel true freedom for the first time without any doubt. He might not have been aware of it, but he had been waiting and preparing his whole life for this moment.

Suddenly, with great gentleness, he felt someone stand right before him and take hold of his arms at the elbows. A feeling of unworthiness began to overwhelm him, but Oliveri kept his eyes closed for he was scared to see what was before him. As he continued to be held by the stranger, he struggled to clear the dryness from his throat.

'Hello, Emmanuel,' the man before him spoke with such love and warmth, the words reverberating deep within Oliveri's chest. 'Please, do not be afraid! Open your eyes.'

Oliveri wanted to explain his fear, but he could not find the words, but that did not matter for something within him led him to believe that if the man was Christ then he could already sense his fear.

'Are you him?' Oliveri managed to murmur.

'I am,' Christ replied, 'And I want nothing more than for you to see me, for I have loved you before you were even conceived in your mother's womb.'

Lowering his head, Oliveri gradually opened his eyes and saw the pure-white robe of Christ that touched the top of his bare feet that bore the wounds from his time on the cross.

'Do not be afraid!' Christ urged, confirming Oliveri's intuition that he could read what he was thinking. 'I only want you to see and feel the love that I have for you.'

Little by little, Oliveri raised his head, noticing the golden cincture tied around Christ's waist and the defined muscles of his chest and the strength in his arms that held him. But as he reached the nape of Christ's neck, he could not bring himself to go any further. Whatever Christ looked like, it clearly was not what he had expected for he could see no beard or locks of hair.

'I can appear in many different ways to people,' Christ spoke, bringing his right hand up to Oliveri's face. 'Before you is my glorified self. Just look up and see how much I love you and how happy I am to meet you face to face.'

As Oliveri felt his chin being lifted, he surrendered to the invitation as he saw the most radiant smile on the clean-shaven face of the most beautiful and perfect man he had ever seen. And as his eyes met Christ's for the first time, Oliveri felt himself connect to the only man who had ever fully understood him.

At first Christ's eyes, were dark and hazel in colour, but the more Oliveri allowed himself to drink them in, his eyes changed into a spectrum of marbled colours and gave out a radiance as they penetrated Oliveri's soul.

'Do not look away,' Jesus said, as his healing eyes gazed upon Oliveri's brokenness. 'Just keep looking at me and allow me to make my home complete within you.'

In that moment, Oliveri felt Christ's Divine Presence enter his being, and like a charge of static electricity he felt His presence swell within his heart. Deep within his soul he repeatedly called out His name, and the more he called it, the deeper the feeling of being wrapped in complete love felt. Taking a deep breath, Oliveri felt the chains of his life fall from his chest, as all his anxiety and trauma, his fear of unworthiness and sinfulness were completely washed away. Time mattered not in that encounter, and Oliveri wished he could look into Christ's eyes for all eternity as he experienced the healing balm that was flowing into him. Like no other love of this world, his being was being renewed with the purest love, and like a refining fire the guilt and the pain of his past was dissolving in the knowing that he meant something to the Son of God.

'You are loved! You are loved! You are so deeply, loved!' Oliveri heard Jesus whisper into his ear, as he brought him closer to him and held him intimately in his warmth and strength of embrace. 'There will be no more darkness in your soul, for I have washed it clean. There is only me. My peace will never leave you, Emmanuel.'

What Oliveri would later describe as a warm healing wave of love washed through his body. Like a rushing tide over the pebbles of a beach, he felt the healing power of Jesus' forgiveness and renewal. Each sin of his life flashed before his eyes, and with each wave they were taken away. Although he would forever remember his offences, they lost their power of guilt, because with each wave he knew that in the eyes of God he was a son who had accepted his wrong and who had been made into a new and perfect creation for the rest of eternity where there would be no more shame.

He did not know the moment his eyes closed or for how long he had been standing there, but when the moment with Jesus came to an end with a gentle awareness that he should open his eyes, Oliveri found himself standing alone in the tomb looking at Dave Mode who sat on the steps watching him, his face glowing and his broad smile revealing the change that had taken place within.

'I think we will be leaving a lot more behind here than you had anticipated,' Mode joked, as he saw Oliveri look around him.

'Where is …' Oliveri stuttered.

'He has taken his leave from us for the time being,' Mode replied, as he re-entered the tomb, 'but I can feel his Spirit very close to me.'

'Your face,' Oliveri said, as he reached out to touch Mode, 'It is radiant.'

'Yours too,' Mode replied. 'I suppose when you look into the face of Jesus, he leaves his mark.'

Oliveri's smile quickly gave way to a nervous chuckle as Mode walked over to hug him.

'What fools we were,' Mode said, as he embraced Oliveri. 'It was true all along and we couldn't see it.'

'Did he speak to you?'

'He did, but most of the time he didn't use words,' Mode replied, as he looked around the tomb. 'I just feel like I'll be forever caught in this feeling of amazement and wonder at what has just happened in here.'

'We must go and tell the others,' Oliveri said, as he reached out to touch the wall of Lazarus's tomb. 'We must let them know that we have seen him.' For a moment Oliveri looked around the tomb for one last time. 'We will never be the same again.'

With those words, Oliveri never looked back and walking towards the exit he climbed out of the tomb and into the chamber, where he waited for Dave Mode before climbing the twisted stairs up to the street above.

As they walked back to their dwelling, they could not stop talking about what they had just experienced and how it had affected them. Every few steps they would stop, turn to one another and with great animation in their voices they would share their joy and desire to see him again.

The people they passed noticed the joy that emanated from Oliveri and Mode. And when people looked into their faces, they could see that they radiated a light that attracted everyone who saw it and the people knew that they had encountered the risen Christ. The further into the city they ventured, the faithful remnant approached them and listened to them talk about what had happened at the tomb of Lazarus. Whilst some stopped and listened to them, others immediately went to see the tomb in the hope of meeting Him there.

There was no hint of jealousy or envy towards them for having had the experience, instead their account gave the people a hope and a desire to understand that they too would one day see him for themselves and have the same moment with him, for such encounters were becoming more frequent for the remnant in Jerusalem.

34.

Since arriving in Jerusalem, Jane Lincoln was content to spend time alone for a few hours each day to gather her thoughts and to try and make sense of the burning question that plagued her, and that was why she was counted amongst the chosen few to survive the horrors of the tribulation.

It was through a chance encounter, when sitting close to the Wailing Wall, that she heard about the viewing terrace on top of the Austrian Hospice, and once she discovered it off the Via Dolorosa, she started to go there every afternoon to sit, watch, pray and think. Plus, the terrace had a great coffee stand and despite the dramatic view over the Temple Mount, it was never too busy and she often found that for significant periods of time she was often alone, and any other visitor to the terrace always recognised her desire for solitude.

Pouring a cup of black coffee, she took her usual seat at the end of the terrace at a white cast iron table, and without fail her former habit of reaching for a cigarette kicked in and for the briefest of moments she wished she could light one up as she sat down to take in the view, but the craving was fleeting as the celestial vision on top of the Temple Mount quickly recaptured her attention.

Despite the coffee being very good, she never finished it. A few sips to settle into the experience was all it took before she completely forgot all about it and would sit for hours gazing in wonder and awe at the choirs of angels flying into and reemerging from the heavenly light. Like everyone else in the city, she pondered what the light concealed but found herself content just to sit and watch. Every now and then, an angel would see her sitting there and would wave at her with the most warming of smiles. This always made her weep, because she felt so unworthy to be in their company and for them to honour her with their presence and respect.

How different it all could have been had Dave Mode decided not to check in on her at her apartment.

It was the rattling of a cup on its saucer as it was sat on her table, that forced her to dry her eyes before she turned to see the young man standing beside her, his warming smile and apologetic eyes revealing his embarrassment that he had broken her moment of contemplation.

'I am so sorry,' he replied, as his right hand held the back of the chair next to her, unsure as to whether he should use the chair or put it back. 'It just got so busy that I thought you wouldn't mind if I sat here for a while.'

So engrossed in her thoughts and focussed on the light, she had not noticed that the terrace had become quite busy with several dozen people sitting around her, watching and commenting on the sight before them. Surprised and a little flustered, she quickly insisted that the young man sit beside her, which he did with much appreciation.

'I'm Joshua.'

'Jane,' she replied, before sipping on her cold coffee.

'Would you like me to get you a fresh one Jane?'

'No, thank you,' she humoured, 'I never finish them. I supposed it just looks silly sitting at a coffee table without any coffee.'

'It's the best coffee in the city,' Joshua replied, as he gently blew across the rim of the cup before bringing it to his lips to taste. 'Where are you from Jane?'

'Rome ... well originally from the United States, but I've lived in Rome for many years.'

'A great city with some of the best restaurants in the world, if you want my humble opinion.'

Jane laughed, as the memory of her favourite restaurant in the Barberini district came to mind. 'Are you well-travelled?'

'I suppose I am,' he replied, before he turned to look towards the celestial vision. 'But, like yourself I was always destined to be here in Jerusalem for this moment in time.'

'It's something else, isn't it?'

'A mere glimpse of what awaits everyone who believes,' Joshua replied. 'God has openly come, and it looks like He is remaining silent no longer!'

His words made her turn to study him very intently as he was transfixed by the sight on the Temple Mount, and she wondered exactly who Joshua was.

'What do you take from what you have found?' he asked.

'At the moment...' she hesitated, before joining him in appreciating the vision, 'a great sense of unworthiness and wondering why I am here?'

'Why not you?' he asked, turning to look at her.

'Let's say I wasn't much of a believer and didn't live the life of a saint.'

'Do you believe now?'

'It's hard not too,' she laughed, as she pointed towards the vision and to the band of angels that were circling a few hundred feet above their heads. 'This would have made it all a lot easier to have believed if we could have seen this all along.'

He smiled.

'Have you always believed, Joshua?'

Nodding his head, he chose to listen rather than speak.

'I lived all my life convinced there was no God,' she finally continued, trusting him with the story she had shared many times with so many people since she departed Rome. 'I suppose He was easier to dismiss than to face in my line of work. Without going into too much detail, let's just say that I did some dreadful things in my time, and yet here I am sharing in this vision, healed of all sickness and surrounded by people who are filled with immense love. That's why I still struggle with it all, because my head is telling me the complete opposite from what my heart accepts.'

'And what is that?' He asked, a few seconds into her silence.

She carefully considered her reply. 'I feel like love is conditional, and that I need to be doing something to deserve it. If you knew my past, you would understand that I have difficulty accepting that I am worthy to be loved.'

Tears quickly filled her eyes as she looked away.

'Sometimes the voices that we allow in our heads are the voices we should expel,' Joshua spoke. 'Especially if they are disturbing our inner peace and making us question our own goodness and self-worth. Your creation is a wonderful and good thing.'

'So I have been told, many times by so many people since I left Rome.'

'Then maybe you need to put on the spirit of grace to relieve you from your spirit of heaviness.'

'What do you mean?'

'Allow yourself to be forgiven,' Joshua replied. 'That is the greatest challenge of the spiritual journey, because only then will you be free to accept the beauty that is you. Don't let the darkness overcome you anymore. Know and accept that you are forgiven and loved.'

'My heart knows that I am loved and forgiven, but in my head I still feel that I cannot be truly loved by a God I will never understand.'

'Perhaps, you are never meant to and never will understand Him,' Joshua replied, as he reached out his hand across the table for her to take hold which she did without any hesitation. 'We will see Him soon enough, but if you are expecting to see a creature or an object then I am afraid you will be disappointed. God is not something that we can name for He is before all being, thought and language. But His presence of love will reveal itself to you, and once it does then your whole creation will become consumed by the creator Himself. That is what you are going to see, and that is what will heal your brokenness. For when you finally get to walk with Him in the cool of the night, only then will you realise that He is everything beyond imagination or word. For no one has seen and no one has heard the glory that awaits you and everyone else, both the living and the dead.'

Now she realised that she had become transfixed on him, as a radiating heat flowed from his hand and into her body. And as she listened to him speak with authority, she did not want the moment to end for she feared that she would lose Him.

'When you were a child, your mother died very suddenly,' he continued as the tears streamed from her eyes as his words touched her heart. 'Alone you had to grieve without family for days until your father arrived back from the air force. The moment he saw you, he knelt as you ran into his arms, and he held you with such a warmth and a love that you have not experienced since. Know that you will see him again very soon and be held not only by him, but held with a greater love that will consume you both.'

Lincoln could almost relive the moment through his words, and the contentment she felt in the safety of her father's arms in that moment of great pain and loss. Yet, as she felt his words touch her, she wondered how he knew the details of such a personal moment in her life, but she could not find the courage to question him for she knew that he had the authority to speak the words that he was speaking.

Before long she was walking with him through the city, heading back to the house she shared with the others. Along the way, they met Dom Colby and Gabriel Roth who were as mesmerised as she was by the young man, as he shared with them his revelation and wisdom.

She tried to hang on to his every word, but in the end, she found that she could remember little of what he had said. Upon reaching their dwelling, Joshua went to take his leave, but they were so eager to spend some more time with him that they begged him to come inside so that he could eat and spend the evening with them.

35.

As they returned to their dwelling with Joshua as their guest, Lincoln, Dom Colby and Roth collected food and drink from the stands that lined the streets to create an evening meal. It was a simple affair of some freshly caught fish which Roth grilled on the barbeque at the rear garden of the house, along with some salad and olives which Dom Colby prepared, whilst Lincoln prepared some cheese and sun-dried tomatoes as Joshua cut the freshly baked bread. All the time, they questioned their guest and listened to him as he spoke.

When Oliveri and Mode arrived home, the excitement that accompanied them was evident for all to see, as they were both eager to tell the others about what they had witnessed inside the tomb of Lazarus, but when they saw Joshua they fell silent, as they did not know who the stranger was.

What amazed the others in the house was the glow that radiated from the faces of Oliveri and Mode, and when Lincoln stated her surprise to them both the others were shocked when Oliveri and Mode pointed out that they too had a glow about them. Lincoln had not noticed it before, but now that it had been pointed out she could see the change on Colby and Roth, and going into the bathroom to look into the mirror she was able to see the change within herself, and it led her to feel more confused about the nature of the day's events.

Over dinner, Mode and Oliveri recalled every minute detail of their encounter with Jesus in the tomb, and how they had both seen the wounds that the crucifixion had made on his wrists and his feet. Mode, who was exploding with excitement, recalled how he was able to leave his past behind him in that tomb and how he now felt like a new man who would give anything to meet with him again. And throughout, Lincoln's intrigue grew.

'Have you ever met with Jesus?' Mode asked Joshua, eventually including him in the conversation.

Joshua shook his head. 'But I have met many who have, and like you they became changed people. Soon, everyone will see him and then his glory will be revealed to all the world. Was it not written that this should be so?'

The five of them fell silent, as they all listened to him speak.

'You and everyone else who is in Jerusalem have been chosen to witness the end of time, and with that the passing of this world,' he continued, as he leaned his elbows onto the table ready to teach them. 'My dear ones, despite the suffering that you have witnessed and the souls that have already departed from this world, you have been ordained to walk with the saviour after he judges the living and the dead and brings with him those who have believed in their hearts that they will see God and dwell in His love for eternity. However, it is not a linear eternity as you would perceive it, instead it is the complete consumption of the soul into pure love. A place where the soul will dwell in peace within His presence.

'Each soul who desires the truth will find that peace and they will not be disappointed. All of this,' he explained, as he waved his right hand above his head, 'will pass too. For the destination to which God is calling you is beyond anything you could perceive through the human eye, or any word could fully explain. It is beyond imagination and out of reach of human understanding.'

No one spoke as they looked at him, wondering in their heart who he was. For Oliveri there was a familiarity about him, a past understanding that he had met him before, and unbeknownst to him, Mode felt the exact same way.

'Are you an angel?' Dom Colby finally asked what they were all thinking, but Joshua could only turn to him and shake his head once more.

'Do you still not know who you are and who I am?' Joshua asked, as he looked at them all individually. 'You are who is not - but I Am who is.'

Then reaching across the table, he took some bread in his hands and tore it apart, and as he did so his skin transformed into a radiant glow as the wounds on his wrists appeared for them all to see, and they realised that he had been sitting amongst them all that time.

Stunned at what she was witnessing, Lincoln looked upon him with complete abandonment as she broke down and cried in the agony of her soul, taking from him the bread.

'I am the one you have been looking for,' he replied, as they watched the radiant light emerge from deep within his wounds before gazing into his eyes that mirrored a collage of indescribable colours. 'I wanted to spend some time with you, just as I am with everyone else in Jerusalem before you all enter the promise of paradise. For you are everything to me.'

Accepting the bread from his sacred hands, Oliveri and Mode recognised him in that moment. Although his appearance was different to what they had seen that morning, the essence of his being shone through, and before him they ate humbly of his body in the bread that he shared.

In his eyes they all saw the love he had for them, and as the time in that room passed gently by, they all had their moment of healing as they looked upon him and felt his touch penetrate through to their souls.

It was a collective moment of peace that brought them all to close their eyes and simply dwell in his presence that was with them in the room. Complete silence surrounded them, as their hearts burned within. Each one wanted nothing more than to go with him in that moment into the paradise he had promised and to dwell there for all eternity. The intensity of his peace grew within them as they breathed him in, knowing they had found the peace they had longed for with all their hearts. A peace this world had never been able to give.

Together, without being told or urged, they opened their eyes and re-entered the room, only to discover that his chair was empty for he had taken his leave. Yet, deep within their souls, they knew he remained close to them and that no one would ever be able to separate them from his love.

36.

Having taken some time to rest, Oliveri felt the peace emanate from deep within his being as he pondered the two encounters he personally had with the risen Lord. He had no idea how long ago those encounters had taken place, for it dawned on him that time no longer had a place or any purpose in the new Jerusalem, for there was no darkness or rising or setting of the sun. Perpetual light from the Temple Mount bathed the city, and for the remnant they lived in the present as everyone basked in the joyful peace that they were experiencing.

The indescribable joy that filled Jerusalem continued to grow as more faithful walked the streets with the distinctive radiant glow on their faces. This made Oliveri smile as he turned to look out the window and into the light of the city, for each story he heard brought such a warmth that he could not get enough from the people he encountered. In those encounters and in the sharing of them, the joy grew as the people longed to see Christ one more time to experience the delight of his presence.

Oliveri appreciated that he would get to see him again, and soon, but for now he lived on the joy of others as they encountered and shared their testimony with everyone who was eager to listen. Again, the image of Christ's eyes filled his thoughts as he remembered the amazing spectrum of colours that emerged from them as his look penetrated deep into his soul during that encounter in the tomb. Oliveri's mind could not process what he had seen, nor make any sense of the connection they had made, but he could still vividly see those eyes turn from the dark hazel into an array that bore pure love for him, and which had left, without any doubt, a mark of the love that Christ had for him. Others had spoken too of experiencing a similar encounter, and it humoured Oliveri that no one had the words to adequately express what they had witnessed, but talking about it filled everyone with such a joy that they wished for nothing more than to see him again.

A slight knock at the bedroom door stirred him from his thoughts, as he beckoned his caller to enter.

'I'm sorry,' Jane Lincoln spoke, when she noticed the cardinal resting on his bed, 'I'll let you be.'

'No, please I was getting up,' he replied, as he got up from the bed without the aches and pains that, until he left Rome, had become the companion of his old age.

'We're about to head out into the city and didn't want to go without you or at least to let you know.'

The prospect of going back into the streets of Jerusalem brought a deep smile to Oliveri's face as he straightened the bedsheets before turning to leave the room. 'How could I not go with you wonderful people?'

The warmth of his words, and his gentle embrace as he took hold of her and kissed her on the forehead, triggered within Lincoln a bolt of love as she connected with the cardinal knowing that for the first time in her life people truly loved her for who she was.

In the hallway the others smiled warmly as they saw Lincoln return with Oliveri. Mode, with the eagerness of a child, was the first to embrace him like he had not seen him for months. Together they all left their dwelling to walk the short distance towards the heart of the ancient city and to see the celestial vision that consumed the Temple Mount.

Breathing in the freshness of the air, Oliveri was just about to comment that it reminded him of a fresh breeze coming off the Atlantic Sea, when Dom Colby spoke of the wonderful fragrance of flowers that filled Jerusalem. This surprised not only Oliveri but the others too, and taking a deep breath just to make sure, Oliveri could not smell any flowers but only the sea air as Lincoln said she could only smell fresh bread, Roth a mixture of coffee and vanilla, before Mode replied that the city smelled like the foyer of a cinema with the smell of buttered popcorn.

'How can we all be smelling different things?' Colby asked, but no one had the answer, and they could only laugh.

'Everything feels so surreal about this place,' Roth spoke, looking around him at the brightness reflecting off the sandstone buildings. 'It is almost as if everything feels more alive.'

'Like you're more tuned in?' Lincoln replied.

'That is exactly it! All my senses feel so clued in. Everything I see appears to be more mesmerising than ever before. I hear joy and love coming from everyone I meet. The warmth of my flesh is so penetrating that I feel no tiredness nor cold. Everything smells amazing and the food and wine, well I have tasted nothing like it.'

'The best there is!' Colby replied, 'Especially the wine!'

'Which does taste good, gives you that little kick but never seems to get you drunk or leave the mark of a cruel hangover,' Mode added. 'And trust me, I could tell you a thing or two about hangovers!'

'Dave, I always knew that the drunk you and sober you were never on good speaking terms,' Lincoln humoured, as she linked him by the arm.

'True! I once drank so much Vodka one night that I woke up the following morning speaking Russian!' Mode replied, slipping into a perfect Russian accent.

The four of them could do nothing but laugh at Mode as he stood up straight, puffed out his chest and acted like a soldier marching through Red Square, talking about comrades and the perils of the vodka bottle. For Lincoln, it was a side of him she had never seen before, in fact she had never heard him once laugh in all the time she had known him in the CIA. Everything about him had become beautiful, and as he acted out his Russian routine still linked to her arm, she loved him more than any one she had ever loved, and for the briefest of moments she pondered how someone so beautiful and perfect in his nature could have been manipulated by her to do whatever she demanded of him. And in her heart, she could only be thankful that they had both been saved from their shared horrible past and the consequences of its murderous actions.

Closer to the Temple Mount, the streets gradually filled with the faithful remnant as they mingled with one another, ate and drank from the stalls that lined the streets and with great excitement in their voices talked of their experiences of having met him as they looked up to the sky and the heavenly array of angels in wonder and awe.

With a glass of red wine in his hand, the variety of grape exquisite but unknown, Oliveri mingled with others and although some had warmly recognised him from his former role at the Vatican and knew of his conversion story, he remained unknown to most and was treated just like everyone else who had come to experience the joy that filled the streets of Jerusalem and to get to know the life stories of the people around him.

In his previous life, Oliveri had little time for mingling and often his eyes would be glancing over the shoulders of people as he spoke to them, looking for someone more important to speak with or wishing he was anywhere but having to listen to such people. No group of people he despised more in meeting than those who publicly proclaimed to be *'on fire for the Lord', especially* the charismatics and those newly fangled with the faith who presumed that as a cardinal he shared their enthusiasm. His secretary knew to never place him in such situations, but they were not always avoidable. Had someone told him a few years ago that he would be gladly walking the streets of Jerusalem, wearing a white robe in his bare feet, and eagerly meeting as many people as he could, just to share in their joy and to listen to the tenderness of their encounters with the risen Christ and to share his with them, he would have thought they were mad. Yet here he was, and here he wished to remain, sharing in this experience, walking the streets of pure serenity and under the majesty of what he knew was only a glimpse of what was to come in heaven.

Truth was spoken like an open confession as people shared their pasts with one another, and no judgement was ever passed, instead only a deep sense of love arose for even the worst of crimes as the power of salvation from the past, and the presence of God in the moment, overwhelmed all guilt and any sense of condemnation.

Oliveri, like every other faithful gathered in Jerusalem, sensed the passing change of this world, and they all knew that soon this would give way to the new heaven and the new Jerusalem that was promised beyond death, yet no one feared the end for they all knew that they were safe and in the hands of God who loved them and allowed them all to feel His burning love swell deep within their souls.

Amid the gladness and the experience on the streets, it felt as if someone was slowly increasing the volume on a music sound system as the heavenly voices of the angels grew louder, forcing the remnant to fall silent and to look up to the sky where the angels had turned towards the Temple Mount. From their mouths came the most beautiful music sung in a language that no one had ever heard, as their wings unfolded behind their backs, and they bowed their heads in reverence towards something that few could see.

The buildings along the streets had blocked the view of the Temple Mount, but instinctively Oliveri knew, as did the rest of the remnant, that they had to move to see what was happening. So, following the faithful through the narrow streets, he walked alongside Mode and Lincoln as they slowly made their way through waves of excitement towards a growing expectation. As the harmony of the angels grew greater and filled them all with a sense of great wonder and awe, a wave of Hallelujahs came from the people who were ahead of them. Surprised by their joyful chorus, Oliveri made the decision that he would respectfully remain dignified no matter what they saw, but that all changed the moment he found himself turning a corner and seeing the magnificence that had remained hidden behind the light on the Temple Mount.

After an initial intake of breath at the sheer sight of the wonder before him, he found that as he exhaled his very soul cried out *Hallelujah* in a burning desire to sing the greatest word of praise. With his heart and soul united together, and joining the choir of the remnant, he sang his praise towards the one who had returned. Each Hallelujah came with pure joy and love, and each one filled him with a peace so great that he could sing it forevermore.

Revealed from behind the light, the man-made structures of the past no longer stood, instead, a series of golden steps ascended to the footstool of Jesus Christ, who sat on a pure white throne. Wearing a golden and jewel encrusted crown, that sparkled in the light of the angels, Christ watched on as the faithful gathered around him. Each one of them he knew, and each one of them he had met, and as he gazed upon them with burning love, glad to have paid the price for their salvation with his own blood on the cross of Calvary, he was now prepared to bring the world to its end, and to judge both the living and the dead.

37.

With tens of thousands gathered and looking upon Christ who had taken his rightful place on the white throne of judgement, Oliveri raised his hands to the one he loved and through whom he had been saved from his wicked and twisted way of life. Witnessing him enthroned, with the angels encircling him with their dazzling light, their worship and praise raising to the hights of heaven, Oliveri proclaimed the Hallelujah from the depths of his being with complete abandonment, allowing the happiness that was overflowing from within him to escape in sweet exaltations of praise.

Close by, Oliveri noticed Mode gazing towards the throne with his arms outstretched in prayer as his own songs of praise poured from his mouth and added to the harmony of the faithful remnant who were transfixed with genuine wonder and awe. Everyone felt the ecstasy grow within them as a sign of their inner connection to the Son of God who had returned just as he had promised. And although the people could have looked upon him and offered him their praise forever, time yet again had no meaning, because in that moment everyone who saw him was consumed by witnessing his presence and no longer desired to do anything else. Without awareness of what was happening, everyone in Jerusalem was coming to the fulfilment of their earthly life.

High above the throne, four angels held aloft a large golden book for all to see, its pages being turned one at a time as the names of those written upon it were read aloud in a language that no human had ever heard before. It was a language that contained a vocal harmony from a scale not of this world but through which the angels understood and communicated with one another. For those who heard it, it was the most beautiful sound they had ever heard as the choirs of angels filled Jerusalem.

Upon the white throne, Christ closed his eyes and listened to every name that was read, and just like he saw upon the cross, the face of each name he heard drew close to his divine heart and he smiled warmly knowing that soon they would join him to see the beatific vision of the love that shone from the presence of his Father. Each named soul he knew intimately, both of their goodness and sinfulness, their struggles and their joys. Yet, he felt the joy radiate around him knowing that through the journey of their lives they had proven their worth and sought to find the meaning of truth. Soon their reward would be granted onto them, and the true purpose of their creation finally revealed once he completed the role which he alone could fulfil.

When the final name was read to the assembled remnant, the rolling rumble of a kettledrum resounded across the earth and it brought them all to complete silence, and with an instinct to reverence his presence among them, each man and woman present in Jerusalem, bowed the knee and knelt before him. Through the vibrations of the drum, they all felt the peace penetrate their being, as they slowly lifted their gaze to see Christ rise from his throne to the sound of angelic trumpets as he stood to speak to them in the language of heaven that they would all understand.

'My dear ones,' his voice resounded throughout the city with great tenderness, 'how I have longed for this day to come so that you might all see the promise that was made to you from the Ancient of Days. Soon this world will come to an end, for it has served the purpose of its creation and together you will all walk with me into the beginning of the new heaven and the new earth.

'In my Father's Kingdom your place for eternity is awaiting you. There you will find the greatest mystery unfold before you and upon seeing His face, you will be brought into the fulness of your nature and forever walk with Him through the endless dawning of days, the joyful heat of eternity and into the cool of the night. You will not fear nor feel the need to hide, but you will be able to approach Him, to see Him and know what it means to be alive in Him. And through Him you will not only see what love is, but you will also see those of this world that you have loved coming into the perfect form of their creation.

'When I came to show you the way, the truth and the life, I could only reveal a fragment of what awaits you. It simply would have been too overwhelming for you to understand. The meaning of life, passing like a vapour, was to find the truth in love. That was the meaning, simply to discover the powerful truth of love for yourself, your neighbour and for God who bore you out of the purest form of love, who brought you into existence through the word and breathed life into you by the Divine Spirit. The journey to find the truth is about to conclude, and very soon you will know what truth is.

'In the new heaven and in the new earth, there will be nothing that you desire that will not be given onto you. You will never tire of seeing the vision of God that is about to reveal itself to you, and your every need, just like here in this city, will be provided for and you will discover the purest of love in those who await you and in those with whom you will walk into heaven.

'You are the living who will never die. Soon, you will pass with me from this world into the next where you will experience the transfiguration of your own earthly bodies into the heavenly perfection of the glorified saints. You have already been judged and found worthy, so you have no need to be afraid. You have all met me by now, and I will forever treasure those encounters in my heart for I got to meet you in the flesh, and you got to experience the deep love that I have for you. Those who have already passed through their own death, their judgement too has taken place. To those found worthy, their souls are already experiencing the eternal joy of love in heaven, awaiting the resurrection of their own mortal remains. For those who have been judged and found wanting, this day has been ordained for them to face the just consequences of how they lived, and that is an eternity cut off from love and trapped within themselves.

'You have been tested by raw evil. You will soon understand why this was allowed to happen, but today is also the day in which evil will face the eternal punishment that is due for rejecting not only the idea of love, but for rejecting the love they had the privilege of experiencing before you were created. I came for you, to save you from them. You are mine and I am yours. They have no place in the world to come and today you will see them receive the just punishment for their pride and their betrayal of heavenly love.'

Taking his place again upon the white throne, a great stillness came across the whole land.

With his words spoken, the four angels who held the book of life closed it and carried it high into the clouds and out of the view of those who remained on bended knee. Upon his throne, the smile upon Christ's loving face faded as the look in his eyes became fixed on the lands north of Jerusalem to which the angels also focused their intent.

It initially sounded like a constant rumble of thunder in the distance, as if a train was entering the limits of the city, but the reverberations grew louder by the second as the remnant stood from their prostrations and looked to the north. From the direction of Armageddon, they could see the darkness approach the city, as a wave of evil screamed and hollered fierce insults to Christ who sat upon the throne.

To where the ring of fire once burned, they were unable to advance any further as the angels of heaven blocked their way, but from there the demons of hell hovered before them and with toxic hatred they spat and roared and hurled every profanity and curse towards the one who had conquered them and, in whose hands, their eternal fate rested. With the power to destroy their existence and remove their dominion forever, their reaction was triggered with the fear over the authority he held over them. Yet they remained defiant and would never seek to submit to the truth they knew, and this frustration reared its head in raw resentment and hatred they felt for him.

With the angels of heaven no longer singing their angelic praises, the noise of the demons became harrowing towards the remnant. Yet throughout it all, each one of the faithful turned to look at Christ, and to trust in him that they were safe and that no harm would come to them.

The angels of heaven did not react to the demons who came up close to their faces and insulted them with the greatest of obscenities they could muster from the pits of their wickedness. Instead, the heavenly host stood ground, ready for the command to execute the just punishment for the betrayal that ultimately led to the saviour being hung upon the cross at calvary.

Then, like a parting wave, the demons opened their flank to allow the prince of darkness, the prince of lies, the one known as Lucifer, to emerge and to face the judgement that even he could not escape.

Suddenly, the screams of the demons ceased as Christ raised his right hand into the sky.

38.

From heaven there descended a cloud that rested above Christ's throne. Across the sky the cloud took its form and every member of the faithful remnant and angels, including Lucifer and his demons, gazed upon it with great expectation. Only Christ chose not to look above him, instead he maintained his thunderous look towards the evil of hell that had gathered before him.

Gradually, the cloud appeared to engulf the remnant as a scent of dust and spices filled the air as screaming voices echoed off the weathered stone walls of the ancient city. Amid the bustling bodies of people from a time gone past, Oliveri, Mode, Lincoln and everyone else became overwhelmed with the many sights and sounds from the people who now appeared around them as they thronged the narrow streets and alleyways; some excited with what was about to come and others crying with despair that it was happening. As traders continued to sell their wares, and as the crowd surged forward to have a better look, it did not take the remnant long to understand what was happening when they saw Christ carry his cross as the Roman Soldiers pressed him onwards towards Calvary, his blood mingling with the rain as it ran onto the cobblestones.

In the distance they could all see Golgotha, where he was called to be the sacrifice for all and to bear witness to the love of his Father. Amid the chaos and confusion, the remnant all followed him to the place of the skull, where the screaming for his blood mingled with the pleas of mercy from the few. Alone now, he was forced to stand as they stripped him naked and exposed him for all to see and to be humiliated before the world. While many ridiculed and mocked him as the soldiers made their final preparations, Jane Lincoln cried out for mercy as did many others, but only the remnant could hear them as they watched on.

Then hearing the hate-filled screams of the demons, Mode and Oliveri turned to look behind them to see Lucifer and his legion watch on as the Son of Man had his feet kicked from below as he fell onto the dirt of Golgotha; the grit and the dust entering into the open wounds of his scourging as he was dragged by two Romans across the ground to the cross that lay waiting for him. Refusing their offer of gall to numb his senses, he instead offered no resistance as they took hold of his right wrist and between the bones positioned the nail.

The sound of the hammer striking the nail reverberated along the earth before the piercing screams of Christ filled Jerusalem, as the Roman executioners drove the nails through his wrists and into the roughly cut beam of the cross. Witnessing the horror, every member of the remnant cried silent tears for the one they knew had loved them unconditionally, as he begged his Father to forgive the world for what it was doing as his feet were nailed to a narrow plinth that would allow him to breathe by pushing the weight of his body up against the cross.

Lifting him high above the ancient city, the Roman's drove the cross deep into the pit where they secured it in place, before attaching the mocking sign of Pontius Pilate above his crowned head proclaiming that he was Jesus the King of the Jews. Unable to move and in complete shock with the immense physical pain that had been inflicted upon his body, Christ gasped for air as the ridicule and the mockery continued. The reality of what had happened shocked everyone as they stood watching. Unable to help, they witnessed the sheer weight of what he suffered press down upon his shoulders as the world dissolved around him as he began to slowly die. Then, slicing through the horror a great silence fell upon the earth.

Moments later, a little child appeared to walk through the cloud and approach the cross. The girl's solitary figure at first gave no hint of who she was or why she was there. Unaware of the crowd, she stood alone, and it quickly became apparent that she was afraid and weeping as she called out for her mother who was nowhere to be seen. Suddenly, she turned to look behind as a soldier appeared and approached her. Terrified she screamed, and for the remnant as they watched on, the man was revealed as a Nazi soldier before the scene behind the cross was transformed into one of horror as a sea of people were gassed to death before flames incinerated them. And it was into these flames that the nazi soldier tossed the young girl without thought.

Like flashing scenes from a movie, the sins of the world flowed into the body of Christ as he carried them upon the cross. Unable to look away, the remnant could only watch as the holocaust gave way to the murderous wars of the world, to the genocides and the innocents who were slain, to the sons and daughters of God captured and brutalised into slavery, the crusades and the inquisitions, from the acts of terror to the barbarity of torture. Every act of murder, torture, rape, molestation, trafficking, abuses, war crimes, corruption, destruction, lies, adultery, violence, discrimination, exploitation, cruelty, manipulation, criminality, sabotage - all flowed into him like a river in flash flood.

Struggling to catch a breath, Oliveri watched on as the dreadfulness of humanity slowly killed Christ upon the cross. Each act of evil he bore without complaint. And as the weight of humanity pulled him deeper into his agony, Christ could only look ahead with those eyes of love as he surrendered to his sacrifice for all of humanity. And that was when Oliveri and the rest saw the face of each human being that ever lived appear before him, and they understood that it was out of love for the Father that Christ was prepared to die.

Yet again no one knew how long the apparition of calvary had taken place, but by the time it concluded the remnant understood why Christ had cried out his prayer of abandonment and questioned why even his Father had forsaken him. When the last sin entered his body, that of a young man walking away from his wife and son to live with another, Jesus took his last breath and gave up his spirit.

Not one sound was heard throughout Jerusalem, even the demons had fallen silent unlike the first time when they jeered and mocked his lifeless body, for they knew what happened three days later. Yet, for now the body remained on the cross for all to see; the corpus to which each living soul owed a debt no man or woman would ever be able to repay. And as the remnant wept for what they had witnessed, they noticed that from the wound on his side that had been pierced at his heart, blood and water flowed along with a luminous light, and from this light a teenage boy appeared in a new vision.

Walking through a busy city, the boy was reaching into his pocket and took out some loose change and looked at it before putting it back, only to take from his wallet a note and without any hinderance he walked over to the homeless man and handed it to him, spoke a greeting of hello and sat next to him for a chat.

Through the light from his side, came the acts of love that people did in his name for the thousands of years since Golgotha. His brothers and sisters who fed the hungry, gave drink to those who thirst, welcomed the strangers into their hearts, who clothed the naked, visited those imprisoned and attended to the sick and the dying. One image after another, of all the good that came from those who had searched for the truth immerged; from people standing up for social justice and equality, to those filled with honesty and integrity, the displays of empathy to those who walked with those who grieved. They were images of self-sacrifice, forgiveness, kindness, healing, comfort, inspiring and choosing to put love above the needs of oneself and accepting others, with their wrongs and flaws without question or condition.

And as the last image, that of an elderly man who held the hand of the one he loved as she took her last breath, appeared before the remnant, Lucifer slowly turned his gaze from the apparition to look into the eyes of his judgement.

With Christ upon the judgement throne, the angels who had been guarding the city parted and some came to rest upon the remnant; one angel for each member of the faithful; for unbeknownst to any of them these angels were their guardians, who had been with them from the moment of conception and who would now stand with them in the final moments of this passing world. For a few moments, Oliveri, Mode and the others, stood side by side with their guardian angels, and although no words were spoken, their loving smiles towards one another expressed all that they needed to convey, for there was indeed a deep familiarity in their connection that everyone could feel and understand.

Suddenly, the sky above was ripped open, and a gap emerged into the heavens from which poured the ranks of the other angels who appeared in their ethereal splendour and with a radiance that transcended, for now, the mortal comprehension of the faithful remnant. Led by Brenard and Hasler as the two witnesses of the end of times, the Seraphim and the Cherubim descended and took their place of honour around the throne of Christ. Next came the ranks of Thrones and Dominions, followed by the Virtue and the Powers, and before the throne they stood dressed in their armours, with their flaming swords of grace, courage and moral excellence, ready to defend the heavenly realms and defeat the demonic forces of the world.

For the remnant the angelic forces were impossible to count, as they filled the entire sky for as far as the eye could see and high into the torn veil that separated this world from heaven. Then to establish the justice that was due to be administered that day, the rank of Principalities came to oversee the Divine Will and the order of the judgement that was to be unveiled for all the living and the dead.

As the demons grew in anxiety and with great fluster, their anger became more and more palpable as they begged Lucifer to allow them to fight knowing they had nothing left to lose, but he remained impassive and stood waiting, for he knew there was one more rank of the angelic hosts to appear, the rank he once controlled when he led the choirs of angels before his fall. Slowly, the ranks of the angels parted and looked up to the torn veil as the archangels descended, before the veil closed behind them.

Together they came to rest above the throne, where they kept their eyes fixed on Lucifer - the one they had once called brother. Gabriel the messenger, stood to the far right with the scroll of judgement day held firmly in his hand. Next to him stood Chamuel who held the love of heaven, ready to administer the inner peace of eternal life to all who had been deemed worthy. On the far-left stood Raphael, with his staff gripped firmly and ready to lead the souls of the dead and those before him into the new heaven which had been prepared for this moment. And next to him stood Uriel who held the burning book of knowledge, ready to bring complete understanding and wisdom to all who had searched for the truth. And in the middle of them stood Michael, clad in the armour of war, and in his right hand he held the heavenly sword of justice and truth, ready to use it in the final confrontation as he led the army of heaven against the forces of hell.

With petrified screams, the demonic legion hissed and spat at the heavenly hosts and the symphony of their heavenly voices that rose in a chorus of praise and adoration to the One who sat on the judgement seat and who did not remove his gaze from Lucifer.

For Lucifer the silence of Christ became too much to bear, and the heavenly chorus of praise was not what he wanted to hear in these final moments. Taking matters into his own control, he took a sword from his side and demanded that his demons did the same. To battle they were called and to battle they would fight. Rising high above his demons, he noticed that neither Michael nor the heavenly forces moved from their positions, instead they all followed with their gaze before doing the one thing Lucifer did not expect them to do.

Upon the command given by Michael, the heavenly hosts and the angels who guarded the faithful remnant, turned their gaze away from Lucifer and in unison they all bowed the knee and turned to face their king, Jesus Christ. At once they acclaimed him as the Son of God, the One who Is, who was and who forever shall be. Their hallelujahs and hosannas filled the entirety of creation from one universe to the next, as the faithful remnant once again took up their exaltations of praise.

With no one looking at him except his demons, Lucifer's anger boiled, and raising his sword high into the air he was just about to give the command to attack when Christ with all the authority given to him, arose from the throne and with his right arm outstretched, he spoke.

'IT IS FINISHED!'

Immediately the earth quaked, and the whole of Jerusalem shook as the vibrations spread throughout the whole earth. Right through the remnant, the earth split open and parted the faithful onto both sides as the gap widened and the core of the earth became exposed for all to see as the heat from its depth issued for all to feel.

Without any word or explanation, the demons were plunged into the fire; screaming as they fell one by one as Lucifer felt the horror come his way and the knowing that this would be his eternity. And as his legion vanished before his eyes, he looked to see the angelic powers for what he knew would be the last time, but they all kept their backs to him, all except one.

For with the authority bestowed upon him, the Archangel Michael with great reverence bowed his head towards the Son of God before slowly turning to face Lucifer with a look of righteous rage written large in the expression on his face. Lifting his sword, he pointed it directly at Lucifer and after making it clear that it was a battle for them both to fight, he leapt from the choirs of angels and flew down to face Lucifer who revealed his own wings and rushed forward to meet him.

The roar that stemmed from the energy of their battle resounded throughout the world, but no one lifted their heads or diverted their eyes to look at what was taking place. Focused entirely on Christ as he sat in judgement, the angelic hosts and the remnant began to sing their praises as the battle took place. Occasionally they saw the battle on the periphery of their vision, but their faith and devotion were never going to shift from the one who had returned.

Michael who was now the most powerful of all the celestial beings, had waited for this moment ever since the fall. With no hesitation but to do the right thing to uphold the rule of heavenly justice and righteousness, he clashed repeatedly with Lucifer in the skies above Jerusalem; their swords crashing and resounding as they fought to the bitter end.

For Lucifer it was a battle he hoped to win before the end, by extinguishing the one who had replaced him in the ranks of the angels and who was called by his name because he was like unto God. With a sword formed from the depths of the earth, Lucifer knew that it was not as powerful as the sword of truth that Michael yielded in his right hand, but with vain hope he defended himself, occasionally able to find a point of entry to the archangel. However, Michael proved too quick and powerful and had the skill to repel each blow of his sword.

In the end it was Lucifer who fell to the earth, and who landed on the land that separated the remnant from the celestial bodies and Christ enthroned. It was his agonising scream that filled the earth that made everyone look, for they knew it was about to end. And as he lay on the ground, a wing fell slowly from the sky as Michael stood with his sword having dealt the crippling blow. Unable to regain flight, Lucifer attempted to take a final stand, but Michael quickly rushed from the sky and with his left foot he turned the body of Lucifer so that it faced the risen Christ, and then bringing his right foot to rest on Lucifer's chest he placed the point of his sword against the temple of his head and looked up to Christ for the final command.

39.

No one reeled from seeing Lucifer fall to the earth for this was how it had to be, for there was no place for the enemy of the good in the new kingdom that awaited those to whom it had been promised. Having seen the brutality that his wickedness had unleashed upon the world, and the suffering many had to endure through the twistedness of sin, no one had any sympathy nor the will to plead for his cause. For they all knew that it was not their call to make, for his damnation had been secured from the moment he rebelled against the love that he once knew.

For the joy of salvation to prevail, Christ needed to extinguish the last residue of evil from the world and to cast the judgement upon those who were deserving of it. With the names already written within the book, with the souls of the righteous saved in his name, he looked up towards heaven, lifted his arms and spoke for all to hear.

'Father, it is to this hour that you have called your children, both the living and the dead, to see the fulness of Your wonder and the joy of the world to come. In my name You have redeemed the sin of the world and have restored the brokenness of sin and conquered the power of evil. The battle is over, and with the love that only you can bring, I will lead them into your presence forever.'

Suddenly, a pulsating light spread across the sky as the remnant looked up and the angels sang out their praises. Then, from the wall below the Temple Mount, an opening appeared that was consumed in darkness, and from its depths came forward a group of people clothed in black whose faces no longer existed. These souls walked with great fear and trembling before the throne of judgement and everyone knew that these were the souls of those who had rejected the love and who had desired to be completely consumed by the darkness of Lucifer's power and dominion.

Oliveri watched on, wondering who they were, but there was no way of telling. However, he was surprised at just how few of them there were; at the most they numbered several thousand as they stood trembling before the Lord of Heaven and Earth.

'I Am Mercy within Mercy,' Christ spoke to the condemned. 'Solemnly I say, depart from me you wicked and faithless souls into the eternal punishment that has been prepared for you and the fallen demons that you serve.'

With the swiftness of a sword falling across the neck of the condemned, a dual wind arose from the east and the west and came to meet them where they stood, and with nothing more to say and with no more need to delay, they were lifted up into the sky until they hovered above the pit of hell, and as they screamed in horror the wind ceased and as dead as they were, they fell into the lake of fire never to see the light again.

In the silence that followed, Christ turned and looked to Michael who stood awaiting the command. Yet, no word was spoken and only a nod was given.

For this final moment Lucifer wanted to yell out his curse of rejection for one final time, but Michael quickly prevented him from doing so by reaching down and grabbing hold of his throat, then he dragged him along the ground until he reached the edge of hell. As the flames roared high from the pit, Michael looked into the eyes of Lucifer for one final time. And as Lucifer watched the smile grow on Michael's face, he felt the humiliation and feared what was about to happen. Suddenly, and with a force unlike any other he had ever felt, Lucifer was lifted high by Michael and tossed into the eternal lake of hell.

As the angels and the remnant saw him fall, his agonising screams and the terror of the wicked and the demons who were cast down with him, filled the whole earth. Suddenly, the flames of hell rose high into the air as they consumed those who had been cast into it like a hunger that would never be satisfied.

With his judgement complete, Christ spoke with an authority to conceal the entrance of hell. Slowly, the opening in the earth closed over, and the screams of the condemned fell silent as the earth was sealed completely shut. And as the remnant all beheld Christ, he turned to look at them and with a love so great he looked up at the most wonderful sight that began to unfold.

Immediately, a pulsating light expanded into a flash of brilliant white, as the remnant witnessed the souls of the faithful departed appear from their place in heaven. With smiles of happiness, they looked down upon the remnant as the angels took to flight and resumed their rightful place within the heavenly realm, once again singing their praises to the love that had consumed them.

It was Lincoln whom Oliveri heard speak first, when she cried out that she could see her mother and father, and then other members of her family before others around him began to say the same. It was only then that Oliveri saw his own parents and grandparents smiling and waving back at him, and in that moment his heart was filled with such a pure joy that the tears of unconditional love streamed from his face, and as he turned, he saw Dave Mode waving up towards those whom he recognised with great excitement and overwhelming wonder.

'I am the resurrection and the life,' Christ spoke, as he descended the steps from the judgement seat and walked on the earth. 'He who believes in me will never die.'

Reaching down, Christ placed the palms of his hands onto the soil of Jerusalem, as a vibration pulsated through the ground and grew to such a magnitude that the soil bounced on the surface of the earth, before that which he had promised began to take place.

From every inch of land and depth of the seas, the remains of those who had fallen asleep in his name and of those who had searched for God with all their hearts, began their own resurrections as the bursts of divine energy from the hands of Christ, brought them up from the darkness of their graves, and like a murmuration of starlings the bodies of the dead ascended from the earth and joined the souls of those who had been waiting for this moment to come. Like bursts of radiation, their bodies connected once again with the souls of the saved, and in the mystery that was unfolding they transfigured one by one into the perfection of their creation in which they would dwell forever in peace and love.

The sight to behold was mesmerising, as the remnant watched in great elation as the greatest miracle that had been promised to mankind unfolded before their eyes. Each one could see the transfiguration take place of those they knew, and it was a happiness that they all knew would never end.

And as this continued, a golden light appeared and drew close to the remnant, and they could see that two golden doors were opening in the middle of the light, and everyone knew that it was beyond this entrance that their eternal happiness lay.

'You will come with me now,' Jesus spoke with great gentleness, as he led them towards the doors. 'Beyond is the New Heaven and the New Earth, for this world in which you now stand will soon dissolve like the snow. Beyond our Father awaits us, and you will see Him face to face as you walk into the eternity of heaven that awaits you. So, do not be afraid!'

And as he stood by the door, he turned to them and with his right hand directed the way into which they should walk. One by one, the faithful remnant passed by him with great joy as they looked deep into his eyes, each one unable to find the words to thank him for the great gift he had given to them in this moment.

It did not take long for them all to pass through, and as Oliveri took hold of Lincoln's and Modes hands they shared in each other's excitement as they sang their praises in a heavenly language. With complete trust they followed the faithful and walked closer to the entrance of heaven, and as Christ stood, he welcomed and embraced everyone by their name as they passed from this life into the next.

It was only as they reached the door that Mode realised that they were the last to walk through. Desperate to hug Christ, Jane Lincoln let go of Mode's hand before Oliveri followed her and embraced the Lord too. Before he could make sense of what was happening, they both disappeared from his sight as they walked through the doors and into the light of the Beatific Vision.

Alone with Jesus Christ, Dave Mode looked deep into his eyes, unable to speak.

Reaching out his hand, Christ took hold of Mode's and turned to look back upon Jerusalem and the world for one last time.

'From the moment of creation, it was always going to be you David,' Christ spoke, as he gripped his hand firmly. 'It was always going to be you!'

'What was, my Lord?'.

'Come and see,' Christ replied, as he led him by the hand.

The End.

Acknowledgements

If you've made it this far, it means you've journeyed with me through the entire *Pontifex Maximus* trilogy—and for that, I owe you my deepest thanks.

As an independent author, without the vast resources of a publishing house behind me, this story could never have reached completion without the support of those who stood beside me. My heartfelt gratitude goes to Daniel for his unwavering encouragement, and to Roisin and Aiden for generously giving their time to read through the manuscript and share their invaluable feedback. Any mistakes that remain are mine alone, and I can only hope they did not diminish your enjoyment of the tale.

If you enjoyed this book, I would be truly grateful if you could write a review on Amazon or Goodreads. Your words make a real difference—not only in supporting my dream of continuing to write, but also in helping other readers discover this story. Though it may seem a small act, the impact of every review is immense.

Now, with this final volume, the *Pontifex Maximus* trilogy comes to a close. Writing it has been an incredible experience, and connecting with readers from across the world—people I've never met, yet who have shared in these characters and their journeys—fills me with amazement and gratitude.

This may be the end of one story, but it is not the end of the journey. I have new projects already taking shape, and I hope you'll continue along with me as they unfold.

From the bottom of my heart—thank you.

Until next time...

Damian North

To contact me:

www.damiannorth.com

x - @Damian_North

Printed in Dunstable, United Kingdom

70253580R00141